Sherlock Holmes Mysteries

Books 1 to 5

Mabel Swift

Copyright © 2024 by Mabel Swift

www.mabelswift.com

All rights reserved.

All rights reserved. No part of this publication may be reproduced in any form, electronically or mechanically without permission from the author.

This is a work of fiction and any resemblance to any person living or dead is purely coincidental.

Contents

Book 1 - Sherlock Holmes and The Missing Portrait 1

Chapter 1 2

Chapter 2 6

Chapter 3 12

Chapter 4 16

Chapter 5 20

Chapter 6 25

Chapter 7 28

Chapter 8 32

Chapter 9 36

Chapter 10 40

Chapter 11 43

Chapter 12 47

Chapter 13	54
Chapter 14	58
Book 2 - Sherlock Holmes and The Haunted Museum	64
Chapter 1	65
Chapter 2	73
Chapter 3	83
Chapter 4	89
Chapter 5	95
Chapter 6	102
Chapter 7	109
Chapter 8	117
Chapter 9	125
Chapter 10	133
Chapter 11	141
Chapter 12	149
Chapter 13	154
Chapter 14	162
Chapter 15	170
Chapter 16	179

Chapter 17	184
Chapter 18	191
Chapter 19	197
Chapter 20	206
Chapter 21	210
Chapter 22	217
Chapter 23	224
Chapter 24	230
Chapter 25	241
Book 3 - Sherlock Holmes and The Hasty Holiday	243
Chapter 1	244
Chapter 2	252
Chapter 3	258
Chapter 4	263
Chapter 5	269
Chapter 6	277
Chapter 7	282
Chapter 8	292
Chapter 9	297

Chapter 10	303
Chapter 11	308
Chapter 12	315
Chapter 13	320
Book 4 - Sherlock Holmes and The Baker Street Thefts	326
Chapter 1	327
Chapter 2	332
Chapter 3	338
Chapter 4	343
Chapter 5	349
Chapter 6	358
Chapter 7	361
Chapter 8	365
Chapter 9	371
Chapter 10	375
Chapter 11	378
Chapter 12	383
Chapter 13	386

Book 5 - Sherlock Holmes and The Lamplighter's Mystery	390
Chapter 1	391
Chapter 2	397
Chapter 3	404
Chapter 4	409
Chapter 5	415
Chapter 6	422
Chapter 7	426
Chapter 8	431
Chapter 9	435
Chapter 10	438
Chapter 11	441
Chapter 12	446
A note from the author	454

Book 1 - Sherlock Holmes and The Missing Portrait

Chapter 1

Inside the upper rooms of 221B Baker Street, Sherlock Holmes reclined in his well-worn armchair, the faint aroma of tobacco lingering in the air as he pored over the daily newspapers. Across from him, his steadfast companion, Dr John Watson, occupied his customary seat, his gaze alternating between the pages before him and the pensive expression upon his friend's countenance.

"It has been an eternity since our last case, Watson," Holmes remarked, his voice tinged with a hint of restlessness as he tossed aside the newspaper, its contents evidently failing to pique his insatiable curiosity. A wry smile played upon his lips, one eyebrow arched quizzically. "Has everyone taken a holiday away from London, perhaps? Or have people taken to solving their own mysteries?"

Watson chuckled. He set aside his newspaper with a contented sigh. "Patience, Holmes," he counselled, a glint of fond amusement dancing in his eyes as he regarded his restive companion. "Trouble has an uncanny knack for finding us, even in the most unlikely of circumstances."

As if on cue, the gentle knock upon the door preceded the entrance of their landlady, Mrs Hudson. Her kindly face crinkled into a warm smile as she made her way into the sitting room, proffering a sealed envelope.

"A message for you, Mr Holmes," she announced, clearly well-accustomed to acting as the intermediary for the various missives and enquiries that found their way to the celebrated detective.

Holmes straightened in his chair, eyes alight with renewed interest as he accepted the mysterious correspondence. Deftly breaking the seal with one long finger, he swiftly scanned the contents of the letter, his expression inscrutable.

"Well, Holmes?" Watson prompted. "What is the nature of this correspondence?"

"It would appear, my dear Watson, that we have been summoned by the Duchess of Rothbury," Holmes replied, his voice tinged with intrigue as he refolded the letter with deft movements. "The esteemed lady requests our assistance in a matter of delicate import and extends a gracious invitation to her stately residence in Mayfair. No doubt the nature of her predicament shall prove a stimulating diversion from the mundanities that have plagued us of late."

Watson's eyes widened in recognition at the mention of the illustrious name. "The Duchess of Rothbury? Why, I have heard many a tale of her lavish soirees and her tireless dedication to the social whirl of London's high society. Indeed, the Duchess has kept herself extremely occupied since the tragic passing of her beloved husband, the late Duke. Her philanthropic endeavours and patronage of the arts are renowned throughout the city's elite circles."

Holmes nodded sagely, his fingers steepled beneath his chin as he pondered the intriguing development. "A most curious summons, to be sure. This matter must be of a delicate nature indeed, to compel her to solicit our services. I must reply forthwith."

He reached for his pen and a fresh sheet of paper. "I shall inform the Duchess that we will pay her a visit this very afternoon."

With a flourish, Holmes inscribed his response, the nib of his pen scratching across the parchment with practised ease. He sealed the missive with a dab of crimson wax from the candle flickering nearby, imprinting it with the distinctive crest of his personal seal. Once the wax had cooled and hardened, securing the envelope's contents, he dashed downstairs in search of Mrs Hudson. He found her in the parlour, dusting the mantelpiece with her customary care and attention.

"Mrs Hudson, might I trouble you to arrange for the prompt delivery of this message?" he inquired, holding out the sealed envelope.

"Of course, Mr Holmes," she replied, taking the letter with a nod. Her eyes widened momentarily with undisguised interest as she glimpsed the name inscribed upon the envelope, but as discreet as always, she didn't voice her curiosity aloud and merely said, "I shall deal with this straight away."

She walked out of the parlour, leaving Holmes to his contemplations about the Duchess of Rothbury and why she needed their help.

Chapter 2

The hansom cab trundled to a halt before the grand façade of the Duchess of Rothbury's stately residence in Mayfair, the hooves of the horses clopping against the cobblestones as they came to a rest. Holmes stepped out first, casting an appraising eye over the imposing edifice before him. Dr Watson followed close behind, unable to entirely conceal his awe at the opulent surroundings.

"Impressive, is it not?" Holmes remarked, his voice laced with a hint of dry amusement as he took in his companion's reaction. "Though I dare say the true interest lies not in the outward trappings of wealth and status, but rather in the delicate mystery that awaits us within."

A liveried footman hastened to usher them into the resplendent foyer. The rich scents of polished wood and beeswax mingled with the faint, floral notes of abundant blooms in vases arranged around the area.

"This way, sirs," the footman intoned as he led them through the labyrinthine corridors towards the parlour, where the Duchess awaited their arrival.

As they entered the sumptuously appointed room, the Duchess rose from her seat, a gracious smile on her face as she extended her hand in welcome. "Mr Holmes, Dr Watson, how good of you to attend with such alacrity," she greeted them warmly. "I do hope the matter at hand proves a worthy diversion from your usual pursuits."

Holmes inclined his head respectfully, his keen gaze sweeping over the Duchess's form as he committed every nuance of her appearance and demeanour to his prodigious memory. "Your Grace," he replied smoothly, "you may rest assured that whatever matter concerns you shall receive the utmost dedication of my humble talents."

The Duchess gestured for them to be seated, her expression growing momentarily pensive as she collected her thoughts. "As I intimated in my missive, the nature of this affair is one of delicate import, requiring the utmost discretion. Early this morning, I received a delivery that has caused me no small degree of consternation."

She rose from her chair and crossed to a nearby side table, upon which rested a large, canvas-wrapped object.

She untied the cords securing the wrappings, allowing the fabric to fall away to reveal the portrait concealed beneath.

Watson's brows rose in surprise as he took in the image depicted upon the canvas. A striking portrayal of a man attired in a business suit, seated in what appeared to be a private library. "You see, gentlemen," the Duchess continued, "this is not, as I had anticipated, a portrait of my own likeness that I had commissioned from the esteemed artist, Julian Devaux. Instead, it depicts a gentleman entirely unknown to me, though I must confess his face does strike a faint chord of familiarity and I wonder if I've seen him at a social gathering recently. More unsettling, though, is the background, for this is my library, and it's the room I choose for my portrait. It's a mystery as to who this man is, and why he should be painted in my library."

Holmes' brow furrowed ever so slightly as he studied the canvas, his eyes narrowing in contemplation. "A most curious development, indeed," he murmured, his gaze flickering briefly towards the Duchess before returning to scrutinise the figure portrayed upon the canvas. "Might I enquire as to the specifics of your commission to Mr Devaux? Any pertinent details, no matter how seemingly insignificant, could prove invaluable in unravelling this perplexing conundrum."

The Duchess said, "Mr Devaux is widely renowned for his unparalleled talent in capturing the essence of his subjects through his exquisite portraiture. Opulent settings and aristocratic subjects have become synonymous with Devaux's name, and he has a long list of clients, some of whom are in my social circles. In the wake of my dear husband's passing, I felt compelled to commission a new portrait of myself in the library. It was a place where I spent many treasured hours with my husband."

Holmes and Dr Watson listened with an occasional nod of understanding.

The Duchess continued, and her eyes took on a distant look as she delved into the recollections. "Mr Devaux and I had several preliminary consultations, during which he would study me intently, committing every nuance of my features and bearing to his sketchpad. Once he had enough information, I chose my required gown and placed myself in the library. Mr Devaux spent many hours painting my portrait, but in line with his requirements, I was not permitted to see any part of the portrait until it was finished." She looked towards the portrait, her expression clearly conveying it was not at all what she'd been expecting.

Watson listened intently; his brow furrowed in concentration as he sought to piece together the puzzle before them. He said, "And yet, despite his meticulous preparations and your explicit commission, the portrait you received bears no semblance to you. A most baffling turn of events, to be sure."

The Duchess inclined her head, a troubled expression flickering across her refined features. "Precisely, Dr Watson," she affirmed. "As you can well imagine, I was quite taken aback upon unveiling this portrayal. Which makes me wonder if my likeness has been captured in another's house, perhaps seated in one of their rooms. As I said, Mr Devaux has a long list of clients, and I'm worried that the workload was too much for him and he made mistakes with his backgrounds and subjects. I sincerely hope someone isn't gazing upon my face instead of their own somewhere in London."

Holmes said sagely, "That's precisely what I am thinking, too."

The Duchess' voice dropped to a hushed tone as she confided her innermost concerns. "I fear the potential ramifications should word of this puzzling substitution become public knowledge. The notion of my true portrait being misplaced, or worse, misused in some untoward manner fills me with no small degree of trepidation. Not to mention, that I now have a portrait of a strange man in my library. What would people think?"

Holmes's eyes narrowed thoughtfully as he regarded the Duchess, his brilliant mind already whirring with potential theories and avenues of investigation. "Fear not, Your Grace," he assured her. "We shall endeavour to unravel this mystery. May I ask, how was the painting delivered to you?"

The Duchess replied, "It arrived at the tradesman's entrance a few hours ago and my butler placed it in here. Another puzzling element is the label that was attached to the outer wrapping. I still have it." She moved over to the sideboard and retrieved a piece of paper. She gave it to Holmes.

He read the words out loud, "'The Duchess of Rothbury's Library'. How peculiar. The painting is addressed to your library and not yourself. This only adds to the mystery. But I assure you, Your Grace, we will solve this puzzle for you."

The Duchess met his gaze levelly, a flicker of relief evident in her eyes. "Mr Holmes, Dr Watson, you have my sincere appreciation. My reputation, and the legacy of my late husband's noble name, rests in your most capable hands."

Chapter 3

With the Duchess' revelations still fresh in their minds, Sherlock Holmes and the good doctor wasted no time in securing the address of Mr Devaux's studio from her ladyship before biding her farewell.

"Come, Watson!" Holmes exclaimed, his long strides carrying him swiftly towards the waiting hansom cab. "The trail grows ever warmer, and we must pursue it with all haste lest it turn cold."

The artistic quarter of London, with its charming array of studios and galleries, proved to be their destination. The cab clattered to a halt before a nondescript edifice, its brick façade weathered by the elements yet exuding an undeniable air of creative energy.

Holmes rapped smartly upon the door of Mr Devaux, but their summons went unanswered. A frown creased his brow as he tried the handle, only to find it firmly secured against unwanted intrusion.

"Most peculiar," he murmured, his keen eyes scanning their surroundings for any clue or indication as to the artist's whereabouts.

It was at that moment that the sound of a door opening nearby caught their attention. A young man, his clothes liberally spattered with vibrant hues of paint, emerged from the neighbouring studio, his brow furrowed in mild annoyance at the disturbance.

"Can I be of assistance, gentlemen?" he inquired.

Holmes replied, "Indeed you can, sir. We are in search of Julian Devaux, the artist whose studio lies just here. Might you have any knowledge of his current whereabouts?"

The young man's expression shifted, a flicker of surprise crossing his features. "Devaux? Why, he departed most abruptly a few hours ago, bundling a few suitcases into a waiting carriage and making off with nary a word of explanation."

Watson's eyebrows rose in surprise at this revelation, and he exchanged a meaningful glance with his companion.

"Abruptly, you say?" Holmes pressed. "Most unlike an artist of such renown, I should think."

The man nodded. "Indeed. I was working intently on my art this morning, and the sudden commotion outside disturbed me. I looked out of my window and saw Devaux, hurrying out into the street with his belongings, hailing a cab with an almost frantic urgency. Most out of character, I must say, the man is usually a picture of composure and decorum."

Holmes' eyes narrowed thoughtfully. "I wonder what made him leave with such haste, and where he was going."

The young artist said, "He might turn up at his exhibition tonight. It's being held at a gallery on Bond Street. It's the unveiling of his latest works, or so I believe. If he's to make an appearance anywhere soon, it would surely be there. Would you like the gallery's name?"

Holmes said, "That would be most appreciated. Thank you."

The young man gave the details and said goodbye before hurrying back into his studio.

As Holmes and Watson retraced their steps towards the awaiting hansom cab, Holmes' expression was pensive, his mind already formulating a strategy for their next move.

"Well, Watson?" he remarked, "it would seem our elusive artist has taken flight, much like a startled bird fleeing its cage. But why? Has he realised what a commotion the delivery of his painting to the Duchess would yield? Was the painting a result of his overworked mind, as the Duchess suggested? We shall make our way to this art gallery this evening and see what truths might be revealed. If luck is on our side, we will meet the elusive Mr Devaux."

With a renewed sense of purpose, the pair climbed into the cab, already discussing why Julian Devaux had undertaken such a sudden departure, and if he would return that evening.

Chapter 4

As Sherlock Holmes and Dr Watson entered the art gallery later that evening, the low murmur of conversation drifted towards them, carrying with it an undercurrent of bewilderment and surprise. The assembled guests, all adorned in elegant attire, were engaged in hushed discussions around the framed artwork, their faces a mixture of confusion and intrigue.

"What was he thinking?" a woman remarked, her voice tinged with disapproval. "This isn't Devaux's usual style at all."

Mutters of agreement met her words.

Holmes' keen ears picked up on the comments. He strode forward, Watson close at his heels, eager to look upon the controversial works that had so captivated the gathered throng.

As they approached the first set of framed sketches, Holmes found himself momentarily taken aback by the stark black-and-white images that greeted him. He had been expecting sumptuous surroundings and noble-looking subjects. In their place were the everyday people of London's poorer districts, their faces etched with the signs of hard living and toil.

Yet, despite the grime and weariness that clung to their features, each subject wore a smile that seemed to radiate from within. More astonishing were the backgrounds that Devaux had sketched. They didn't convey the person's expected surroundings at all and were a mix of seemingly impossible environments.

"Extraordinary," Holmes said, his gaze roving over the assembled portraits. "Devaux has captured the people with an almost whimsical touch and he's placed them in entirely new environments. But why would he undertake such an enterprise?"

Dr Watson replied, "Perhaps his subjects asked him to. Maybe they wanted him to represent whatever dreams filled their sleeping hours."

Holmes nodded. "You could be right in that assumption. But let's continue looking and find evidence to support your theory."

Dr Watson pointed to the next framed image. "Why, Holmes, isn't that Sarah, the flower seller from Covent Garden?"

Indeed, there she was, the young woman's likeness rendered in exquisite detail. But instead of the bustling streets and market stalls that usually formed her backdrop, Sarah was depicted in a sprawling garden, surrounded by lush plants and towering trees. In her hands, she clutched a set of plans, the intricate designs hinting at landscape design.

Holmes smiled and said, "Having chatted with Sarah on a few occasions, I do recall that she often spoke about being a landscape designer. Yet, she always laughed as soon as she said those words as if it were an impossible dream. Perhaps she voiced those same words to Julian Devaux, hence the reason for creating this particular background. I wonder what Sarah thought of this image?"

"Maybe she never saw the finished sketch," Watson said. "But I'm sure it would be something that would bring a smile to her face."

As they moved further along the gallery wall, another familiar face caught their attention. Billy, the young chimney sweep who often delivered messages to their Baker Street lodgings, grinned up at them from the canvas, his soot-streaked face alight with joy.

But instead of the grime and detritus of his trade, Billy was on a stage and surrounded by the trappings of a magician's art—top hat, playing cards, and mysterious boxes hinting at illusions and magic.

"It appears the boy dreams of magic," Holmes mused. "I wouldn't put anything past Billy; he's a bright young man."

Watson chuckled softly, his heart warmed by the sight of Billy's infectious grin. "A noble aspiration, to be sure. And one that Devaux has captured with remarkable sensitivity."

As they continued their circuit of the gallery, Holmes and Watson found themselves confronted with portrait after portrait, each one a window into the hidden hopes and dreams of London's forgotten citizens. Seamstresses and factory workers, street urchins and labourers - all were represented, their faces suffused with a quiet dignity that belied their humble circumstances.

"One thing puzzles me," Watson said. "Why would Devaux choose to focus on these subjects, so far removed from his usual fare? And to have them display here for all to see?"

Holmes replied, "Questions that beg an answer, my dear Watson. And one that I suspect may lie at the very heart of our mystery."

Chapter 5

Holmes' eyes narrowed at the sound of the sneering voice that cut through the quiet murmurs of the gallery. He turned to find himself face-to-face with a man whose countenance seemed etched with bitterness and disdain.

"Mr Bartholomew Grange, I presume?" Holmes said coolly, recognizing the man who penned scathing critiques in many newspapers. It was said Bartholomew was a failed artist, and instead of taking up a new craft, he had taken the easier route of unleashing his frustrated anger upon others instead. His published words had earned him a certain notoriety in artistic circles.

Grange's lips curled into a contemptuous sneer as he raked his gaze over the assembled portraits. "So, you've deduced who I am, Mr Holmes. How utterly thrilling for you."

Watson bristled at the man's mocking tone, but Holmes raised a hand, forestalling any retort from his faithful companion.

"I take it you have some insight into Devaux's motivations for this particular exhibition?" he asked, his tone deceptively mild.

Grange snorted derisively. "Motivations? The man has clearly lost what little talent he possesses. For years, I told him that his work had grown stale, predictable. An endless parade of simpering aristocrats and vapid society beauties, all rendered with the same lifeless precision."

People turned around at his rising voice, giving him looks full of disgust.

That didn't stop Bartholomew Grange. His eyes glittered with a mixture of scorn and perverse delight as he gestured at the nearby sketches. "I dared him to produce something different, something that would actually stir the soul instead of lulling it to sleep. And this," he said, his voice thick with contempt, "is what he offers in response. Pathetic renderings of the unwashed masses, their vulgar grins mocking the very notion of art itself."

Holmes regarded the critic with a steady, appraising gaze. "I find your assessment somewhat lacking, Mr

Grange. To my eyes, Devaux has captured something far more profound than mere portraiture."

Grange opened his mouth to protest, but Holmes pressed on, undeterred.

"These sketches offer a glimpse into the lives and dreams of those often overlooked by polite society. The flower seller who longs to shape and cultivate gardens of beauty. The young chimney sweep whose spirit yearns for the magic and wonder of the stage." He gestured at the nearby images of Sarah and Billy, their faces alight with hope and aspiration. "Devaux has given voice to their dreams and captured them on canvas. Is that not the true purpose of art; to elevate the human spirit, to capture those fleeting moments that might otherwise be lost to the relentless march of time?"

Grange seemed momentarily taken aback by Holmes' impassioned defence, his mouth working soundlessly for a moment before he regained his composure.

"Pretty words, Mr Holmes," he sneered. "But who wants to gaze upon such commonplace subjects? Art should inspire, should elevate the viewer to loftier realms, not wallow in the squalor of the gutters."

A ghost of a smile played across Holmes' lips. "Ah, but therein lies the true genius of Devaux's work, my dear sir.

He has shown us that beauty and inspiration can be found in the most unexpected of places, if one only has the eyes to see it."

With that, Holmes turned away from the sputtering critic, his attention once more drawn to the portraits of Billy and Sarah. A thoughtful expression settled over his features as he studied the sketches, his mind already formulating a plan.

"Watson," he said, beckoning his friend closer. "I find myself quite taken with these particular works. I should like to purchase them, if the gallery owner is amenable."

Watson's brow furrowed in surprise. "But whatever for, Holmes?"

A warm smile spread across the detective's features, softening the usual sharp lines of his countenance. "Why, to gift them to young Billy and dear Sarah, of course. A small token, a reminder that their dreams and aspirations are worthy of being celebrated, no matter how lofty or fanciful they might seem."

As Holmes walked towards the gallery owner, Watson cast a fond smile at his friend. Despite Holmes' sometimes cold and calculating demeanour, there lay a warm-heartedness that often surprised him.

And as they departed the gallery, the carefully wrapped sketches tucked under Holmes' arm, Watson asked in which direction their investigation should take next. All he received from Holmes in reply was an enigmatic smile.

Chapter 6

Upon arriving at Covent Garden the next morning, Holmes scanned the bustling throngs with a keen eye until he espied the familiar figure of Sarah, the flower seller. Her bright smile lit up her face as she hawked her wares to the passing crowds.

"Good day to you, Miss Sarah," Holmes called out, drawing her attention.

"Why, Mr Holmes! And Dr Watson too," she replied, bobbing a little curtsy. "Whatever brings you here this morning? Would you like some flowers? I have plenty to choose from."

Holmes declared, "We shall acquire some blooms during our visit, but our purpose here is of a more delightful nature." He extracted one of the framed portraits tucked securely under his arm and offered it to her. "I believe this rightly belongs in your possession. Mr Devaux exhibited it in a gallery the previous evening, and I could not resist purchasing it for you."

Sarah gasped, her eyes growing wide as she took in the exquisite image of herself amidst a lush garden, plans clutched in her hands. "Oh, Mr Devaux...he did capture my dream so beautifully, didn't he?" She blushed, averting her eyes shyly. "When he asked if he might sketch me a few weeks ago, I'll confess I was flattered, but thought little of it at the time. But as he worked, he asked about my life and my hopes for the future. I found myself admitting how I longed to design landscapes one day. I had no idea he was going to put this background in his sketch. He did ask if I'd give him permission to display the sketch in public. I said yes, but I thought he was jesting, because who would want to see me?"

Holmes gave her a slight bow. "Many people would, and many people did last night. In my opinion, it is one of the most exquisite pieces of art that I have ever set my eyes upon, and it's down to Mr Devaux's talent and the sparkle in your eyes, Miss Sarah."

Sarah smiled. "Thank you, Mr Holmes." She looked at the image and sighed wistfully. "If only this picture was real. If only this was how my life could be."

Watson smiled warmly at the young woman. "And why can't it be? All great works start with a dream, Miss Sarah."

"Quite so," Holmes agreed with a nod. "I do hope this portrait shall serve as inspiration to pursue your dreams. The world is in sore need of more beauty."

Her blush deepened, but her eyes shone with renewed determination. "You're right, Mr Holmes. Seeing this picture makes it seem more real somehow. I'll do what it takes to make it happen. I don't know what or how! But I'll make a start. Thank you so kindly for buying this for me, Mr Holmes."

With a smile, the detective dismissed her gratitude, remarking, "The pleasure is mine. Now then, which floral arrangements shall we buy from your offerings today?"

Upon concluding their acquisitions, Holmes and Dr Watson bid Sarah farewell and commenced their quest to locate Billy, the youthful chimney sweeper. Regrettably, he proved elusive, but after inquiring about his whereabouts from his companions, they were assured Billy would be told of their inquiries and would seek them out in due course.

Chapter 7

Later that morning, Holmes rapped the brass knocker against the Duchess of Rothbury's front door with a decisive hand. Whilst awaiting a response, he turned to his companion. "What do you make of those sketches I bought from the gallery last evening, Watson?"

"Quite remarkable, Holmes," replied Watson, admiring the bouquet of flowers in his hand that they had purchased from young Sarah earlier. "Devaux has an extraordinary talent for capturing the human spirit, does he not?"

Before Holmes could respond, the door swung open, revealing the Duchess' maid. "Good day, sirs. I'm afraid her Grace is not at home at present."

"I see. We have arrived unannounced, and please, forgive us for disturbing you," Holmes said with an apologetic smile. "Could we leave a message with you? Please inform the Duchess that Sherlock Holmes and Dr Watson called to provide an update on the matter she hired us to investigate. Additionally, we would be most obliged if we could take another look at the painting that the Duchess received yesterday. If you have the time, of course."

The maid's eyes widened slightly at the request, but she nodded. "Very well, Mr Holmes. If you'll follow me."

They were led into the Duchess' parlour, where the mysterious portrait was leaning against the wall. Holmes wasted no time in crossing the room and examining it intently through his lens.

"Anything of interest?" Watson inquired, joining his companion.

"Indeed, Watson." Holmes' eyes narrowed as he focused his keen gaze on a small detail upon the subject's lapel. "Do you see that insignia there? A badge of some sort, it would seem?"

Watson leaned in closer, squinting slightly as he attempted to discern the minute detail his friend had noticed. "Why, yes, I do believe you're right, Holmes. A curious emblem of sorts adorns the lapel."

"I recognize that emblem," Holmes declared. "It belongs to the elite Lionsgate Club, one of London's most prestigious and exclusive gentlemen's establishments. Membership is strictly by invitation only, but I may be able to secure our admittance if needs be. We should go there immediately and search out this gentleman."

Prior to their departure from the residence, Dr Watson expressed his gratitude to the maid and presented her with the floral arrangement, asking if she could give it to the Duchess. She dipped into a respectful curtsy and affirmed that she would carry out the request.

She hesitated before turning away, and Holmes sensed she wished to tell them something.

He smiled kindly and asked, "Is there something you wish to say to us?"

"Yes, Mr Holmes," she replied hesitantly. "I hope I'm not speaking out of turn, but the Duchess showed me that unusual portrait, and I recognised the man because I used to work for him a few years ago. I told the Duchess his name, and she said she would let you know his identity when you next called on her. Would you like to know the man's name now? Or should that be something that the Duchess tells you?"

Holmes broke into a wide smile. "My dear girl, it would save us a lot of time and trouble if you could give us his name now. I'm sure the Duchess would appreciate your assistance with our investigation."

The maid gave him a smile of relief. "Thank you, Mr Holmes. His name is Sir Reginald Baxter, and he's usually at his club at this time of the morning."

Holmes and Watson thanked the maid for her invaluable help. They took their leave and hailed a hansom cab to transport them across London to the club's grand headquarters.

Chapter 8

Holmes and Watson arrived at the grand entrance of the Lionsgate Club, an imposing structure that exuded an air of exclusivity and refinement. With a confident stride, Holmes approached the doorman, who regarded them with a scrutinizing gaze.

"Good afternoon, gentlemen," the doorman said, his voice polite yet firm. "May I inquire as to your business here?"

Holmes produced a calling card from his pocket and handed it to the doorman. "Sherlock Holmes and Dr John Watson. We are here to see Sir Reginald Baxter on a matter of some urgency."

The doorman examined the card, his eyebrows raising slightly in recognition. "Ah, Mr Holmes. Please wait here while I inform Sir Reginald of your arrival."

As they waited in the foyer, Watson marvelled at the grandeur of the surroundings. "I say, Holmes, this is quite an impressive establishment. How did you manage to secure our admittance?"

Holmes smiled enigmatically. "Let us just say that I have cultivated certain connections over the years, Watson. Ah, here comes Sir Reginald now. I recognise him from the painting."

A distinguished-looking gentleman approached them, his face a mixture of curiosity and puzzlement. "Mr Holmes, Dr Watson, you wanted to see me?"

Holmes wasted no time in explaining their purpose. "Sir Reginald, we are here on behalf of the Duchess of Rothbury. She recently received a painting from the artist Julian Devaux, depicting a man who bears a striking resemblance to yourself, seated in her library. She was most astonished as she was expecting a portrait of herself."

Sir Reginald's eyes widened in surprise. "How extraordinary! I must confess, I am both puzzled and intrigued by this revelation. As it happens, I also commissioned a painting from Devaux, and only yesterday, I received that portrait, but it was not at all what I expected."

Holmes leaned forward. "Pray tell, Sir Reginald, what did this portrait depict?"

"A young woman, seated in my office chair, wearing a striking red dress. I have never seen her before in my life. I had a lot of explaining to do to my dear wife, I can tell you! There was something strange thing about the label that came with the delivery. It was addressed to, 'Sir Reginald Baxter's Office', which I considered to be rather formal and not in keeping with Devaux's friendly manner."

Holmes exchanged a glance with Watson. "Sir Reginald, might we impose upon you to view this portrait? I believe it may shed some light on the mystery at hand."

Sir Reginald readily agreed. "Of course, gentlemen. My residence is nearby. Please, accompany me, and I shall show you the painting."

A short while later, they arrived at Sir Reginald's impressive home. As they entered the study, Holmes's glance immediately went to the portrait in question. A flicker of recognition crossed his face as he examined the image of the young woman in the red dress.

"Why, that is Miss Clara Simmons, a rising star in London's theatre scene," Holmes declared. "Dr Watson and I had the pleasure of attending one of her performances recently. She is quite talented."

Sir Reginald looked at Holmes in astonishment. "You know this woman, Mr Holmes?"

Holmes nodded. "Indeed, I do. And I believe I may have an inkling as to why Devaux chose to depict her in your portrait."

Holmes proceeded to recount their discoveries about the sketches Devaux had made of other people, and how he'd captured their dream lives. Sir Reginald listened intently, a smile gradually spreading across his face.

"How fascinating," he mused. "I must admit, I had often spoken to Devaux about my desire for a simpler life, one where I could sit in a library with nothing to do but read books. It seems he has taken those conversations to heart and incorporated them into his art, albeit in a painting that was meant for the Duchess of Rothbury. I would quite like to see that portrait, even purchase it if that's possible. I will send the Duchess a message and request a visit."

As they took their leave, Holmes and Watson felt they were one step closer to unravelling the mystery behind the Duchess's painting and the enigmatic artist behind it.

Chapter 9

Holmes and Watson made their way to the theatre where Miss Clara Simmons was currently rehearsing. Upon their arrival, they were greeted by the bustling activity of the stage crew and the distant echoes of performers practising their lines.

After a brief conversation with the stage manager, they were directed to Miss Simmons' dressing room. Holmes rapped gently on the door, and a melodious voice called out, "Come in!"

As they entered, Miss Simmons looked up from her script. "Mr Holmes, Dr Watson! To what do I owe the pleasure of your visit?"

Holmes smiled politely and began to explain the purpose of their visit. "Miss Simmons, we are here on a rather peculiar matter involving the artist Julian Devaux and a series of paintings he has recently completed."

Miss Simmons gave them a confused look. "Devaux? Why, I recently received a painting from him. What a coincidence. But what does that have to do with you, Mr Holmes?"

Watson stepped forward, his voice gentle. "It appears that Devaux has been creating portraits that depict his subjects in rather unexpected settings, often reflecting their innermost desires or aspirations."

Holmes nodded in agreement. "Indeed, and it seems that you, Miss Simmons, have been featured in a painting commissioned by Sir Reginald Baxter, depicting you seated in his office chair."

Clara's eyes widened in surprise, and a bemused smile played upon her lips. "Me? In Sir Reginald's office? How extraordinary! I must admit, I've always dreamed of being a businesswoman and having my own office one day. It was something I discussed with Devaux during our sittings."

Holmes's eyes sparkled with intrigue. "I thought that might be the case, as you have often mentioned that particular aspiration to me. The painting that was delivered to you, Miss Simmons, might we see it?"

Clara nodded eagerly and led them to a corner of her dressing room where a large canvas was propped up against the wall. As Holmes and Watson examined the painting, they saw a woman who was clearly not Clara, relaxing in a dressing room similar to the one they were currently standing in.

"Why, that's Lady Lavinia Ashford!" Watson exclaimed. "The renowned botanist! She works at Kew Gardens."

Clara laughed. "Indeed, it is! I was quite surprised when I first saw it as I was expecting to see myself in the painting. But now, hearing about my appearance in Sir Reginald's painting, it all makes sense. He's been placing his subjects in the life they dream of, rather than the life they are living. And isn't it strange how someone else's normal life can be the subject of another person's dream?"

Holmes smiled. "How astute of you. Miss Simmons, did Devaux share much about himself during your sittings?"

Clara shook her head. "No, he was quite the listener, but he rarely spoke about himself. He seemed more interested in understanding his subjects and their innermost thoughts."

Watson smiled warmly. "It seems Devaux has a gift for not only capturing the likeness of his subjects but the rare gift of really listening to a person."

Clara nodded in agreement. "Indeed, he does. I would love to have that painting of myself in Sir Reginald's office.

It could inspire me to think seriously about my ambitions. I shall contact him and see if he will sell it to me."

Holmes clasped his hands together. "A splendid idea, Miss Simmons. Having met him recently, I am sure he will readily agree. One more question, if I may? Do you still have the label for the painting?"

Clara shook her head. "Sorry, I don't. I've already disposed of it. The wording was ever so peculiar. What was it now? Oh, yes. The words were, 'Miss Simmons' Dressing Room'. But now that you've told me what's happened, it makes sense. I think!"

Holmes smiled as if it was precisely the information he was expecting.

As Holmes and Watson took their leave, they thanked Miss Simmons for her time and assistance, their minds already racing with the possibilities of what they might discover when they met with Lady Lavinia Ashford.

Chapter 10

Holmes and Watson stepped out into the crisp London air, their minds awhirl with the revelations gleaned from their conversation with Miss Simmons. As they navigated the bustling streets, dodging carriages and passers-by, Watson gave voice to the doubts plaguing his thoughts.

"I must confess, Holmes, I harbour a growing unease that we may be embarking on a wild goose chase," he remarked. "If Devaux has delivered a multitude of new paintings in recent weeks, we could find ourselves lost in an extensive search for the Duchess's elusive portrait. The prospect of spending countless days, or even weeks, tracking down each and every one of his commissions is a daunting one indeed!"

Holmes replied, "Worry not, my dear Watson. We shall follow one clue at a time, and the truth will reveal itself in due course. Our task may seem daunting, but with perseverance and a keen eye for detail, I have no doubt that we shall locate the Duchess's missing portrait."

Their next stop was the resplendent Kew Gardens, where they sought out the esteemed Lady Lavinia Ashford. The renowned botanist, known for her extensive knowledge of exotic flora, was overseeing the installation of a new and highly anticipated exhibition when the intrepid duo approached her. After explaining the peculiar situation surrounding the proliferation of Devaux's portraits and the curious case of the Duchess's missing likeness, Lady Ashford smiled knowingly, her eyes gleaming with a hint of intrigue.

"Ah, yes, I too had the pleasure of commissioning Mr Devaux to paint my portrait," Lady Ashford revealed, her eyes twinkling with fond memories. "During our sittings, we engaged in the most delightful conversations about my secret dreams and aspirations. I've always harboured a deep-seated desire to take to the stage, perhaps not as a full-time pursuit, but rather as an occasional indulgence. It was a whimsical fancy I felt compelled to share with him, knowing that he would understand the yearning of an artist's soul."

Holmes, his curiosity thoroughly aroused by Lady Ashford's revelation, leaned forward slightly. "Lady Ashford," he began, his voice low and conspiratorial, "have you, perchance, been the recipient of an unusual portrait yourself? One that might shed light on the mystery at hand?"

The accomplished botanist's eyes sparkled with barely contained mischief, her lips curving into an enigmatic smile. "Indeed, I have, Mr Holmes," she confirmed. "However, I believe it would be most prudent if you and your esteemed colleague, Dr Watson, were to pay a visit to my home later on today, perhaps around six this evening? I'm afraid I cannot, in good conscience, divulge the intriguing details of the painting in such a public setting, lest we attract unwanted attention."

Watson, his curiosity growing by the second, exchanged a meaningful glance with Holmes, silently communicating his intrigue. He said, "Of course, Lady Ashford. We shall most certainly call upon you later, at the appointed hour."

Chapter 11

Sherlock Holmes and Dr John Watson arrived at the stately home of Lady Ashford later that evening. Holmes reached out a slender finger and pressed the bell, which echoed with a sonorous chime inside the grand house. After a brief moment, the large oak door swung open, revealing a stern-faced butler who greeted them with a curt nod and ushered the detective and his companion inside.

As Holmes and Watson followed the butler into the drawing room, a sense of anticipation hung in the air. The room was dimly lit, with the flickering glow of the fireplace casting dancing shadows on the walls. In the centre of the room stood an easel, upon which a portrait was covered by a simple white sheet.

Lady Ashford smiled at Holmes and Watson. "Gentlemen," she began. "Thank you for coming to see me. I must confess that I know the identity of the person in this portrait. However, I hesitated to contact her, considering the nature of the image."

Holmes raised an eyebrow. "Please, do go on, Lady Ashford. We are most intrigued."

Lady Ashford continued, "You see, the sketches for this portrait were done in the small garden of my country cottage about a month ago. It's a rather secluded spot, and I'm afraid I took the liberty of wearing trousers, which, as a lady, I'm not supposed to do. But I often do things that are not expected of me, and quite honestly, I seldom give a hoot about other's opinions. But I must admit, trousers are terribly comfortable and I couldn't resist wearing them for my painting. As the portrait was intended to be hung only in the bedroom of my country home, I instructed Mr Devaux to sketch me in my leisurely attire—the trousers and a comfy shirt."

With a flourish, she removed the sheet, revealing the portrait beneath. Holmes and Watson took in every detail. The painting depicted the Duchess of Rothbury standing beside an apple tree in a charming garden, clad in trousers and a comfortable shirt. The Duchess's expression was one of relaxation and contentment, a stark contrast to her usual societal persona.

"The Duchess of Rothbury!" Watson exclaimed. "I must say, I never imagined her in such garments."

Holmes, however, remained focused on the portrait, his keen eyes studying every brushstroke. "Lady Ashford," he said, turning to face their host, "am I correct in assuming that you and the Duchess are close friends?"

Lady Ashford nodded. "Yes, Mr Holmes, we are. And I fear that she will be quite shocked to see herself portrayed in such a manner. It is not something she would typically allow."

Holmes stepped closer to the portrait, his mind already working through the implications. "Lady Ashford, with your permission, I would like to take this painting with me. I assure you, I will use the utmost tact when explaining the situation to the Duchess."

Lady Ashford hesitated for a moment, then nodded her assent. "Of course, Mr Holmes. I trust your judgment in this matter. Please, do what you think is best."

As Holmes carefully removed the portrait from the easel, Dr Watson turned to Lady Ashford, a question forming on his lips. "Lady Ashford, if I may ask, why did you choose to have your portrait painted in such an unconventional manner and not in a more formal setting such as your lovely home here?"

The lady smiled, a wistful look in her eyes. "Dr Watson, sometimes we all yearn for a bit of freedom from the constraints of society. The garden at my country cottage is my sanctuary, a place where I can be myself without fear of judgement. When Mr Devaux asked to paint my portrait, I saw it as an opportunity to capture a moment of true happiness and comfort. I wonder if he actually did complete that image of me in my garden. I would love to see it. Mr Holmes, would that be something you could look into for me?"

Holmes, having secured the portrait, turned to face Lady Ashford once more. "Of course. If such a painting exists, I will ensure it is delivered to you."

With that, Sherlock Holmes and Dr Watson bid their farewells to Lady Ashford and stepped out into the cool night air, the portrait of the Duchess of Rothbury safely in their possession. As they made their way back to Baker Street, Holmes' mind was already racing, piecing together the clues and forming a plan to unravel the mystery of the misplaced portraits to their client.

Chapter 12

Early the next morning, just as the sun was beginning to peek through the curtains of 221B Baker Street, Holmes sent an urgent message to the Duchess of Rothbury to see if they could call upon her as soon as possible as they had some important information to impart to her. Whilst waiting for her reply, Holmes and Watson enjoyed a breakfast together, sipping their tea and musing over what the Duchess's reaction would be when she laid eyes upon the painting of herself clad in such unusual, and possibly shocking, attire.

A reply arrived within two hours from the Duchess, inviting Holmes and Watson to visit her that very afternoon at her Mayfair residence.

A few hours later, Holmes gathered the painting, safely shrouded by the white sheet, and the two companions set off for the Duchess's home, eager to share their discovery with her.

Upon their arrival, the Duchess greeted them warmly; her smile was genuine though a hint of anxiety played across her fine features as she glanced at the wrapped object in Holmes' possession. She ushered them into her lavish drawing room, offering them a seat and a cup of tea.

"Mr Holmes, Dr Watson, thank you ever so much for coming. I trust you have some news regarding my missing portrait?"

Holmes nodded as he regarded the Duchess with concern. "Indeed, your Grace. We have successfully located your portrait, but I must warn you, it one you are expecting. I'm afraid the circumstances surrounding its appearance and subsequent recovery are rather unusual, to say the least." He placed the covered portrait against the wall.

The Duchess frowned. "Unusual? In what way, Mr Holmes?"

Holmes said, "I have reached the conclusion that during your sittings with Mr Devaux, you may have discussed your dreams of a simpler life, away from the constraints and expectations of society. Am I correct in my assumptions?"

The Duchess averted her gaze. "Well, yes, I suppose I did," she admitted. "One does tend to chat during those long hours of posing, to pass the time and ease the tedium.

But what has that to do with my missing portrait, Mr Holmes?"

Watson cleared his throat. "Your Grace," he began, "it appears that Mr Devaux took those intimate conversations to heart and decided to paint you not as you are, but as you might wish to be."

The Duchess looked from one man to the other. "I don't understand. Please, do explain more."

With a flourish, Holmes removed the sheet, revealing the Duchess in her casual attire, standing amidst the picturesque garden. The vibrant colours of the blooming flowers and the lush greenery seemed to come to life on the canvas, creating a stunning backdrop for the Duchess's unconventional portrait.

The Duchess gasped, her delicate hand flying to her mouth. "Oh, my word!" she exclaimed, her voice trembling. "Is that me? Am I truly wearing trousers in that portrait?"

Holmes nodded sagely, his keen eyes observing the Duchess's reaction. "It appears that Mr Devaux desired to immortalise you in a moment of genuine happiness, one he imagined as a result of your conversations with him."

The Duchess continued to stare at the painting, her expression a complex mix of emotions that seemed to shift and change with each passing second. "I see. But the potential repercussions if this portrait were to be seen by the wrong eyes! The scandal it could ignite would be catastrophic."

Watson's voice was reassuring as he said, "Your Grace, if I may be so bold, the painting was discovered in the safekeeping of your dear friend, Lady Ashford. She had no intention of revealing it to anyone else, and we can assure you that its existence will remain a closely guarded secret."

The Duchess nodded slowly. "That was most kind of her." Her attention was still fixed on the painting. A slow smile began to form on her face. "Mr Devaux painted me as I truly yearned to be, didn't he? Not the Duchess, not the stately society matron, but simply me. The real woman beneath it all. A woman who would love to relax and unwind in a beautiful garden in wonderful solitude."

Holmes nodded slowly, his own gaze studying the painting with a keen appreciation. "It appears so, your Grace. It is a rather striking likeness indeed. Mr Devaux has captured your essence most exquisitely."

A wistful expression spread across the Duchess' elegant features. "I look happy in that painting. Truly, genuinely happy. As if a great weight has been lifted from my soul and I am finally free to be myself once more. I haven't seen myself looking like that in years."

A hush descended upon them as they contemplated the intricacies of the portrait.

The Duchess of Rothbury turned to face Holmes and Watson, her eyes glistening with the sheen of unshed tears. "I cannot begin to express my gratitude, Mr Holmes, Dr Watson. Not merely for your diligence in locating this portrait, but for opening my eyes to the realisation that perhaps it is not such a terrible thing to dream of a different life, even if that life only exists within the brushstrokes of a painting."

Holmes bowed his head respectfully. "It was our distinct pleasure to be of service, your Grace. And if I may offer you a small piece of wisdom? Hold fast to that dream, nurture it deep within your heart. For it is the capacity to dream, to imagine a better world, that makes us fundamentally human, after all."

The Duchess smiled softly. "I shall most definitely take that to heart. Moreover, this portrait has sown the seeds of change within my very soul. Perchance the time has arrived for me to embrace a simpler existence, in some tranquil rural haven. I am moved to embark upon this path forthwith. To seize the day while my courage is strong, as it were." A soft laugh escaped her. "Perhaps I shall even request that my seamstress fashion me a pair of trousers. They have the appearance of being exceedingly comfortable."

Her statement brought forth warm smiles from Holmes and Watson.

The Duchess asked, "I must thank Mr Devant immediately. Have you managed to speak to him? Did you catch him at his studio?"

"Alas, he has made a sudden departure from his place of work," Holmes advised. "But we shall track him down and find out why he decided to create this painting."

The Duchess nodded. "When you do find him, please express my sincere gratitude to him for painting this wonderful image of me."

Holmes assured her they would. He added, "If Mr Devant completed your original commission, would you like us to arrange the delivery of it?"

The Duchess looked back at the painting leaning against the wall. "I would like that, Mr Holmes. Yet, in all honesty, I prefer the one you have brought to me today. I may even find the courage to display it in my hallway, just to see the look on my guests' faces! My goodness, what sort of a woman am I turning into?" Her smile was carefree and lit up her face.

Holmes and Watson smiled at the Duchess, who looked much happier than when they had first met her.

As they departed the residence and strolled down the street, Watson enquired, "If Mr Devant captured you within a canvas, how would you be occupying yourself? What vision would your ideal existence resemble?"

A wistful expression passed fleetingly over Holmes's angular features. "My dear Watson," he began, his rich baritone voice warm with fondness, "I am already living it. A challenging career that engages my mind and tests my abilities. A faithful companion who stands steadfastly by my side through every twist and turn. And the endless mysteries of London waiting at my very doorstep, each one a new puzzle to unravel. In truth, what more could a man possibly ask for? Now, let's continue with our investigation as all the loose ends have not yet been tied up."

Chapter 13

As Holmes and Watson strolled briskly along the street, a young soot-faced boy came running up to them, his worn shoes slapping against the stones.

"Mr Holmes! Dr Watson!" the lad called out excitedly as he caught up with the two gentlemen, a big grin spreading across his grimy face. "My pals down the way, said you were looking for me. Do you need my help with one of those grand investigations of yours? I'm always keen to lend a hand, I am!"

Holmes smiled warmly at the eager young lad. "Billy, my boy, you're just the person we were hoping to see. Indeed, we have a gift for you, a token of appreciation for your invaluable assistance in our investigations. But first, let us retire to the comfort of our humble abode on Baker Street, where we can discuss matters further."

Billy's eyes widened with a mix of excitement and trepidation. "But Mr Holmes, sir, I'm not fit to be seen in a fine house like yours. I'm covered in soot from head to toe, I am!"

Holmes chuckled. "Nonsense, Billy. A little soot never hurt anyone. In fact, I daresay it adds to your charm. Now, come along, and we'll explain everything in no time."

The trio made their way to 221B Baker Street, with Billy chattering excitedly about the possibilities of his mysterious gift.

Upon entering the house, Holmes called out to their landlady. "Mrs Hudson, would you be so kind as to provide young Billy here with a sheet to sit upon? We wouldn't want to soil your lovely sofa."

Mrs Hudson appeared, a warm smile gracing her features. "Of course, Mr Holmes. I'll fetch one right away. And perhaps a spot of tea and biscuits for our young guest?"

"Capital idea, Mrs Hudson," Holmes replied, as Billy grinned from ear to ear.

Once Billy was settled on the sofa, a sheet beneath him and a cup of tea on the table in front, Holmes retrieved the sketch from his desk. "Billy, my lad, Dr Watson and I came across this at an exhibition featuring the works of one Julian Devaux. We thought you might like to have it."

He handed the sketch to Billy, whose eyes grew wide with wonder as he took in the image of himself, surrounded by the tools of a magician. "Blimey, Mr Holmes! That's me, that is! But I'm dressed like a proper magician, with all them fancy props and whatnot. How did this happen?"

Holmes smiled knowingly. "It seems, Billy, that Mr Devaux has a keen eye for the aspirations of others. He asked about your dreams, did he not?"

Billy nodded, still transfixed by the sketch. "He did, sir. We often chatted when I met him on the streets. I told him how I'd love to be a magician, performing on stage and making people smile. But I never thought he'd go and draw me like this!"

"Well, Billy," Holmes said, "perhaps this is a sign that you should pursue your dream. I'll put in a good word for you at the local theatre. Every great magician needs to start somewhere, and an assistant's role could be just the ticket."

Billy's face lit up with joy. "You'd do that for me, Mr Holmes? Oh, thank you, sir! Thank you!"

Dr Watson, who had been observing the exchange with a fond smile, spoke up. "Billy, did Mr Devaux happen to mention anything about his own dreams or aspirations?"

Billy thought for a moment, then nodded. "He did, Dr Watson. He spoke of a cottage in Cornwall, where he hoped to retire someday. Said he'd paint pictures of the sea, just for his own pleasure. But he reckoned he might never get there, being so busy with work and all."

Holmes and Watson exchanged a meaningful glance. "Cornwall, you say?" Holmes mused. "Did he mention a specific location, by any chance?"

Billy shook his head. "No, sir. Just that it was in Cornwall and he looked right happy when he talked about it. I hope he gets to go there someday."

Holmes leaned back in his chair, steepling his fingers beneath his chin. "A cottage in Cornwall, a dream of painting the sea. Intriguing. It seems our Mr Devaux is a man of many layers, Watson."

Watson nodded in agreement. "Indeed, Holmes. And perhaps this information could help us solve the final parts of this mystery."

Chapter 14

Billy lingered a while longer with Holmes and Watson, eagerly discussing his aspirations of becoming a magician and how he planned to make that dream a reality. With a twinkle in his eye, he vowed that once he had achieved fame and success, he would always ensure that they had complimentary tickets to his performances. His infectious enthusiasm soon had Holmes and Watson chuckling along with him, caught up in his excitement.

Before long, however, it was time for Billy to take his leave. Mrs Hudson, ever the thoughtful hostess, kindly provided Billy with a sheet to carefully wrap up the painting for safe transport. She also pressed a wrapped packet of biscuits into his hands, insisting that she had baked far too many and that Billy would be doing her a great favour by taking them off her hands. Billy expressed his gratitude, his eyes shining with pure delight at her generosity.

A few minutes later, as Holmes and Watson settled into their chairs, a nervous-looking man was shown into the room by Mrs Hudson. He introduced himself as Albert, Julian Devaux's long-time assistant, and explained that he had heard they were looking for Mr Devaux and he assumed it was due to the recent delivery of some unusual paintings. With an agitated air and a slight tremble in his voice, he confessed that the unfortunate mix-up of the portraits was entirely his doing, and he was deeply remorseful for the trouble it had caused.

"You see, Mr Holmes," Albert began, wringing his hands anxiously, "Mr Bartholomew Grange's relentlessly harsh words and scathing critiques had finally gotten to Mr Devaux. In a rare moment of daring, he decided to paint two portraits for each of his paying clients—the expected formal one and a second, more intimate piece capturing their secret dream life. He intended to keep the latter hidden away in his studio, hoping to one day discreetly approach his clients and offer them the additional portrait as a surprise gift."

Holmes kept his keen eyes fixed on Albert. "And what happened then, Albert?"

"I'm afraid I delivered the wrong portraits, Mr Holmes," Albert admitted, his voice trembling with remorse. "In my haste to distribute the paintings, I didn't read the labels properly and I mixed up the formal portraits with the intimate ones, delivering the wrong ones to the unsuspecting clients. When Mr Devaux realised the dreadful mistake, he was overcome with panic and decided to leave London. He said that everyone would blame him for the embarrassing mix-ups and not me. He sent me a telegram a few hours ago from a cottage in Cornwall, saying he has decided to stay there indefinitely and enjoy a simpler life, far away from the chaos and potential scandal he left behind in the city."

Albert looked so utterly distraught that Holmes felt compelled to offer some words of comfort. He said, "Albert, it seems your mistake may have inadvertently led to a positive change in the lives of the people who commissioned those paintings. So, in hindsight, your mistake has turned into an interesting form of fate, guiding them towards the lives they always yearned for but never dared pursue."

The relief was visible upon Albert's face. "Really? You think everything has turned out for the best?"

Holmes nodded. "I do. Albert. How many unusual paintings did Mr Devant create?"

Albert replied, "There were four. He was going to do more but, well, because of my error, he's left London."

Holmes said, "You'll be relieved to know that we have seen all four of those paintings and spoken to the recipients. Everything is in order, and really, you have no need to be concerned. May I ask, do you still have the keys to Mr Devant's studio?"

"I do," Albert replied.

"Would you be kind enough to deliver the portraits that were commissioned by Mr Devant's clients? The expected ones, that is, for now. I know Lady Ashford is keen to receive hers."

"Of course, Mr Holmes. I'll go to the studio straight away. Is there anything else I can do? I feel so guilty about what happened. Poor Mr Devant has had to leave London." Albert shook his head in dismay.

"Ah," Holmes said. "I do believe that is a blessing in disguise. We have it on good authority that Mr Devant had dreams of retiring to Cornwall, and through this unfortunate, or should I say, fortunate, series of events, he has now achieved his dream."

"I suppose he has," Albert said, a smile appearing on his face. "Shall I let him know that everything has turned out alright, Mr Holmes? I've got his address in Cornwall from that telegram."

"No need," Holmes replied. "I will contact him. He will be given the full details of our investigation, and if he so wishes, he could return to London knowing his reputation is still intact. But I rather suspect he will stay in Cornwall."

"I think so, too," Albert replied. "I'll miss him. I might go and visit him in Cornwall. Maybe I'll move there as well. I've never seen the sea or been on a beach."

Watson said, "You must go, Albert. You'll love it."

Albert grinned. "I will go! But I'll deliver those other portraits before I dash off to the seaside." He gave his heartfelt thanks to Holmes and Watson for their help, and left the room looking much more cheerful than when he'd arrived.

"Well! What do you think about this case?" Watson asked, a bemused expression on his face.

Holmes replied, "It has been a case that ended with how it began, in a manner of speaking. I believe that by painting images of others living their dream lives, Julian Devant has inadvertently achieved his own dream life. I will send him a brief telegram today to put his mind at rest and let him know his clients are happy with their unexpected portraits. Watson, would you be so kind as to write a detailed letter to him about our investigation? Your way with words far surpasses my own."

Watson nodded. "Of course. I shall pen the letter and explain the peculiar portrait situation to Mr Devaux."

As Watson began to write, Holmes leaned back in his chair. "It's quite remarkable, Watson, how a simple act of artistic rebellion has led to such an intriguing series of events. The power of dreams and the desire for a different life can be a potent force indeed."

Watson glanced up from his writing, a twinkle in his eye. "And to think, Holmes, all of this began with a portrait of a strange man in the Duchess of Rothbury's library!"

Holmes chuckled, his laughter echoing through the cosy confines of 221B Baker Street. "Indeed, Watson. The Duchess's portrait has certainly provided us with a most unusual case."

As Watson continued to write, Holmes allowed his mind to wander, reflecting on the curious nature of the human spirit and the lengths to which people would go to pursue their dreams. It was cases like these, he mused, that made his chosen profession all the more fascinating. He was eager for more mystifying cases to come their way.

Book 2 - Sherlock Holmes and The Haunted Museum

Chapter 1

Sherlock Holmes gazed pensively out of the window of his Baker Street lodgings, his keen, grey eyes surveying the bustling London street below. His brilliant mind, ever active and hungry for stimulation, pondered the next perplexing case that would inevitably find its way to his doorstep. Dr Watson, his stalwart companion and chronicler of their many adventures together, sat in his customary armchair by the crackling fire, the morning paper spread across his lap as he perused the day's news with a thoughtful expression.

"I say, Holmes," Watson remarked. "Listen to this peculiar headline: 'Ghostly Activities at Waxworks Museum.' Apparently, there have been numerous reports of strange and inexplicable occurrences at that museum of wax figures not far from here. You know the one; it opened about a year ago, I think."

"I know the one," Holmes replied without turning around. "Although, I haven't visited the place as yet. Perhaps I'll get around to it soon."

Watson said, "Would you like me to read this article out loud? About the strange occurrences that are happening? Some visitors claim the museum is haunted."

Holmes held up his hand. "You can stop there, Watson. I have no interest in such sensational claims. There is always a rational explanation for such so-called hauntings and supernatural activities. We have proved this many times using the power of logic and deduction."

Watson chuckled, folding the paper neatly and setting it aside on the side table. "Right, you are, Holmes. I'll read it later. No doubt the famous medium, Madam Rosalind, will make a grand appearance at the museum to commune with the alleged spirits that haunt its rooms. Doesn't she always appear at such times as these?"

At the mere mention of the medium's name, Holmes's face darkened. "She does, and with more regularity than I care for. Whenever there are claims of ghostly goings-on, Madam Rosalind is never far behind, offering her services. I would be quite content to never cross paths with that infernal woman again. Her constant attempts to offer her so-called psychic services whenever we take on a new case are most unwelcome and distracting. She has a calculating look in her eyes. One I've seen in hardened criminals. There's something untrustworthy about that woman."

With a smile, Watson said, "There will be no more talk of Madam Rosalind and her calculating eyes."

Holmes continued to gaze out of the window. His eyes narrowed as he studied the passersby. "I wonder when our next case will present itself. It feels like an eternity since we last had a mystery to unravel."

Watson replied, "It's only been a week since we concluded the affair of the missing crown. Surely you can't be growing restless already?"

"Ah, but you know me," Holmes replied. "My mind rebels at stagnation. Give me problems, give me work, give me the most puzzling mystery possible, I am in my proper atmosphere. But this inactivity is something I cannot abide."

Rising from his armchair, Watson joined his friend at the window, his eyes following Holmes's gaze to the bustling street below. "Perhaps there are new mysteries to be found right here, amongst the ordinary lives of London's citizens."

Holmes's eyes sparkled with interest. "Indeed, Watson. Take, for example, that young woman hurrying along with a bundle clutched tightly to her chest. What secrets might she be carrying?"

Watson studied the woman in question, taking note of her furtive looks and how she seemed to shrink away from the other pedestrians. "Perhaps she's fleeing from an unhappy marriage, or maybe she's stolen something valuable and fears being caught."

"Very possible," Holmes said, his attention already shifting to another figure on the street. "And what about that elderly gentleman, walking with a pronounced limp and a faraway look in his eyes?"

"A war veteran, I'd wager," Watson replied, his own military background allowing him to recognise the tell tale signs. "Haunted by the memories of battles long past, and perhaps nursing a wound that never fully healed."

Holmes nodded, a hint of admiration in his voice. "Your medical expertise serves you well, my dear friend."

As they continued to observe the passersby, Holmes's keen eyes alighted upon a young man who seemed to be in a great hurry, his face pale and his hands trembling. "Now, Watson, what do you make of that fellow?"

Watson furrowed his brow, studying the man intently. "He appears to be in a state of great agitation, Holmes.

Perhaps he's just received some terrible news, or maybe he's fleeing from some sort of trouble."

"Ah, but look closer, Watson," Holmes urged. "Notice the ink stains on his fingers, the slight bulge in his coat pocket that suggests a small notebook, and the way he glances left and right, as if searching for someone or something."

"A journalist, then?" Watson ventured, beginning to see the clues that Holmes had so easily discerned.

"Precisely, Watson. And not just any journalist, but one who has stumbled upon a story of great importance. The question is, what could have made him so unsettled?"

His tone deliberately solemn, Watson suggested, "Is it possible there's been a development in that perplexing haunting at the museum? Maybe our dear acquaintance, Madam Rosalind, is due to pay a visit there at any moment and despatch any impish phantoms. And our young journalist out there doesn't want to miss a second of this latest development."

Holmes let out a loud laugh that startled Watson. "You could very well be correct! I've half a mind to run after that fellow and see where he is going."

"Even if it leads to Madam Rosalind?" Watson jested.

"Ah, you have a point. We'll leave the fellow alone." He looked left and right. "Now, who else do we spy out there?"

As they continued to observe the street below, a particular figure caught Holmes' eye. A man, dressed in a fashionable hat and an expensive-looking overcoat, was pacing back and forth in front of their building, his movements erratic and hesitant.

"Watson," Holmes said, "do you see that man down there? The one in the hat and overcoat?"

Watson leaned closer to the window, squinting to get a better look. "Yes, I see him. He seems rather agitated, doesn't he?"

"He does," Holmes agreed, his attention never leaving the man. "His behaviour is most peculiar. It's as if he's wrestling with some internal dilemma, unsure of whether to approach our door or not."

They watched as the man took a few determined steps towards the entrance of 221B Baker Street, only to abruptly turn away at the last moment. He walked a short distance, then paused, his shoulders slumping as if in defeat.

"He's changed his mind," Watson observed. "But why? What could be troubling him so?"

Holmes replied, "I suspect we may have a potential client on our hands. A man who is grappling with a problem so perplexing, so overwhelming, that he fears to even seek our assistance. Notice the way he keeps glancing at our windows, the tension in his shoulders. There is something troubling him. Something he needs to share with another person."

As if on cue, the man turned around once more, his steps now filled with a newfound determination as he approached the door of 221B Baker Street. Holmes and Watson watched as he raised his hand, hesitating for the briefest of moments before finally knocking.

The sound echoed through the house, a sharp and insistent rap that seemed to hang in the air. Moments later, the door was opened and Mrs Hudson's muffled voice could be heard as she greeted the visitor.

"Well, Watson," Holmes said, a glint of excitement in his eyes, "it appears our lull in activity is about to come to an end. Shall we see what mystery this gentleman brings to our doorstep?"

Holmes dashed to his chair, urging Watson to do the same, insisting they must be seated before their guest's arrival, lest he suspect they had been peering at him through the window.

Watson looked as if he might say that they had been doing exactly that, but thought better of it and instead hurried to his own chair, swiftly arranging himself in a posture of studied indifference.

They waited as Mrs Hudson's footsteps grew louder, accompanied by the heavier tread of their mysterious visitor. The door to their sitting room opened.

Chapter 2

Mrs Hudson entered the sitting room, followed closely by the visitor. "Gentlemen," she said, "this is Mr Alfred Chamberlain. He's here to see you about a matter of some urgency."

The man took off his hat and overcoat and gave them to Mrs Hudson, who already had her hands extended towards him.

Holmes rose from his chair, extending his hand in greeting. "Mr Chamberlain, welcome. I am Sherlock Holmes, and this is my colleague, Dr John Watson. Please, come in and have a seat."

Mr Chamberlain was a portly man in his late fifties. He had bushy eyebrows and a jovial face, and was dressed in a tailored suit that strained slightly at the buttons. His handshake was firm. "Pleased to meet you, both of you."

Mrs Hudson turned to Holmes. "Shall I bring up some refreshments, Mr Holmes?"

"Yes, thank you, Mrs Hudson. That would be most appreciated," Holmes replied with a nod.

Mrs Hudson left the room, closing the door behind her. Chamberlain was invited to take a seat. A light sheen of perspiration lay upon his brow.

"Now, Mr Chamberlain," Holmes began, settling back into his own chair, "what brings you to our doorstep today? I can see that you are troubled by something."

Chamberlain cleared his throat, his glance darting between Holmes and Watson. "Well, Mr Holmes, it's a bit of a delicate matter. I'm not quite sure how to begin."

Holmes said, "Mr Chamberlain, I assure you that no problem is ever too delicate for our assistance. Please, feel free to speak freely."

Chamberlain nodded, taking a deep breath. "You see, gentlemen, I am the proprietor of a waxworks museum. It opened over a year ago, and we've been doing quite well. That is, until recently."

Watson, who had been listening intently, suddenly sat up straighter. "I say, Mr Chamberlain, your museum wouldn't happen to be the one mentioned in this morning's paper, would it? The one with the alleged ghostly activity?"

He held up the newspaper, the headline clearly visible. Chamberlain's face reddened, and he shifted uncomfortably in his seat.

"Yes, Dr Watson, I'm afraid that is indeed my establishment. I don't know how the press got news of it. But I must stress that I do not believe in the supernatural whatsoever. There must be a logical explanation for the strange occurrences."

Holmes' eyes lit up with interest. "Ah, I am glad to hear that your views on the supernatural match my own. I'm eager to learn more of these strange occurrences you speak of. Please, Mr Chamberlain, do go on."

Chamberlain settled back in his chair. "It started recently. Small things at first. Objects moving on their own, strange noises suddenly filling the air, ghostly figures moving through the corridors. But then it escalated."

"I see," Holmes said. "Please, continue."

Chamberlain paused, as if steeling himself for what he was about to say next. "One of our most popular exhibits, a wax figure of William Shakespeare, had disappeared, leaving only his quill behind. He turned up later, standing next to Captain Blackbeard. The two figures had been turned towards each other as if in cahoots. You should have heard the complaints we received about that, especially from a local historian who had decided to visit us that day. And then, just two days later, a figure of Jack the Ripper vanished entirely from its usual position, only to reappear in a different part of the museum which was created for our younger visitors. Some of the smallest children erupted into tears when they saw the menacing look on Jack's face. Oh! The complaints I received from furious parents that day!"

Watson's eyes widened. "Good heavens!"

Holmes, however, remained impassive. "Forgive me for asking, Mr Chamberlain, but are these merely pranks or publicity stunts? I'm not saying they were committed by you, but maybe someone you employ?"

Chamberlain shook his head vehemently. "The people I employ would never stoop to such a thing. I trust them implicitly, no doubt about that. What troubles me, is how the newspapers have labelled this as ghostly activity. That isn't good for my business and visitor numbers are already falling. I know there must be a reasonable explanation behind these strange events, but I'm at a loss to think what that could be."

At that moment, Mrs Hudson returned with a tray of tea and biscuits. She set it down on the table, casting a curious glance at Chamberlain before leaving the room once more.

As Holmes poured the tea, he said, "Mr Chamberlain, I am pleased to hear that you seek a logical explanation for the strange occurrences at your museum. From the details I have so far, I suspect a human hand is behind these, and not that of a spectral nature."

He handed a cup to Chamberlain, who accepted it with a grateful nod. "Thank you, Mr Holmes. I knew coming to you was the right decision, even though it took some courage to knock on your door, considering the nature of my problem. I was so embarrassed at the prospect of asking you to look into my supposed haunted museum. Will you help me get to the bottom of this mystery?"

Holmes smiled. "My dear Mr Chamberlain, nothing would give me greater pleasure. Dr Watson and I will be happy to lend our assistance."

Watson, who had been helping himself to a biscuit, looked up in surprise. "We will?"

Holmes shot him a smile. "Of course we will, Watson. A case like this, where we get to debunk supernatural rumours, is just the sort of challenge I relish." He turned back to Chamberlain. "Now, Mr Chamberlain, please tell us everything you know about these activities. Leave out no detail, no matter how insignificant it may seem."

Chamberlain, looking visibly relieved, began to recount his tale in earnest. "It all started about three weeks ago," he said. "A young lady, quite distressed, came rushing to me, claiming that one of the waxworks in an exhibit room had moved."

Holmes said, "Moved, you say? In what manner?"

"She said it had shifted slightly to the left, right before her eyes. The poor girl was convinced it had come to life. She let out a scream that echoed through the entire museum. She ran out of the exhibit room in a state of sheer terror. It was that scream that made me run towards her. She looked as if she was about to faint."

Watson's eyebrows rose in surprise. "That must have been quite a shock for her."

Chamberlain nodded, his expression grim. "At the time, I tried to reassure her, suggesting that perhaps a sudden, strong gust of wind had caused the movement. After all, these things do happen in old buildings like ours."

Holmes, however, seemed unconvinced. "A gust of wind? Was the waxwork figure in an enclosed exhibit room or near a doorway?"

Chamberlain shifted uncomfortably in his seat. "It was in an enclosed room, and, well, it was the only explanation I could think of at the moment. I didn't want to alarm the young lady further."

"Understandable," Holmes said, his tone neutral. "Please, do go on."

"I thought nothing more of it," Chamberlain continued, "until I started receiving other complaints. More visitors claimed to have seen the waxworks moving, and then there were the sounds..."

"Sounds?" Watson asked.

"Yes, Dr Watson. Eerie noises, coming from all directions. Whispers, creaks, and even the occasional moan. It was as if the museum itself had come alive."

Holmes asked, "And when did these sounds begin?"

"A few days after the first incident with the young lady," Chamberlain replied. "It wasn't long before rumours started circulating that the museum was haunted. Visitor numbers began to fall, and then the newspaper got wind of the story and those rumours have increased tenfold."

"I can well imagine," Holmes said in understanding.

Chamberlain continued, "Mr Holmes, if these rumours persist, I fear my museum will be forced to close its doors. I simply cannot afford to lose any more business."

Holmes nodded, his expression one of deep thought. "I understand your concerns, Mr Chamberlain. Now, do you have any suspects in mind? Someone who would like to see the closing of your museum?"

Chamberlain looked up, his eyes wide. "Yes, Mr Holmes. There is someone who I believe would like to see my museum fail and take great joy in it."

"And who might that be?" Holmes asked.

Chamberlain said, "Marcus Bramwell. He's my ex-business partner. I'm almost certain he's the one behind this."

"What makes you suspect him?" Holmes asked.

Chamberlain sighed. "We had a falling out three years ago over a financial matter. I'd rather not go into the details, but suffice it to say, it was a messy affair. Bramwell has been out for revenge ever since."

Watson frowned. "Revenge is a powerful motive. Has he made any direct threats?"

"Not directly, no," Chamberlain admitted. "But I wouldn't put it past him to employ people to sabotage the museum on his behalf. He's a cunning man, and he knows how to cover his tracks."

Holmes nodded. "Interesting. And where might we find this Marcus Bramwell?"

Chamberlain said, "He's set up a rival tourist attraction, Bramwell's Hall of Scientific Marvels. It's probably receiving all the tourists who no longer visit the waxworks museum."

Holmes said, "Bramwell's Hall of Scientific Marvels? I've heard of it. It's been gaining quite a reputation of late."

"Yes, it has," Chamberlain said, his tone bitter. "While my museum struggles, his thrives. It's as if he's stealing my customers right from under my nose."

Watson looked at Holmes. "What do you think, Holmes? Could Bramwell be behind these disturbances?"

Holmes tapped his chin, deep in thought. "It's certainly a possibility, Watson. A man with a grudge and a rival business. It's a classic motive. Mr Chamberlain, Dr Watson and I will pay a visit to your ex-business partner and see what he has to say for himself. After that, I would like to visit your museum, to examine the scene of these disturbances firsthand."

Chamberlain nodded eagerly. "Of course, Mr Holmes. I'll give you a personal tour. When would be convenient for you?"

Holmes glanced at the clock on the mantelpiece. "Shall we say, three o'clock this afternoon? That should give us ample time to speak with Mr Bramwell and then make our way to your establishment."

"Three o'clock it is," Chamberlain agreed, rising from his seat. "Thank you, Mr Holmes, Dr Watson. I can't tell you how much I appreciate your help."

Holmes also stood, shaking Chamberlain's hand. "We'll do our best to get to the bottom of this mystery, Mr Chamberlain. You have my word."

With that, Chamberlain took his leave, the relief on his face palpable. As the door closed behind him, Watson turned to Holmes.

"Well, Holmes, what do you make of it all?" he asked.

Holmes picked up his pipe, turning it over in his hands. "It's a curious case, Watson. There is much to unravel here, one of them the intriguing matter of the financial dispute between the two businessmen. I would like to find out what happened there. It could be related to what's occurring at the museum now. Let's speak with Marcus Bramwell and see what he has to say."

Watson nodded, reaching for his hat and coat. "Then let's be off, Holmes. The game, as they say, is afoot."

Holmes laughed. "Indeed, it is, Watson. Indeed, it is."

Chapter 3

Holmes and Watson hailed a hansom cab and made their way to Bramwell's Hall of Scientific Marvels. As they approached the building, they couldn't help but be impressed by its modern design. The clean lines and large, plate-glass windows stood in stark contrast to the gothic architecture of the surrounding buildings. Electric lights framed the entrance, beckoning visitors to come and witness the marvels of technology within.

After paying for their tickets, they entered the impressive building and found themselves in a sleek and utilitarian interior, designed to showcase the exhibits rather than the architecture itself. The main hall was filled with interactive displays and machines, each demonstrating the latest technological advancements of the era. A working model of a steam engine caught Watson's eye, while Holmes was drawn to the early electrical devices on display.

It was clear that Bramwell's attraction appealed to the public's fascination with science and innovation, offering a glimpse into the future that was both exciting and awe-inspiring.

As they were examining a particularly intricate display, a tall and distinguished figure approached them. With his neatly trimmed beard and penetrating blue eyes, the man exuded confidence and intelligence. His salt and pepper hair lent him an air of distinguished maturity, while his impeccably tailored dark suit spoke of his success and status.

"Ah, Mr Sherlock Holmes and Dr John Watson, I presume?" the man said, his voice smooth and charming. "I am Marcus Bramwell. I saw you through the window of my office and recognised you immediately from photographs that have appeared in the newspapers. May I ask, is your visit one of pleasure or of business?"

Holmes said, "Our visit is of a business nature, Mr Bramwell. We were hoping to have a word with you regarding a matter of some importance."

Bramwell smiled, but there was a coldness behind it. "Of course, gentlemen. Please, follow me to my office, where we can speak more privately."

As they followed Bramwell to his office, Holmes noticed the approving looks the man received from several women they passed. It was clear that Bramwell's charm and enigmatic nature made him a favourite among the fairer sex.

Once they were seated in Bramwell's office, the man leaned back in his chair. "So, gentlemen, what brings you to my humble establishment?"

Holmes explained, "We're here on behalf of Mr Alfred Chamberlain, the owner of the waxwork museum across town."

Bramwell's smile tightened almost imperceptibly. "Ah, yes. Poor Alfred. I heard he's been having some trouble lately."

Holmes continued, "He believes that someone may be deliberately sabotaging his business. As a result, his visitor numbers have dwindled."

Bramwell raised an eyebrow. "And he thinks the person responsible for the sabotage is me?"

Holmes didn't answer immediately, instead studying Bramwell's reaction. After a moment, he said, "He mentioned that you two had a falling out some years ago."

Bramwell waved a hand dismissively. "A minor disagreement, nothing more. Certainly nothing that would drive me to sabotage his business."

Watson spoke, his tone curious. "Mr Bramwell, is it possible that your establishment has benefited from the misfortunes of Mr Chamberlain's museum?"

Bramwell's eyes flashed, but his voice remained calm. "Dr Watson, success in business is often a matter of seizing opportunities when they arise. If Alfred's misfortune has driven more customers to my doors, well, that's simply the nature of competition. Was there anything else? I've got a busy day ahead of me."

Holmes said, "Mr Bramwell, would you like to know the specific acts of sabotage that have taken place at Mr Chamberlain's establishment? Aren't you the least bit curious?"

Bramwell retrieved a folded newspaper from the side of his desk, a knowing smile on his face. "I'm already aware of what's happened, at least according to the press." He tapped the newspaper with his finger.

"And what do you make of the gossip that the troubles are of a supernatural nature?" Holmes asked.

Bramwell scoffed, his eyes narrowing. "Not likely. I don't believe in any of that nonsense."

Watson asked, "Do you have any theories about what might be behind these incidents, Mr Bramwell?"

Bramwell answered, "It could be an insider job."

Holmes raised an eyebrow. "Mr Chamberlain assured us that his staff are loyal."

A cold smile spread across Bramwell's face. "That isn't the case with some of them. I suggest you talk to the staff more closely, especially one of the sculptors who has been overheard in a public house complaining about how he's been treated by Mr Chamberlain."

"And do you have a name for this disgruntled sculptor?" Holmes asked.

Bramwell shrugged. "I've no idea. Isn't it your job to find that out, Mr Holmes? You are a detective, after all."

Holmes stood, buttoning his jacket, not appreciating the mockery in Bramwell's voice. "Thank you for your time and the information you've provided. It has been most enlightening."

Watson stood as well, nodding to Bramwell. "Yes, thank you, Mr Bramwell."

As they left Bramwell's office and walked away, Holmes turned to Watson, his brow furrowed in thought. "I believe there's more to this than meets the eye. Bramwell's demeanour and his readiness to point the finger at Chamberlain's staff raises some interesting questions."

Watson nodded. "You think he might have ulterior motives?"

"It's a possibility we can't ignore," Holmes said, his pace quickening as they exited the Hall of Scientific Marvels. "We need to speak with Chamberlain's staff, particularly this sculptor Bramwell mentioned. But we must also keep an open mind. There could be other factors at play here."

They hailed a cab and asked the driver to take them to Mr Chamberlain's Waxwork Museum. As they settled in their seats, Holmes' mind was already filling with questions and theories. He was determined to solve the mystery as soon as possible.

Chapter 4

A short while later, Holmes and Watson approached the imposing façade of Chamberlain's Waxwork Museum. Holmes sensed there was an air of unease hanging over the building. A small queue had formed at the entrance, and as they took their place in line, snippets of worried conversation reached their ears.

"I heard it's haunted," whispered a young woman to her companion. "People say there are restless spirits roaming around the displays. And there are strange sounds like the dead calling out for help."

Her friend nodded, glancing nervously at the museum's darkened windows. "They say the wax figures come to life at night and walk around. I hope they don't come to life when we're inside. I can't be doing with anything spooky. If we see anything like that, I'll leave and I won't be coming back, I can tell you."

Holmes and Watson exchanged a knowing look but didn't say anything.

They soon reached the ticket booth.

Holmes stepped forward, offering the woman behind the counter a charming smile. "Good morning, madam," he greeted, his tone warm and friendly. "We would love to visit this fine establishment, but I have to say, I overheard some rather intriguing rumours about this place whilst waiting in line. Is it true the museum is haunted?"

The woman's face, already lined with worry, seemed to fall even further at Holmes' question. She shook her head, her voice strained as she replied, "No, sir, it isn't. I've been told to inform any patrons that if they have complaints about their visit, they should direct them to Mr Chamberlain himself."

Holmes studied her for a moment, taking in the dark circles under her eyes and the tension in her shoulders. "It must be quite a burden," he said gently, "having to deal with these rumours day in and day out."

The woman's eyes widened in surprise, and for a moment, her guard seemed to drop. "It is," she admitted in a low voice. "Jobs are hard to come by these days, and I can't afford to lose this one. But with all this talk of ghosts and hauntings..." She trailed off, shaking her head.

Watson stepped forward, his kind eyes filled with sympathy. "Rest assured, we're not here to cause any trouble. We simply wish to enjoy the marvels of the museum."

The woman managed a weak smile, clearly appreciating Watson's reassurance. She handed them their tickets. "I hope you enjoy your visit, gentlemen," she said, her voice a little stronger now. "And please, if you do experience anything unusual, let Mr Chamberlain know."

Holmes and Watson thanked her, then turned to enter the museum proper. As Holmes and Watson ventured deeper into the museum, the atmosphere seemed to shift. The grand foyer, with its chequered marble floor and crystal chandelier, gave way to dimly lit corridors lined with velvet ropes and dark wood panelling. The air grew thick with the scent of dust and the faint, persistent odour of chemicals used in the preservation of the wax figures.

The exhibits themselves were a testament to the skill and artistry of their creators. Each scene was meticulously crafted, the wax figures so lifelike that one almost expected them to breathe. In one alcove, King John sat hunched over the Magna Carta, his barons gathered around him in a tableau of historic significance. The figures' faces were painted with such detail that every wrinkle, every line of worry or contemplation, was visible.

As they walked on, Holmes and Watson overheard the hushed conversations of the other visitors. A group of older women huddled together, their glances darting left and right.

"Did you hear about the ghost of an old king?" one of them asked. "They say he moves the figures around at night, rearranging the scenes."

Her friend nodded. "I had heard that. And I'd heard about the strange sounds, too. The moans and whispers. It's like the figures are trying to communicate with us."

Holmes and Watson carried on, passing a display of famous authors. Charles Dickens sat at his desk, pen in hand, his face a mask of concentration. Next to him, a glass case contained a first edition of "A Christmas Carol," open to the page where Marley's ghost first appears to Scrooge.

As they turned a corner, they nearly collided with a man who was hurrying towards the exit, his face pale and his hands shaking.

"Excuse me," Watson said, steadying the man. "Are you all right?"

The man shook his head, his eyes wide with fear. "No," he said, his voice hoarse. "No, I'm not. I saw...I saw something. In the special exhibits room."

Holmes stepped forward. "What did you see, exactly?"

The man swallowed hard, glancing back over his shoulder as if he expected to be followed. "It was in the Egyptian area," he said. "The Sphinx. I swear, I saw it move. And its face changed! Right in front of me. It looked right at me. And then, it smiled. A chilling smile, like it was mocking me."

With that, the man pulled away from Watson's grasp and hurried off, leaving the two investigators standing in the corridor.

"Increasingly intriguing," Holmes mused. "It does make one ponder whether the chap actually witnessed something, or if his imagination, fuelled by the rumours that are widespread in this place, created the alarming visions of its own accord."

They made their way to the special exhibits room, which was currently hosting a display on the wonders of the ancient world. The centrepiece was a scale model of a Sphinx set against a background of scaled-down pyramids, all set on a layer of golden sand. Holmes and Watson approached it, examining it closely.

"I see no signs of movement," Watson said, peering at the model. "And the face looks like those I've seen on such structures before. I can't see anything out of the ordinary here."

Holmes nodded, but his eyes were still scanning the room, taking in every detail. "Perhaps not," he said. "But there's something off about this room. Something is not quite right."

Before Watson could ask him to elaborate, a scream rang out from somewhere deep within the museum. The sound was high and shrill, filled with terror. Around them, visitors began to murmur and shift uneasily.

"Stay here," Holmes told Watson, his voice low and urgent. "Keep an eye on this room. I'm going to investigate."

With that, the Holmes slipped away, disappearing into the shadows of the corridor. Watson watched him go, then turned back to the model of the Sphinx, a frown creasing his brow.

Chapter 5

Holmes followed the echoes of the scream, his footsteps swift and purposeful against the polished wood floor. The sound led him to an exhibit area where the waxworks of kings and queens stood in regal poses, their faces frozen in expressions of power and authority. Among them, the imposing figure of Henry the Eighth loomed, his broad frame and stern countenance dominating the scene.

At the foot of the display, a pale-faced woman sat on a chair, her hands trembling as her friend wafted a bottle of smelling salts under her nose. Holmes recognised them as the same women who had been ahead of them in the queue earlier. He approached them.

"Pardon me, ladies," he said, "but I heard some screams of distress. Did those screams come from you? If so, might I offer my assistance?"

The seated woman looked up at him, her eyes wide and frightened. "Oh, thank you, sir," she said, her voice quavering. "I'll be all right in a moment. It's just, oh, it was so terrifying."

Holmes knelt beside her. "What happened, exactly?"

The woman took a deep, shuddering breath. "It was the waxwork," she said, pointing a shaking finger at the figure of Henry the Eighth. "I was walking past it, and suddenly I felt this cold draft on the back of my neck. And then...then I heard a voice. It said 'beheaded,' clear as day. It was coming from the figure, I swear!"

Her friend nodded vigorously, her own face pale. "It's true!" she exclaimed. "I heard it too. It must be the ghost of the king who haunts this place. He's threatening to behead any woman who passes by!"

Holmes listened to their story, his expression thoughtful. He knew the power of suggestion could be strong, especially in a place like this where the atmosphere was carefully crafted to unsettle and unnerve. But he kept his thoughts to himself, not wanting to dismiss the women's fears outright.

"That must have been a truly frightening experience," he said, his tone sympathetic.

Just then, a member of the museum staff rushed over, his face etched with worry. "Is everything all right here?" he asked, looking from the women to Holmes.

The seated woman shook her head. "No, it's not," she said, her voice rising. "We were just verbally attacked by the ghost of Henry the Eighth. He threatened to behead us!"

The staff member's eyes widened. "I'm so very sorry," he said. "Is there anything I can do?"

The woman's friend declared, "We want to leave this instant! And you can be sure we'll be telling all our friends about this. This museum is not a safe place to visit, not at all! And we demand a refund."

The employee nodded, helping the seated woman to her feet. As he led the frightened women away, Holmes could hear their voices echoing down the corridor, the dramatic retelling of their experience growing more embellished with each step.

Holmes approached the waxwork of Henry the Eighth, his keen eyes scanning every detail of the figure. The king stood tall and imposing on the raised platform, his broad frame draped in rich velvet and ermine, his face set in a stern expression. Holmes leaned in closer, examining the figure's hands, the folds of its clothing, the texture of its skin. He was looking for anything that might explain the strange occurrence the women had reported.

But try as he might, he could find nothing amiss. The waxwork was expertly crafted. The skin looked almost lifelike; the clothing was historically accurate, and the pose was regal and commanding. There were no obvious signs of tampering, no hidden wires or mechanisms that might account for the ghostly voice. None that he could see, at least.

Frowning, Holmes stepped back and surveyed the other figures in the room. There were other kings and queens here, each standing in line on the same platform. He moved from one to the next, examining each in turn, looking for any anomaly or inconsistency that might provide a clue.

But again, he found nothing. The figures were all of the same high quality as the Henry the Eighth waxwork, their features and clothing rendered with meticulous attention to detail. There were no hidden speakers, no signs of anything unusual.

Holmes stepped back, his brow furrowed in thought. He turned slowly, taking in the entirety of the room. It was a large, high-ceilinged space, with ornate mouldings, heavy velvet drapes, and highly patterned wallpaper. The lighting was dim and atmospheric, designed to showcase the waxworks to their best advantage. And yet, something about the room was bothering him, nagging at the back of his mind.

He couldn't quite put his finger on it, but there was something...off. Something that didn't quite fit. He was about to examine the room more closely, but he heard Watson calling out his name.

"Holmes! Come here! Quickly!"

Holmes rushed into the special exhibit room. He found Watson standing in front of the Sphinx model, his face pale and his eyes wide with shock.

"Watson, what's the matter?" Holmes asked.

Watson raised a trembling finger and pointed at the figure. "I saw it move, Holmes. It shifted slightly to the right, and then...then I saw its face change. From the weathered one that you see now, to a human one. It was a ghostly human face, staring right at me. And, just like that man said earlier, the new face smiled at me; such a chilling smile. The face vanished a moment later."

Holmes frowned, stepping closer to examine the model. "A human face?"

"Yes, I'm certain of it. It was there, as clear as day, and then it was gone." Watson's voice was shaky, but there was a note of anger in it, too.

"And you're sure the Sphinx itself moved?" Holmes asked, looking for disturbances in the sand surrounding the model and finding none.

"Quite sure. It was a subtle movement, but I saw it. I'm certain of that."

Holmes turned to face his friend. "And what do you make of this matter? Has this incident convinced you the museum is haunted?" He waited to hear what the good doctor would say.

All fear left Watson's face. He said, "I don't believe it's haunted whatsoever. This is some kind of trick, an illusion. Something you'd see on the stage. It's all smoke and mirrors, in my opinion."

"I'm glad to hear that," Holmes said. "And whoever is behind this incident is very skilled. They've managed to unsettle even a man of your steadfast nature. If only for a short while."

Watson bristled. "Well, I don't appreciate being the subject of their tricks, skilled or not. It's not right, playing with people's fears like this."

"I agree. And it's our job to expose the truth behind these supposed hauntings. To shed light on the shadows, as it were. Let's examine this room thoroughly, looking for any sign of trickery at work. And we'll talk to the staff, see if anyone else has witnessed these strange occurrences. Also, we need to locate the sculptor with a grudge against Mr Chamberlain, and talk to him."

Watson said, "And what about Mr Chamberlain? Should we inform him of what I saw?"

Holmes paused, considering. "Not yet. I'd like to have a clearer picture of what's going on before we talk to him. For now, we keep this between ourselves."

Watson nodded, trusting his friend's judgement. Together, they began their search, scouring the room for any clue that might shed light on the mysterious events that had just occurred.

Chapter 6

Holmes and Watson meticulously examined the exhibit room. But despite their thorough search, they found nothing out of the ordinary.

As they moved through the room, Holmes couldn't shake the feeling that he was missing something. It was like a puzzle piece that refused to fit, a clue that danced just beyond his grasp. He frowned as he tried to pin down the elusive thought.

Watson, meanwhile, was growing increasingly uneasy. He kept glancing over his shoulder, his glance darting to the shadowy corners of the room. "Holmes," he said, his voice low and tense, "I feel that we're being watched."

Holmes looked at his friend. He hadn't felt the same sense of unease, but he trusted Watson's instincts. "You think someone is observing us?" he asked.

Watson nodded, his face pale in the dim light. "I can't explain it, but I just have this feeling."

Holmes considered this for a moment. While he didn't share Watson's sense of being watched, he respected his friend's intuition. "Very well," he said. "Let's move on to another exhibit. Perhaps a change of scenery will ease your mind."

They made their way out of the exhibit room and into the next part of the museum, which was a reconstruction of a Victorian street. But this was no ordinary street. It was a dark, grimy alleyway, the kind where criminals and ne'er-do-wells plied their trade. The lighting was dim and flickering, casting eerie shadows on the walls. The air was thick with the smell of fabricated smoke and decay.

Watson looked around, his eyes wide with surprise. He said, "I'm not sure this particular change of scenery has eased my mind at all. I must say, I'm astonished that this is an exhibit. It's all a bit too close to home, isn't it? All the crime and squalor that we see every day in London."

Holmes nodded, his eyes scanning the street with a detective's precision. "Indeed, it is a grim reminder of the underbelly of our city," he said. "But perhaps that is the point. People have a morbid curiosity about the criminal underworld. This exhibit allows them to safely indulge that curiosity, to peer into the shadows without actually stepping into them."

Watson considered this, then nodded slowly. "I suppose you're right. Still, it's an unsettling sight. And this eerie atmosphere... it would be the perfect place for hauntings and spooky noises, wouldn't you say?"

Holmes agreed. "It would. If I were a ghost, or rather, someone pretending to be a ghost, this is precisely the kind of place I would choose to haunt."

They began to walk down the reconstructed street, their footsteps echoing on the cobblestones. On either side, the façades of dilapidated buildings loomed over them, their windows dark and empty. Here and there, shadowy figures could be seen lurking in doorways or crouching in nooks and crannies.

As they moved deeper into the exhibit, Holmes and Watson saw scenes of criminal activity playing out before them. A pickpocket was lifting a wallet from an unsuspecting victim. A con artist was luring a mark into a game of three-card monte. A burglar was jimmying a lock, preparing to break into a shop.

The waxwork figures were incredibly lifelike, their faces etched with malice and greed. Watson shuddered as they passed a particularly menacing figure, a brute of a man with a scar across his cheek and a knife in his hand.

"It's all very impressive," Watson said, "but I must say, it's making me rather uncomfortable. It's like we've stepped into the pages of a penny dreadful."

Holmes, however, seemed fascinated by the exhibit. He was studying each scene with intense concentration, his attention darting from one detail to the next. "Look at the craftsmanship," he murmured. "The attention to detail. These figures are remarkably realistic."

As they turned a corner, they found themselves in a small, dimly lit square. In the centre was a gallows, its noose swaying gently in a breeze. A waxwork figure stood on the platform, a hood over its head, its hands bound behind its back.

Watson swallowed hard. "Good Lord," he whispered. "This is ghastly."

Holmes, however, seemed unperturbed. He approached the gallows, examining the figure with a critical eye. "Fascinating. The sculptor has captured the moment of imminent death with incredible precision. The slump of the shoulders, the limpness of the limbs... it's as if we're looking at a real man."

Watson shook his head, turning away from the grim sight. "I've seen enough," he said. "Let's move on, shall we?"

Holmes and Watson moved away from the grim spectacle of the gallows and made their way back to the dimly lit street.

Despite the unsettling atmosphere, Holmes smiled at the waxwork figures they passed.

"You know, Watson," he said, his voice tinged with amusement, "I'm quite certain I recognise some of the faces portrayed in these criminal waxworks. I think we've helped track down a few of them in our time. I'm sure that man in the long coat over there was responsible for the theft of a racehorse. I wonder if these figures are based on real-life people."

Watson, however, was too nervous to respond. "Holmes," he whispered. "I don't like this at all. It feels like someone is going to jump out at any second."

Holmes opened his mouth to reassure his friend, but before he could speak, a figure suddenly leapt out at them from the shadows. It was the waxwork of Jack the Ripper, his face twisted into a menacing snarl, his knife glinting in the dim light.

Watson let out a scream, stumbling backwards in terror. For a moment, it looked as if he might turn and run, but Holmes quickly placed a steadying hand on his shoulder.

"Easy, old chap," he said, his voice calm and reassuring. "It's all part of the museum's set-up. Look here." He pointed to a section of the street where some of the cobblestones were slightly higher than the others. "When we stepped on these stones, it activated the waxwork of Jack, causing him to move."

Watson let out a nervous laugh, his face flushed with embarrassment. "Of course," he said, shaking his head. "I should have realised."

They watched as the figure of Jack the Ripper retreated back into the shadows, ready to leap out at the next unsuspecting visitor.

Watson shuddered. "Do you think the police will ever catch him, Holmes? Jack the Ripper, I mean."

Holmes considered the question for a moment. "They might," he said, "if they enlisted the help of professional detectives. But I fear Jack is a cunning and elusive quarry. It will take more than the usual methods to bring him to justice. People don't even know what he looks like. But that figure we've just seen could be a reasonable representation."

They continued down the street, the eerie silence broken only by the sound of their footsteps. As they neared the end of the exhibit, Holmes turned to Watson, a curious expression on his face.

"Do you still feel like we're being watched?" Holmes asked.

Watson paused, considering the question. "No," he said, after a moment. "The feeling seems to have passed."

But Holmes shook his head. "On the contrary, Watson," he said, his voice low and serious. "We are being watched. And I know exactly where our observer is."

Chapter 7

Holmes and Watson emerged from the reconstructed street.

Holmes walked purposely towards a woman standing nearby who was wearing a simple black dress, a white apron, and a white cap atop her soft brown hair, which was tied back in a neat bun. In her hand, she held a cleaning cloth, but she was standing as still as a statue, her eyes wide with wonder as she stared at Holmes.

Holmes smiled at her. "Hello," he said, his voice warm and friendly.

The woman blinked, as if coming out of a trance. "I can't believe it," she whispered, her voice filled with awe. "You're Sherlock Holmes; the great Sherlock Holmes. Right here. Right in front of me. Am I dreaming?"

Holmes smiled and assured she wasn't.

The woman cast a shy smile at Watson, who had joined them and said, "Dr Watson, I've read all your stories. You have such a wonderful way with words. It's such an honour to meet you both."

Watson returned her smile, bowing his head slightly. "The pleasure is ours, Miss..."

"Mrs Eliza Morton," she said, bobbing a curtsey. "I work here at the museum as a cleaner. I suspect you've already worked that out, Mr Holmes, what with your impressive detective skills."

Holmes nodded. "Your attire does give you away, Mrs Morton." He took a moment to study her and placed Eliza Morton in her early forties, with a slim frame and kind, gentle eyes. Her hands were rough from years of work. There was a sadness about her, a sense of loss that seemed to cling to her like a shroud.

Mrs Morton looked from one man to the other, muttering, "I can't believe it, I just can't. The great Sherlock Holmes and Dr Watson. The world's most famous detectives."

Holmes waved away her praise, though he did feel some modicum of pleasure at her words.

She continued talking, "I'm sorry for staring at you so much. It's just that when I saw you both in that street behind you, I thought for a moment that you were waxworks. I was thinking to myself that the sight of you would draw the crowds in for certain, even with all these rumours about hauntings and the suchlike."

Holmes nodded. "We have heard about the rumours. But can you tell us any more about them, Mrs Morton?"

Eliza hesitated, glancing around as if to make sure no one was listening. "Well," she said, lowering her voice, "there have been some strange things happening here at the museum. Visitors have been complaining about feeling cold spots, hearing strange noises, even seeing things move on their own."

Holmes said, "We have heard of similar things. Is there anything else?"

Eliza swallowed nervously. "I shouldn't really be telling you anything. I might lose my job if Mr Chamberlain finds out I've been saying things about his museum. And he's been so kind to me, giving me this job. I lost my husband, Charlie, three years ago to influenza, and working here takes my mind off my grief and my loneliness. I'd be lost without it." Tears sprang to her eyes.

Holmes placed a gentle hand on her shoulder. "I am very sorry to hear about the passing of your husband, Mrs Morton. I wouldn't want to jeopardise your job in any way. It may ease your mind to know that we are here in an official capacity. Mr Chamberlain hired us to investigate the strange activities."

Eliza blinked back her tears. "Oh, Mr Holmes, that is a relief, I can tell you. No doubt, you'll have this mystery cleared up in no time, and then everything can go back to normal."

Holmes retrieved his hand, smiling kindly at the woman. "Now then, Mrs Morton, could you tell us what else you know about the supposed hauntings? If that is okay with you, of course."

Eliza smiled. "It is most certainly okay, Mr Holmes. Well, let me tell you what I know. Only yesterday, I heard a visitor telling her friend that she saw a waxwork figure turn its head and look right at her. Another woman said she heard whispering coming from an empty room. And just the other day, one of the staff found a trail of wax droplets leading from one of the exhibits to the back door. It looked as if someone had carried a melting candle through the museum, but someone said it was a ghost that had left its mark there."

Holmes listened intently. "And have you experienced anything unusual yourself, Mrs Morton?"

Eliza shook her head. "No, sir, and I hope I never do. But I've heard plenty from the other staff. They're all on edge, jumping at shadows and whispering about ghosts and curses. It's not good for business, I can tell you that much."

Dr Watson asked, "And do you believe that these events are paranormal in nature? Do you believe in ghosts, Mrs Morton?"

She shook her head. "I don't. I never have. And anyway, if ghosts were real, and the spirits could talk to us from the other side, wouldn't my Charlie have been in touch with me? Given me a word of comfort or two? But no, once people have passed away, they are gone forever and all they leave behind are the memories we carry in our hearts." She blinked back fresh tears that had appeared.

Holmes smiled kindly at the woman. "Well, Mrs Morton, I must thank you for your candour. I do hope our questions haven't upset you too much. The information you have given us is invaluable."

Eliza beamed, her sadness replaced with pride. "Oh, it's my pleasure, Mr Holmes. Truly, it is. I've always been a great admirer of your work. The way you solve those impossible cases, the way you see things that no one else can...it's just incredible."

Holmes smiled, a rare genuine smile that softened his sharp features. "Thank you, Mrs Morton," he said. "If I may take the liberty of asking you more question, please?"

"Of course." Eliza stood a little taller.

Holmes said, "May I ask which parts of the museum you are responsible for cleaning?"

Eliza's eyes widened slightly at the question, but she answered readily enough. "Why, everywhere, Mr Holmes. From the grand entrance hall to the darkest corners of the exhibits. Even that gruesome street behind us." She shuddered slightly. "I don't much like cleaning there, truth be told. It gives me the shivers, it does."

Holmes nodded. "I can imagine it must be quite unsettling, working in such an atmosphere. Tell me, Mrs Morton, would you be willing to assist us in our investigation?"

Eliza's hand flew to her chest, her face paling. For a moment, it seemed as though she might faint. "Me?" she whispered. "Assist the great Sherlock Holmes?"

Holmes smiled reassuringly. "Indeed, Mrs Morton. You see, in your role as a cleaner, you are uniquely positioned to observe things that others might miss. People tend to overlook those they consider invisible, like yourself, and I mean that with no disrespect whatsoever. People may speak more freely and let their guard down, even though you are nearby."

Eliza nodded slowly, understanding dawning in her eyes. "I see what you mean, Mr Holmes. Yes, people do tend to talk as if I'm not there. As if I'm just another piece of furniture."

"Precisely," Holmes said. "Which is why I believe you could be invaluable to our investigation. I would ask that you keep your eyes and ears open. If you notice any suspicious activity, any odd conversations, anything at all out of the ordinary that you think could help us, I would be most grateful if you could report it to me."

Eliza gave him a firm nod, a look of determination settling over her features. "Of course, Mr Holmes. I'll do whatever I can to help. You can count on me."

Holmes reached into his pocket and withdrew a small card. "Here is my address. Please, feel free to call upon me at any time, day or night, if you have something to report."

Eliza took the card reverently, holding it as if it were a precious gem. "Thank you, Mr Holmes. I'll guard this with my life."

Holmes chuckled. "I don't think that will be necessary. But I do appreciate your dedication."

With a final nod and a smile, Holmes and Watson bade farewell to Eliza Morton and continued on their way through the museum.

As they walked away, Watson looked at his friend. "Holmes, why did you ask Mrs Morton for her help? Surely we can handle this investigation on our own."

Holmes smiled enigmatically. "My dear Watson, you heard what Mrs Morton said. In her role, she is practically invisible. People speak around her as if she's not there. That kind of invisibility can be a powerful tool in our line of work. Never underestimate the power of those who are often overlooked, Watson. They see and hear far more than most people realise. And even I can miss things. That's why it's always good to have an extra set of eyes and ears on a case."

Watson said, "Well, I hope Mrs Morton does hear or see something useful. The sooner we can get to the bottom of this mystery, the better."

Holmes agreed. "But for now, let us continue. I think we have seen enough of the museum for now. It's time to find that sculptor who has a grudge against Mr Chamberlain. I'm interested to hear what he's got to say."

Chapter 8

Holmes and Watson prepared to seek out the disgruntled sculptor. They didn't get very far before the sound of hurried footsteps echoed through the museum's corridors. They turned to see Alfred Chamberlain approaching them with a look of concern upon his face.

"Mr Holmes, Dr Watson!" Chamberlain called out, his voice tinged with relief. "I've been searching for you, gentlemen. I heard you were in the building."

Holmes raised an eyebrow, his keen eyes taking in Chamberlain's nervous demeanour. "Mr Chamberlain, I trust everything is all right?"

Chamberlain swallowed nervously. "I know I promised you a tour, but might we proceed directly to my office? I'd like to discuss what you've discovered thus far."

Watson exchanged a glance with Holmes, who nodded almost imperceptibly. Watson said, "Of course, Mr Chamberlain. Lead the way."

The trio made their way through the winding corridors of the museum. They soon arrived at Chamberlain's office, a spacious room lined with bookshelves and adorned with various curiosities from around the world. A large mahogany desk dominated the centre of the room, its surface cluttered with papers and ledgers.

Chamberlain gestured for Holmes and Watson to take a seat in the plush armchairs facing his desk. He sank into his own chair, his shoulders sagging as if under a great weight.

"Mr Chamberlain," Holmes began, his voice calm and measured, "Dr Watson and I paid a visit to your ex-business partner, Marcus Bramwell, earlier today."

"And what did he say?"

Holmes said, "Mr Bramwell denies having anything to do with the strange activities occurring in your museum. However, I must confess, I am not entirely convinced of his innocence in this matter."

Chamberlain nodded. "I agree, Mr Holmes. These incidents, they are escalating at an alarming rate. I've had numerous complaints today alone. I fear that if this continues, someone might get physically hurt, and then I'd have no choice but to close the museum immediately. Something that would please Marcus."

Watson said, "Mr Chamberlain, you have our assurance that we will do everything in our power to get to solve this mystery."

Chamberlain managed a weak smile. "Thank you, Dr Watson. I appreciate that more than you know. I need all the help I can get to put a stop to these disturbances, and as quickly as possible."

Holmes studied their client intently. "Mr Chamberlain, I sense there is something weighing on your mind. Something you have not yet shared with us."

Chamberlain shifted uncomfortably in his seat, his eyes avoiding Holmes's penetrating gaze. "I...I don't know what you mean, Mr Holmes."

Holmes said, "Mr Chamberlain, if we are to assist you to the best of our abilities, it is imperative that you are completely honest with us. Even the smallest detail could prove crucial in unravelling this mystery."

Chamberlain's shoulders slumped, and he let out a heavy sigh. He seemed to be wrestling with some internal dilemma.

After a few moments, he reached for a telegram on his desk. He held it up and said, "Mr Holmes, Dr Watson, this arrived less than an hour ago. It's from a woman named Madam Rosalind."

At the mention of the name, Holmes let out a snort of disgust. "I didn't think it would be long until she got in touch," he said, his voice dripping with disdain.

Chamberlain looked at Holmes, curiosity piqued. "I'm aware she's a famous medium, but that's all I know. What can you tell me about her, Mr Holmes?"

Holmes replied, "Madam Rosalind, in my opinion, is nothing but a charlatan, albeit a very skilled one. She has fooled many people into believing she possesses genuine talents, preying upon their grief and vulnerability with her cleverly crafted illusions."

Watson added his thoughts, "I've heard stories of her supposed abilities, but I've always been sceptical. It seems to me that she merely tells people what they wish to hear, offering false comfort for her own gain."

"What does the telegram say, Mr Chamberlain?" Holmes asked.

Chamberlain glanced down at the telegram. "Madam Rosalind claims to have heard about the hauntings and has offered her services to rid the museum of the spirits. She wants to hold a séance."

Holmes raised an eyebrow. "And does she intend to charge for that?"

"No, she doesn't mention any fee," Chamberlain replied, scanning the telegram again. "However, she does request that the press be at the séance. And that I'm to organise that."

A look of understanding dawned on Holmes's face. "Ah, so she's after fame, then. Maybe her present fame isn't enough, and she craves more. Now, this new information makes her a suspect in my eyes."

Watson asked, "You think she might be behind these disturbances, Holmes?"

"It's a possibility we cannot ignore, Watson," Holmes said. "Madam Rosalind has much to gain from associating herself with a high-profile case like this. If she is after fame, as I suspect she might be, Madam Rosalind could have orchestrated this whole affair from the very beginning. She could have asked some of her loyal clients to visit your museum, Mr Chamberlain, and pretend to have seen and felt something strange."

"Ah, I see," Chamberlain said. "But is she capable of such deceit?"

Holmes raised one eyebrow. "Her profession is built on deceit."

Dr Watson cleared his throat, and said, "If I may, Holmes, don't forget what I experienced earlier. I am certainly not working for Madam Rosalind."

Chamberlain asked, "What happened earlier?"

Watson explained about seeing the Sphinx move, and then how the face changed and smiled at him.

"That must have shaken you up, Dr Watson," Chamberlain said. "I'm sorry you had to experience that."

Holmes gave Mr Chamberlain a direct look. "If Madam Rosalind has employed people to discredit your museum, she could also have hired someone working on the inside to help her, too. Someone employed by you."

"Absolutely not!" Chamberlain declared. "I told you earlier that my staff are trustworthy and loyal, and I stand by that."

Holmes thought it wise not to push that point further. Instead, he looked at the telegram and said, "Perhaps you should ask Madam Rosalind to proceed with the séance."

"But why?" Chamberlain asked. "After what you've told me, I'm not sure I want her here."

Holmes nodded. "I agree with you. But by asking her here, the public will see you are doing all you can to put an end to these hauntings. And, more importantly, if she does have people helping to stage these strange occurrences, she may bring them along to the séance and we could catch them in the act."

"Oh, yes, I see what you mean," Chamberlain said with a smile. "I assume you and Dr Watson would like to be at the séance, too?"

Holmes grimaced. "As much as it pains me to say this, yes, I would like to be at the séance held by Madam Rosalind. Could you organise that, Mr Chamberlain?"

"I will reply to her telegram immediately." Chamberlain visibly relaxed. "Is there anything else you can tell me about your investigation so far? Apart from Marcus Bramwell, and now Madam Rosalind, do you have any other suspects?"

"Not yet," Holmes said. He stood up. "But we would like to continue having a look around. I must say, I am extremely impressed with the quality of the waxworks. I'd love to know how they are created. Would it be possible to speak to the sculptors who are behind such works of art?"

"Of course," Chamberlain replied. "My main sculptor is a wonderful chap called Thomas Hargreaves. You'll find him in the workshop area. Let him know I sent you. I'm sure he'll be delighted to tell you more about his work."

He gave Holmes and Watson directions to the workshop and promised to be in touch soon with details of the upcoming séance.

Holmes and Watson walked away from his office.

As soon as they were out of earshot, Watson said, "I wonder if this Thomas Hargreaves is the same sculptor Bramwell told us about, the one who resents Mr Chamberlain. He doesn't sound like it going by Mr Chamberlain's kind words about him."

Holmes smiled at his friend, and said, "We'll soon find out."

Chapter 9

Holmes and Watson navigated their way through the museum, following the directions provided by Mr Chamberlain. They soon found themselves standing before a sturdy wooden door marked 'Private'. Holmes rapped his knuckles against the door, the sound echoing in the quiet hallway.

Moments later, the door swung open, revealing a man with a friendly face. His eyes crinkled at the corners as he smiled at the two gentlemen. "Good afternoon, sirs. How may I assist you?"

"Good afternoon. I am Sherlock Holmes, and this is my associate, Dr John Watson. We are at the museum on a private matter, and asked Mr Chamberlain if we could learn more about the waxworks and how they are created. He said we should stop by this workshop. We are looking for Thomas Hargreaves."

The man's smile widened. "I'm Thomas Hargreaves. I've worked for Mr Chamberlain since he opened this museum. Before that, I worked for various other museums. Please, come in." He stepped aside, gesturing for them to enter.

As they entered the workshop, Watson let out a gasp. The room was filled with an array of wax figures in various stages of completion. Some were mere skeletons of wire and wood, while others were so lifelike, they seemed poised to draw breath.

"I must say, Mr Hargreaves," Holmes began, his keen eyes scanning the room, "the quality of the waxworks in the museum is truly remarkable. The level of detail and craftsmanship is extraordinary. You are extremely talented."

Thomas beamed with pride. "Thank you, Mr Holmes. I pour my heart and soul into each and every one of these figures. It's not just a job for me; it's a passion."

Holmes nodded. "I can certainly see that. Tell me, how do you go about creating these marvels?"

Thomas clasped his hands together. "Ah, well, the process varies depending on whether the subject is a living person or a historical figure. For living subjects, we begin by taking precise measurements and creating a plaster cast of their face and body."

He led them over to a workbench where a partially completed figure lay. "Once we have the cast, we use it to create a wax positive. This is where the real artistry begins. We sculpt the wax, adding in every detail, from the lines on their face to the texture of their skin."

Holmes leaned in closer, examining the figure. "Fascinating. And what about historical figures?"

"For those, we rely on paintings, photographs, and written descriptions to capture their likeness. It's a bit more challenging, as we have to interpret the information and bring it to life in three dimensions."

Watson pointed to a figure in the corner, dressed in regal attire. "Is that Queen Victoria?"

Thomas nodded. "It is, Dr Watson. Whilst Her Majesty hasn't yet paid a visit to our museum, we are ever hopeful that she will one day. I spent months researching her features and mannerisms to ensure I did her justice."

Holmes circled the figure, his brow furrowed in concentration. "The attention to detail is astounding. The folds of her dress, the expression on her face—it's as if she could step right off the pedestal."

"That's the goal, Mr Holmes," Thomas said, his chest puffing out slightly. "We want our visitors to feel as though they are in the presence of the real person."

Watson turned to Thomas. "How long does it typically take to complete a figure?"

"It varies, but on average, it takes several months. There are many stages involved, from the initial sculpting to the painting and costuming. Each step requires precision and patience."

"And the hair?" Watson asked. "It looks so realistic."

Thomas grinned. "Ah, yes. That's a painstaking process. We use real human hair, which is inserted strand by strand into the wax scalp. It's a time-consuming task, but it makes all the difference in the final product."

As they continued to tour the workshop, Thomas regaled them with stories behind each figure, his enthusiasm infectious. Holmes and Watson listened intently, asking questions and marvelling at the skill and dedication that went into creating these waxen wonders.

"Mr Hargreaves," Holmes said as they prepared to take their leave, "your work is truly exceptional. The museum is fortunate to have an artist of your calibre."

Thomas bowed his head, a slight flush colouring his cheeks. "You're very kind, Mr Holmes. I am grateful for the opportunity to pursue my passion and bring these historical figures to life. I have worked in other museums before this one, but I must say that working for Mr Chamberlain is a real privilege."

Holmes regarded Hargreaves with a thoughtful gaze. "Mr Hargreaves, I hope you don't mind me broaching a rather delicate subject."

Thomas's brow furrowed slightly, but he maintained his friendly demeanour. "Of course not, Mr Holmes. Please, go ahead."

Holmes clasped his hands behind his back, choosing his words carefully. "You might not be aware, but Mr Chamberlain has asked Dr Watson and myself to look into the peculiar occurrences that have been plaguing the museum as of late. The supposed hauntings, if you will."

Thomas replied, "Yes, I have heard the rumours. It's most unsettling for everyone involved."

Watson chimed in, "Have you personally experienced anything unusual, Mr Hargreaves?"

Thomas shook his head. "No, I can't say that I have. You see, I spend most of my time here in the workshop, engrossed in my work. I'm rarely out on the museum floor, except when placing the new figures into place, so I haven't witnessed any of the alleged hauntings first hand."

Holmes said, "And what is your opinion on the matter? Do you believe there could be any truth to these claims of supernatural activity?"

Thomas held up his hands in a gesture of dismissal. "Absolutely not, Mr Holmes. I am a man of reason and logic. I don't put any stock in ghost stories or tales of the paranormal. There must be a rational explanation for whatever is happening."

Holmes nodded. "I agree with you, Mr Hargreaves. Dr Watson and I have always found that the truth lies in the realm of the tangible, not the fantastical. There is another matter I wish to discuss with you. Dr Watson and I recently visited Mr Marcus Bramwell, who is Mr Chamberlain's former business partner. Our visit was in relation to the supposed hauntings."

Thomas's eyebrows shot up in surprise. "Mr Bramwell? I have heard Mr Chamberlain mention him a few times. I'm assuming you considered him a suspect if you visited him. May I ask, what did he have to say?"

Holmes studied Thomas's reaction closely as he continued. "Mr Bramwell made a rather curious claim. He said that a sculptor who worked at this museum was overheard in a public house speaking ill of Mr Chamberlain. I was wondering if you might have any knowledge of this incident."

Thomas's face fell, and he shook his head vehemently. "No, Mr Holmes, I can assure you that I know nothing of the sort. It pains me to think anyone would speak badly of Mr Chamberlain. He has been nothing but kind and supportive to me and my work."

Watson said gently, "We don't mean to imply that you were involved, Mr Hargreaves. We're simply trying to gather all the information we can."

Thomas met Watson's gaze. "I appreciate that, Dr Watson. And I want you both to know that I would never engage in such behaviour. I have the utmost respect for Mr Chamberlain, and I would never dream of disparaging him, especially not in a public setting. That's outrageous!"

Holmes said, "We believe you, Mr Hargreaves. Your dedication to your work and your loyalty to Mr Chamberlain are evident."

Thomas continued, "I can also assure you that I never frequent public houses, as I don't partake in drinking. My evenings are spent here, working on my craft or at home with my family."

Holmes nodded, his expression thoughtful. "Mr Hargreaves, your insight has been invaluable. Before we take our leave, I was wondering if you might have any ideas about who could be behind the strange activities at the museum."

Thomas's brow furrowed, and he seemed to hesitate for a moment. "Well, Mr Holmes, I don't like to speak ill of others, but there is someone who has been quite vocal about his dissatisfaction with the museum as of late."

Watson asked, "Who might that be, Mr Hargreaves?"

"To explain who that might be, I need to take you into another part of the museum," Thomas answered. "It isn't a pleasant area, and it's somewhat ghoulish. Would you like to go there?"

Holmes smiled. "We would, Mr Hargreaves. Please, lead the way."

Chapter 10

Thomas Hargreaves led Holmes and Watson through the workshop, navigating between the workbenches and shelves laden with tools and supplies. At the back of the room, they reached a large, heavy wooden door.

"Gentlemen," Thomas said, "beyond this door lies a room that some of the employees have taken to calling 'The Crypt'. I must confess, I find the name rather distasteful, but I suppose it does capture the essence of the place."

He reached for the iron handle and pulled the door open with a creak. A gust of cold air rushed up from the depths below, causing the gas lamps on the walls to flicker. Watson shivered involuntarily, pulling his coat tighter around himself.

"I say, it's rather chilly down there, isn't it?" Watson remarked.

Holmes, however, seemed unperturbed by the drop in temperature. His keen eyes were fixed on the stone steps that descended into the darkness. "Shall we?" he said, gesturing for Thomas to lead the way.

Thomas nodded and began the descent, the sound of his footsteps echoing off the damp walls. Holmes and Watson followed close behind, the cold air nipping at their faces as they ventured deeper into the bowels of the museum.

At the bottom of the stairs, Thomas lit several more lamps, illuminating the vast cellar. Watson's eyes widened as he took in the sight before him. The room was filled with an assortment of waxwork figures in various states of disrepair. Some stood intact, their blank eyes staring into the void, while others were mere torsos or disembodied limbs scattered across the stone floor.

"Good Lord," Watson breathed. "It's like a macabre version of a sculptor's studio."

Thomas nodded, a wry smile playing on his lips. "This is where we store the figures that are no longer needed for display. Some will be repurposed, their parts used to create new characters. Others, I'm afraid, are destined for the melting pot, their wax to be reused in future creations."

Holmes moved through the room, his keen eyes taking in every detail. He paused beside a table where several wax heads were lined up, their expressions frozen in various states of emotion.

"Fascinating," Holmes murmured, lifting one of the heads to examine it more closely.

Thomas joined Holmes at the table, ready to answer any questions he might have.

Watson, meanwhile, had wandered to the far end of the cellar, where a group of figures stood in a semicircle, their poses suggesting they had once been part of a larger tableau. As he approached, a floorboard creaked beneath his feet, the sound echoing through the cavernous space. He froze, his heart pounding in his chest. "This place is rather unsettling," he called out to Holmes and Thomas. "It's as if the figures are watching us, even in their current state."

Holmes chuckled softly. "Come now, Watson. You know as well as I do that these are merely inanimate objects, devoid of any real consciousness."

Despite Holmes's reassurance, an expression of unease settled on Watson's face.

Thomas, sensing Watson's discomfort, offered a sympathetic smile. "I understand your apprehension, Dr Watson. It takes some getting used to, being surrounded by these figures. But I assure you, there is nothing to fear down here."

Holmes, having completed his inspection of the heads, turned to face Thomas. "Mr Hargreaves, you mentioned earlier that there was someone who had been vocal about their dissatisfaction with the museum. I believe you were about to tell us who that might be."

Thomas Hargreaves led Holmes and Watson to a corner of the cellar where a solitary figure stood, its features obscured by shadows. As they approached, Thomas reached out and turned the figure to face them, revealing the waxen likeness of a man in a tailcoat and top hat, his hands poised as if in the midst of a magic trick.

"Gentlemen, allow me to introduce you to Quentin Silverstone," Thomas said, a note of weariness in his voice.

Holmes studied the figure. "Ah, yes. The stage magician, Quentin Silverstone. I've seen his name emblazoned on playbills around the city, though I must confess I've never attended one of his performances myself. I assume there must be a reason why his likeness has now been placed down here."

Thomas explained, "Mr Silverstone was quite popular when the museum first opened. His figure was prominently displayed, and visitors were drawn to his likeness.

However, something happened at the theatre where he performed recently that caused his popularity to wane."

Watson raised an eyebrow. "What sort of incident, Mr Hargreaves?"

Thomas shrugged. "I'm not entirely sure of the details, Dr Watson. Rumours circulated about a trick gone wrong, or perhaps a scandal involving Mr Silverstone. Whatever the case, the theatre-goers began to avoid his shows, and Mr Chamberlain decided it was time to remove his figure from the main exhibition."

Holmes circled the waxwork. "And how did Mr Silverstone react to this decision?"

Thomas replied, "He was furious, Mr Holmes. He came to the museum and caused quite a scene in front of the visitors. He demanded to speak with Mr Chamberlain, and when he arrived, Quentin threatened him with all sorts of dire consequences if his figure wasn't reinstated immediately."

Watson's eyes widened. "He threatened Mr Chamberlain? In public?"

Thomas nodded. "He did. It was a most unpleasant spectacle. Mr Chamberlain tried to reason with him, explaining that the museum had to adapt to the changing tastes of the public, but Mr Silverstone wouldn't hear of it."

Holmes paused in his examination of the figure. "And has Mr Silverstone returned to the museum since then?"

"Oh, yes," Thomas said. "He comes back every day, demanding to see if his figure has been returned to its former place of honour. Each time, he grows more agitated when he discovers it hasn't."

Watson shook his head. "It sounds like the man has quite the temper. Holmes, do you think he could be responsible for the strange occurrences in the museum?"

Holmes tapped his chin thoughtfully. "It's a possibility, Watson. A man with a wounded ego and a flair for the dramatic could certainly be capable of staging such events. But we mustn't jump to conclusions just yet. Mr Hargreaves, what do you intend to do with Quentin's figure now that it has been removed from display?"

Thomas glanced at the waxwork, a hint of uncertainty in his eyes. "To be honest, Mr Holmes, I'm not entirely sure. It's possible that the figure will be repurposed, its parts used to create a new character. Or, if Mr Chamberlain decides it's no longer needed, it may be melted down, and the wax reused for future projects. Going by how upset Mr Chamberlain was after Quentin yelled at him, this waxwork is most likely to be melted."

Holmes said, "I see. And does Mr Silverstone know of these potential fates for his likeness?"

"No, sir," Thomas replied. "Given his current state of agitation, we thought it best to keep such details private. But considering what has been going on in the museum, these so-called hauntings, I wonder if Mr Silverstone has already found out and is taking revenge."

Watson shifted uneasily. "Holmes, if Mr Silverstone were to discover his figure might be destroyed, it could push him over the edge. A man with his temperament, faced with the prospect of his own destruction, even in effigy…"

"It's a delicate situation and one we must handle with the utmost care," Holmes said. "Mr Hargreaves, I trust you will keep this information about Quentin's waxwork confidential for the time being?"

Thomas nodded solemnly. "Of course, Mr Holmes."

Holmes asked, "Do you have any other people in mind who could be behind the activities, apart from Quentin Silverstone?"

Thomas shook his head. "None that I know of."

Holmes gave Thomas a card and said, "If you do think of anyone, please let us know. And if you discover any information that may be relevant to our enquiries, we would appreciate it if you could call on us."

Thomas said he would.

Holmes thanked him for his time, and with Watson at his side, they ascended the steps and entered the relative cheeriness of the workshop again.

A few minutes later, Holmes and Watson left the museum and walked away from it.

Watson shivered and said, "No wonder they call that cellar, 'The Crypt.' What a dreadful place. Where shall we go now, Holmes? Seek out Quentin Silverstone, I presume?"

Holmes came to a sudden stop, his attention on someone across the road. He said, "We will visit Mr Silverstone in due course, but first, I would like to speak to that person across the street there."

Watson looked at where Holmes had his attention. "By Jove! What is he doing here?"

Chapter 11

Holmes and Watson studied the man across the street. It was Marcus Bramwell. He was intently focused on a notebook, his hand moving deftly across the page. Holmes' keen eyes narrowed as he observed the scene.

"Watson," he said, "it appears that Mr Bramwell is sketching something. His attention appears to be on Mr Chamberlain's Waxwork Museum, but I could be mistaken. I suggest we approach him discreetly from behind to ascertain the subject of his drawing."

Watson nodded, and the two men crossed the road, careful to remain out of Bramwell's line of sight. As they drew nearer, they could see the unmistakable outline of the Waxwork Museum taking shape on the page. However, there was one striking difference: the name 'Alfred Chamberlain' had been replaced by 'Marcus Bramwell'.

Before either of them could comment, Bramwell spoke without turning around. "Good day, Mr Holmes, Dr Watson. I trust you're both well?"

Holmes raised an eyebrow. "You recognised us without even turning around, Mr Bramwell. Impressive."

Bramwell tapped the ground with his foot, indicating the shadows cast by the detective and his companion. "Your silhouettes are quite distinctive. Now, to what do I owe the pleasure of your company?"

"We were about to ask you the same question," Holmes replied, stepping forward. "What brings you to this area, and why have you replaced Mr Chamberlain's name with your own in your sketch?"

Marcus closed his notebook and turned to face them. "Ah, straight to the point, Mr Holmes. I admire that about you."

Watson interjected, "Are you planning to force Mr Chamberlain to sell you the museum, Mr Bramwell? Are you drawing up plans for the changes you will make once it is yours?"

Bramwell laughed. "Dr Watson, you do have a vivid imagination. No, I have no intention of forcing anyone to do anything. However, I do believe this conversation should be continued in a more private setting. Might I suggest we adjourn to The King's Arms? It's just around the corner, and they serve an excellent pint."

Holmes studied Bramwell for a moment, trying to discern his true intentions. The man's demeanour was calm and collected, giving nothing away. Finally, he nodded. "Very well, Mr Bramwell. We will go with you."

A short while later, they entered The King's Arms, a cosy establishment with a warm, inviting atmosphere. Bramwell led them to a quiet corner table and signalled to the barman for a round of drinks.

Once they were settled, Holmes said, "Now, Mr Bramwell, perhaps you could enlighten us as to your interest in the Waxwork Museum and your reasons for altering Mr Chamberlain's name in your sketch."

Bramwell replied, "I have always been a man with an eye for opportunity. The Waxwork Museum is not reaching its full potential under Alfred's management. I believe that with my expertise and vision, I could elevate it to new heights. With all the rumours of hauntings taking place within the building, I suspect Mr Chamberlain will be forced to close the museum soon. That will give me the perfect opportunity to purchase it. And when that happens, I will use all my business expertise to make sure I get it at a low price. I'll make Mr Chamberlain an offer that he can't refuse, not in the circumstances."

Holmes said, "Would you be responsible for those rumours?"

Bramwell shook his head. "My old friend, Chamberlain, has brought this on himself. As you will find out if you ever solve this case and discover who is benefiting from these disturbances. I assume you are further on in your investigation, Mr Holmes? Or could this be the case that finally stumps the great Sherlock Holmes?"

Watson bristled at Bramwell's mocking words and retorted, "I assure you, Mr Bramwell, that Holmes is more than capable of solving this case. He has tackled far more complex mysteries with great success."

Holmes, however, remained unperturbed. He studied Bramwell with a calm, analytical gaze. "The case is proceeding quite well, Mr Bramwell. However, your professional history with Mr Chamberlain intrigues me, in particular, why you are no longer business partners. Any information you could provide on that matter would be most appreciated."

At that moment, their pints arrived, carried by a young barmaid with rosy cheeks and bright eyes. Bramwell flashed her a charming smile, causing her to blush deeply.

"Thank you, my dear," he said smoothly, his smile lingering as she hurried away.

Bramwell took a long, slow sip of his pint, savouring the flavour. He set the glass down and fixed Holmes with a condescending look. "Very well. I shall enlighten you about my falling out with Chamberlain, if only to aid your clearly floundering investigation."

He leaned forward, his elbows resting on the table. "Alfred and I were once partners, as you know. We created many small businesses that performed well. It soon came to our attention that a waxworks museum could be extremely lucrative, so we began to take steps to make that happen. We had grand plans to create the most spectacular and innovative museum London had ever seen. However, it soon became apparent that Chamberlain lacked the vision and ambition necessary to achieve true greatness. He was content with mediocrity, satisfied with the status quo. I, on the other hand, saw the potential for much more. I wanted to push the boundaries, to create displays that would astound and amaze the public. But Chamberlain, in his narrow-mindedness, refused to see the merit in my ideas."

Holmes and Watson remained silent, waiting for Marcus Bramwell to continue talking.

And talk he did.

Bramwell took another swig of his pint, his eyes narrowing. "We argued constantly, our differing philosophies driving a wedge between us. Finally, I could take it no more. I severed our partnership and struck out on my own, determined to prove that my vision was the true path to success. To my great annoyance, he used the plans that we had drawn up together as the basis for his new waxworks museum, thus bringing some parts of my vision to life without giving me any credit. Which is why I never went ahead with my own waxwork museum and settled on creating a science-based one instead. Chamberlain betrayed me. Something I'll never forgive him for."

Bramwell fell silent and looked into his nearly empty glass. A slow smile spread across his face.

Holmes said to Bramwell, "I sense you have something else you wish to share."

Bramwell looked up, a malicious gleam in his eyes. "I am still furious with that man. And yet, it warms my heart to know that Chamberlain's business is floundering, while mine is thriving. It is only a matter of time before he is forced to sell, and when he does, I shall be there to pick up the pieces and mould them into something truly magnificent."

"I see," Holmes said. "And you believe that these rumours will be the undoing of Mr Chamberlain's museum?"

Bramwell chuckled. "Undoubtedly. The public is fickle, Mr Holmes. They crave sensation and spectacle, but they are easily frightened. It won't be long until they will stay away in droves. And when Chamberlain is desperate, I shall swoop in and acquire the property for a fraction of its true value."

Watson frowned. "That seems a rather underhanded way to go about business, Mr Bramwell."

Bramwell shrugged, unconcerned. "Business is not for the faint of heart, Dr Watson. One must be ruthless if one wishes to succeed. I make no apologies for my methods."

He drained the last of his pint and set the glass down with a thud. "Now, if you'll excuse me, gentlemen, I have other matters to attend to. I trust our conversation has been enlightening, and I wish you the best of luck in your investigation. Though, from what I've seen, you'll need more than luck to solve this case."

With a final, arrogant smile, Bramwell rose from his seat and strode out of the pub, leaving Holmes and Watson to ponder his words.

Before Holmes and Watson could discuss their conversation with Bramwell, an older man with ruddy cheeks approached their table looking apprehensive. He said, "Mr Holmes, is it?"

Holmes nodded. "It is. Can I help you?"

The man glanced toward the door. "Mr Bramwell spotted me on his way out. We know each other. He comes in here sometimes, and we often have a chat, setting the world to rights, that sort of thing. Well, just now, Mr Bramwell said I was to come over here and talk to you. He said I know something that will help you."

Chapter 12

"Please, have a seat," Holmes said. "And your name is?"

The man sat down and said, "George. George Smithson."

Holmes smiled. "A pleasure to meet you, Mr Smithson. Now, what is it you wish to tell us?"

George began, "Well, it's about a friend of mine, Thomas Hargreaves. He works at Mr Chamberlain's Waxworks Museum."

Holmes' brow furrowed. He described Thomas Hargreaves as they had met him earlier - a genial, welcoming man who took pride in his work. "Is this the same Thomas Hargreaves?"

George nodded. "The very same. He comes here almost every night, right after work. But not tonight. His wife put her foot down, demanded he come home early and spend time with the family for a change."

Watson said, "But Thomas told us he never drinks."

George burst into laughter, the sound ringing through the pub. "Never drinks? That's a good one. Thomas is here more often than not, complaining about his job over a pint or three. The more he drinks, the more he complains."

Holmes said, "And why did Marcus Bramwell ask you to speak with us?"

George shifted uncomfortably in his seat. "Like I said, Thomas is always going on about how terrible it is working at the museum. He says Mr Chamberlain is a right tyrant, never appreciating the work Thomas does. I mentioned it to Bramwell a while back during one of our chats. He seemed mighty pleased to hear that Chamberlain's employees were unhappy. I didn't give him Thomas' name because I didn't want Thomas to get into trouble. But I did tell Mr Bramwell that it was a sculptor at the museum who'd been complaining. Afterwards, I felt so bad talking about Thomas like that. But it's the beer, you see, it always loosens my tongue."

"I understand, George," Holmes said. "Could you tell us exactly what Thomas told you? Mr Bramwell is right that it would help us."

George hesitated, but under Holmes' unwavering gaze, he relented. "He was always going on about how he's the real talent behind the waxworks, but Chamberlain takes all the credit. Says his sculptures are the only reason people come to the museum, but Chamberlain treats him like dirt and it would serve him right if Thomas left."

"Anything else?" Holmes prompted.

Charlie said, "Well, Thomas talked about getting his revenge on Chamberlain. Saying things like 'Chamberlain will get what's coming to him' and 'One day, he'll regret treating me like this'. It's all a bit unsettling, if you ask me."

Holmes and Watson exchanged a meaningful glance. This information shed new light on the case, suggesting that the disturbances at the museum might not be the work of a rival, but of a disgruntled employee after all.

"Has he ever mentioned anything specific?" Watson asked. "Any plans or ideas about how he might seek this revenge?"

George shook his head. "No, nothing specific. Just a lot of dark muttering and ominous statements. I always thought it was just the drink talking, but with all these strange things happening at the museum. Well, it makes you wonder, doesn't it?"

"Thank you, Mr Smithson," Holmes said. "You've been most helpful. We may need to speak with you again. Is there a way we can contact you?"

George waved his arm around the pub. "You'll usually find me here. This is a second home to me, that's what my wife says, anyway. You'll find Thomas here tomorrow night, too. Shall I tell him I've been talking to you?"

"I'd rather you didn't," Holmes replied. "We'll be talking to Mr Hargreaves soon about his threats, but we won't let on it was you who told us."

"I appreciate that," George said. He stood up and walked away, slightly unsteady on his feet.

As Holmes and Watson made their way out of the pub later on, Holmes said, "It seems our Mr Hargreaves has been leading us a merry dance. I wonder what else he has been lying about."

Watson nodded. "Do you think he's behind this haunting business?"

"He could very well be," Holmes surmised. "Let's see if we can catch him at the museum now and have another chat with him. Although, I fear the museum may now be closed at this late hour."

Holmes was correct, and it was with dismay that they stopped outside the museum's door and looked at the 'Closed' sign.

"Never mind," Holmes said briskly. "Hargreaves told us that Quentin Silverstone could be a suspect in this matter.

We shall visit Mr Silverstone now and see what he tells us. However, it could turn out that Mr Hargreaves lied about him, too."

Chapter 13

Holmes and Watson made their way through the bustling theatre district, the streets lined with grand, ornate buildings and the air filled with the excited chatter of theatregoers. Billboards and posters adorned the walls, announcing the latest shows and the brightest stars of the stage.

After a few minutes of searching, they found the theatre they were looking for. 'Quentin Silverstone: The Final Curtain,' it proclaimed in bold, red letters on a poster outside the building.

"Looks like we're just in time for his last performance," Holmes remarked as they approached the ticket booth. "I wonder if he's taking early retirement, or if there is something else in play here."

"Two tickets for Quentin Silverstone's show, please," Watson said to the cashier. "And if possible, we'd like to speak with Mr Silverstone after the performance."

The woman in the ticket booth handed over the tickets, but before she could speak, a man standing nearby stepped forward and introduced himself. "Reginald Barclay, theatre manager. May I ask why you wish to speak with Mr Silverstone?"

"It's a private matter, Mr Barclay," Holmes replied politely. "We have some questions for him regarding an ongoing investigation."

Barclay nodded, then gestured for them to follow him to a quieter corner of the lobby, away from the bustling crowd of eager theatregoers. "I must warn you, gentlemen," he said in a low voice, "Mr Silverstone is not in the best of moods. I'm not sure he will even speak to you. This is to be his final performance, and it weighs heavily upon him."

"We noticed it was his final show from the poster outside," Watson said. "Could you tell us why?"

Barclay sighed. "His act has been slipping as of late. Too many mistakes on stage, and he's lost his touch with the audience. They no longer gasp in wonder at his illusions; instead, they whisper and laugh when he falters. The younger magicians, with their new tricks and daring stunts, are outshining him, and he knows it all too well."

"Has he said anything about this?" Holmes asked.

"Oh, he never stops complaining," Barclay said, shaking his head in exasperation. "Always going on about how these young upstarts don't know true magic, and how they've stolen his tricks. It's a constant refrain with him these days. And he's been particularly bitter about his waxwork figure being removed from that museum not far away. You'd think the manager of it had personally insulted him, the way he carries on about it. But I suppose when your star is fading, every slight cuts a bit deeper."

"His waxwork figure?" Watson asked in all innocence.

Barclay's expression turned sombre as he recounted the events. "Yes, he used to have a figure in Chamberlain's Waxwork Museum. Was quite proud of it, too. But they took it down in recent weeks. He's been in a foul mood ever since. Quentin has worked for me for years and I feel awful about letting him go. But I had no other choice. The audience complained after his every performance and demanded refunds. And my other acts also complained because they were on the receiving end of Quentin's constant criticism."

"Interesting," Holmes said. "Well, thank you for your time, Mr Barclay."

Barclay gave them a grim smile. "Enjoy the show, gentlemen. Though I fear it may not be the grand finale Mr

Silverstone had hoped for. Out of respect for Quentin, I will be watching it, too."

Holmes and Watson made their way into the theatre. The auditorium was sparsely populated, with only a handful of people scattered among the seats. They found their places just as the lights began to dim.

Mr Barclay took a standing position at the side of the seats, his face set in a frown.

The curtains slowly opened, revealing a stage set with various pieces of equipment. A sense of anticipation hung in the air, tinged with a hint of unease.

As the spotlight illuminated the centre of the stage, Holmes leaned over to Watson. "Let's see just how bad this performance will be," he whispered. "And more importantly, what it might tell us about our Mr Silverstone's state of mind."

Watson nodded, his eyes fixed on the stage as they waited for the magician to make his appearance.

The theatre lights dimmed a little and Quentin Silverstone made his grand entrance. He strode onto the stage with a confident smile, his tailored suit and top hat impeccable and his eyes gleaming with anticipation. Despite the sparse audience, Quentin greeted them warmly, his voice carrying through the auditorium with a practised ease.

"Ladies and gentlemen, I thank you for parting with your hard-earned money to witness the wonders I have in store for you tonight," he said, his tone both gracious and assured. "I promise you an evening of magic and illusion that will leave you breathless."

Holmes and Watson exchanged a glance, both surprised by Quentin's confident demeanour. They had expected a bitter, resentful man, but the magician before them exuded a professional air that belied the rumours of his decline.

As the show began, Quentin launched into a series of mesmerising tricks that held the small audience spellbound, with Holmes being the one exception.

Quentin started with a classic sleight of hand, producing a flurry of playing cards from thin air. The cards danced between his fingers, vanishing and reappearing in a dizzying display of dexterity. The audience gasped and applauded, their eyes wide with wonder.

Next, Quentin called for a volunteer from the audience. A young woman, her face flushed with excitement, made her way to the stage. Quentin presented her with a simple wooden box, inviting her to examine it closely. Satisfied that it was indeed ordinary, she handed it back to him. With a flourish, Quentin closed the lid and tapped it three times with his wand. When he opened the box again, a couple of white doves burst forth, their wings fluttering as they soared over the audience's heads. The young woman clapped her hands in delight, and the audience erupted in applause.

Quentin's performance continued, each illusion more impressive than the last. He conjured bouquets of flowers from empty vases, levitated a table with a mere gesture, and even made his assistant disappear and reappear on the other side of the stage. Throughout the show, Quentin's confidence never wavered. His movements were precise, his patter engaging, and his illusions flawless.

In the audience, the theatre manager watched with a look of growing astonishment. It was clear he had expected Quentin to falter, to make the mistakes that had plagued his recent performances. But tonight, the magician was in top form, his act as polished as it had been in his prime.

As the show reached its climax, Quentin announced his final trick—escaping from the water torture cell. A large, glass tank was wheeled onto the stage, filled to the brim with water. Quentin's assistant helped him into a straitjacket. With a dramatic flourish, Quentin was lowered into the tank, the lid locked above him.

The audience held their breath as they watched Quentin struggle against his bonds, bubbles rising from his mouth as he fought to free himself. Seconds ticked by, turning into minutes. Just when it seemed all hope was lost, the lid of the tank burst open, and Quentin emerged, gasping for air but triumphant. The straitjacket hung loosely from his shoulders, proving his skill as an escape artist.

The small audience leapt to their feet, their applause thunderous despite their few numbers. Quentin took his bows, his face beaming with pride. As he exited the stage, the theatre manager rushed towards the backstage area, grinning with delight.

Watson exclaimed, "Well! That was quite a show. Not at all what I was expecting."

Holmes nodded. "I don't think the manager was expecting that either. Did you see the way he dashed towards the backstage area? No doubt, after that performance, he will be asking Quentin Silverstone to stay."

"But why the sudden change in his performance?" Watson wondered.

Holmes stood. "That's what we are going to find out. Come, Watson, let's make our way to Mr Silverstone's dressing room."

"Do you think he could be responsible for those occurrences at the museum?" Watson asked as he followed

Holmes. "He certainly knows enough tricks to create such effects, I would imagine."

"We should certainly consider him a suspect, but let's hear what he's got to say about the museum first. I'm also intrigued as to why his performance was better than what everyone, including the manager, was expecting."

Chapter 14

Holmes and Watson went backstage. They were greeted by a bustling scene of activity. Performers of all kinds were preparing for their time in the spotlight. Acrobats stretched and limbered up, their sequined costumes glinting under the dim lights. Jugglers practised their routines, the colourful balls and clubs arcing through the air with precision. Dancers applied their stage makeup, turning their faces into works of art.

Amidst this whirlwind of preparation, Holmes and Watson spotted Quentin's dressing room. The door was slightly ajar, and the sound of animated conversation spilled out into the corridor. They approached cautiously, positioning themselves just out of sight, their ears straining to catch every word.

"Quentin, my dear fellow!" Mr Barclay's voice was effusive with praise. "That was a magnificent performance! I must admit, I had my doubts, but you've proven me wrong in the most spectacular fashion."

Quentin's laughter was warm and genuine. "Thank you, Mr Barclay. I know my recent performances have been lacking, and I apologise for that. But I've had a change of heart, a new perspective on life and my craft."

"Well, it's working wonders! The audience was absolutely enthralled. I haven't seen a response like that in years."

Quentin said, "It's all thanks to a wise woman who helped me see things differently. She made me realise that my bitterness and resentment were holding me back, both on stage and off."

Mr Barclay replied, "A wise woman? Who is she? Do I know her?"

"Ah, that's a story for another time, my friend. Suffice it to say, she helped me remember why I fell in love with magic in the first place. The joy of creating wonder, of making the impossible seem possible, if only for a moment."

"Well, I'm glad she did. And I'm glad you've found your passion again. Which brings me to my next point. Quentin, I know we had discussed this being your final performance, but after tonight, I simply can't let you go.

The theatre needs you, the audience needs you. Would you consider staying on?"

There was a pause, and Holmes could almost picture Quentin's thoughtful expression.

"Mr Barclay, I would be honoured to continue performing here. And I promise, from this moment on, I will give every show my all. No more half-hearted efforts, no more bitter complaints. I will be the magician this theatre deserves."

"Excellent! I couldn't be happier to hear that. And Quentin, I want you to know that I understand the pressures of this business. If you ever need to talk, my door is always open."

"Thank you, I appreciate that. And I want to apologise for my behaviour these past few weeks, perhaps months! I know I've been difficult to work with, and I've likely upset quite a few people. I intend to make amends, to apologise to everyone I've wronged."

"That's a noble sentiment, Quentin. I'm sure they will appreciate it. Now, I must be off. I have a theatre to run, after all! But again, congratulations on a stunning performance. I look forward to many more."

The sound of footsteps approached the door, and Mr Barclay emerged, a broad smile on his face. He nodded to Holmes and Watson as he passed, his eyes alight with satisfaction. He said, "I'm sure Mr Silverstone would love to talk to you. He's in excellent spirits!"

The manager hastened away, still smiling.

Holmes knocked on the open door and entered the room with Watson at his side. The dressing room was a cosy space, filled with the trappings of a magician's trade. A large mirror adorned one wall, surrounded by bright bulbs. Costumes hung on a rack, their sequins and silks catching the light. A table was littered with an assortment of props - playing cards, silk scarves, and mysterious boxes with hidden compartments.

Quentin, now changed into dry clothes following his escape from the water tank, greeted them with a smile. "Ah, Mr Holmes and Dr Watson! I thought I recognised you in the audience. What brings you backstage?"

Holmes returned the smile. "Mr Silverstone, we were hoping you could help us with an investigation we are dealing with."

Quentin's eyes sparkled with interest. "But of course! I would love to be of assistance. Please, take a seat." He gestured to some plush armchairs.

As they settled in, Holmes began, "We are currently dealing with a case that involves so-called hauntings. There have been reports of ghostly figures, objects moving on their own, and disembodied voices."

Quentin nodded. "Hauntings? How fascinating."

Holmes proceeded to give more details. "In one instance, a statue-like figure was reported to have moved its head and spoken. In another, a cold wind was felt, and a threatening message was heard. What I'm curious about, Mr Silverstone, is whether someone with your skills, say an experienced magician, would be capable of achieving such things."

Quentin sat back, a thoughtful expression on his face. "It's certainly possible, Mr Holmes. We magicians are masters of illusion, after all. While I can't give away my secrets, I can tell you that those effects you mentioned could be achieved through clever staging and misdirection."

"Please, do elaborate," Holmes encouraged.

"Well, take the moving figure, for example. With the right mechanisms hidden inside the figure, or around the outside, it could be made to move subtly. A hidden phonograph could provide the voice. As for the cold wind and the message, a well-placed fan and a concealed speaker could create that illusion."

Watson looked impressed. "That's ingenious!"

Quentin smiled modestly. "It's all part of the craft, Dr Watson. We magicians spend years perfecting these techniques to create the illusion of the impossible."

Holmes nodded. "And what about the ghostly figures that have been sighted?"

"Ah, there are several ways to achieve that effect. Pepper's ghost illusion is a classic; using angled glass and carefully placed lighting to create a ghostly apparition. Or, with the right costume and makeup, an actor could pass for a spectral figure in the right setting."

"Fascinating," Holmes said. "This sheds new light on our investigation."

Quentin leaned forward conspiratorially. "Mr Holmes, if you don't mind me asking, where exactly are these hauntings taking place?"

"At the Chamberlain Waxworks Museum," Holmes responded.

Quentin's expression shifted, a flicker of discomfort crossing his features. He leaned back in his chair, a sigh escaping his lips. "Ah, the Chamberlain Waxworks Museum," he said, his voice tinged with regret. "I must confess, gentlemen, I have made quite a spectacle of myself there recently.

"The museum used to have a waxwork figure of me, a representation of my craft and my fame. I was proud of it, perhaps too proud. But some weeks ago, I discovered that it had been removed, replaced by a figure of a new and upcoming magician. I was furious, absolutely livid. I demanded that my figure be reinstated, that my legacy be respected. I'm ashamed to admit it now, but I caused quite a scene. My behaviour was unacceptable, and I deeply regret it. I intend to visit the museum soon, to apologise to everyone I've upset, including Mr Chamberlain himself."

Holmes said, "That's admirable of you. I'm sure Mr Chamberlain and his staff would appreciate your apology. Mr Silverstone, we spoke with your manager, Mr Barclay, before your performance. He warned us that your performance would not be up to your usual standard, hence the reason for it being your last performance. But Mr Barclay was impressed by your act, as were the audience. I couldn't help but overhear his conversation with you just now, and how he has asked you to stay at the theatre. Might I ask what prompted this transformation in yourself that has led to your renewed success?"

Quentin's face softened. "Ah, Mr Holmes, it's all down to an amazing woman. She has shown me the error of my ways, helped me see the world in a new light. She has been my saviour."

Holmes said, "Really? And who might this enigmatic woman be?"

Quentin's gaze drifted towards the open door of his dressing room. "She's here now, as a matter of fact."

Chapter 15

Holmes and Watson turned to look at the person behind them.

Quentin rose, held out his hands and said, "Madam Rosalind, what a delight to see you again so soon."

Madam Rosalind entered the room, the silver embroidery on her flowing purple dress sparkling brightly. Her long, dark hair framed her striking face and intelligent green eyes. A large crystal pendant hung from her neck, catching the light as she moved with otherworldly grace.

"Quentin, my darling man," Madam Rosalind said as she placed her delicate hands in his, her voice smooth as silk and imbued with a captivating charm. "Your performance was absolutely mesmerising. The audience was spellbound by your illusions and the mastery with which you executed them. I have no doubt that your star will rise higher than ever before, and your name will be spoken with reverence in the halls of magic."

Quentin beamed at her praise, his eyes alight with gratitude and a touch of pride. "Thank you, Madam Rosalind. Your guidance has been invaluable to me. I could not have achieved such a change without your wisdom and support. I am forever in your debt."

Madam Rosalind bestowed a gracious smile upon Quentin and smoothly removed her hands from his. She turned her attention to Holmes, a smile playing on her lips. "Ah, the famous Sherlock Holmes. It has been far too long since our paths last crossed. I have missed you. And Dr Watson, is it my imagination or have you become more handsome since we last met."

Watson cleared his throat and said stiffly, "Good evening, Madam Rosalind."

Holmes said nothing at all; his face was devoid of any emotion.

Madam Rosalind said softly, "My dear Sherlock, as I walked down the hallway mere moments ago, I overheard your conversation about Chamberlain's Waxwork Museum. I believe I may be the one to solve this mystery of yours."

Holmes raised an eyebrow. "Is that so? May I ask how?"

She stepped closer, her robes swishing around her ankles. "I have offered to hold a séance at the museum, to communicate with the restless spirits and guide them to move on. Mr Chamberlain has graciously accepted my offer. I received a telegram from him about an hour ago."

Quentin looked intrigued. "A séance. How fascinating!"

Madam Rosalind nodded. "The spirit world is a mysterious and complex realm. It takes a skilled medium to navigate its depths and bring peace to troubled souls."

Holmes remained sceptical as ever. "And you believe you possess such skills, Madam Rosalind?"

She laughed, a melodic sound that filled the room, her eyes sparkling with amusement and perhaps a touch of mischief. "I have been communicating with the spirit world for many years. It is my life's calling, you see. I have helped countless individuals find closure and solace, guiding them through the veil that separates our world from the next. I am quite confident in my abilities. The spirits and I, we have an understanding, a connection that transcends the boundaries of the physical realm."

Quentin said, "Madam Rosalind is truly gifted, Mr Holmes. Her insights have been invaluable to me." He glanced towards the enigmatic woman, admiration in his eyes.

Holmes' gaze focused intently on Madam Rosalind, searching for any tell-tale signs of deception or trickery.

But the medium met his scrutiny with an unflinching stare, her striking green eyes sparkling with amusement and perhaps a touch of defiance.

"The séance will be held tomorrow," she announced. "You and Dr Watson are welcome to attend, of course. But I must warn you, Mr Holmes, to leave any scepticism or negative energy at the door. The spirits can be sensitive to such vibrations." Her words hung in the air, a gentle admonition and a challenge all at once, as if daring the great detective to step into her world of the supernatural.

Watson said, "We wouldn't miss it for the world, would we, Holmes?"

Holmes replied, "We certainly wouldn't."

Madam Rosalind smiled enigmatically. "I look forward to seeing you there, gentlemen. I have a feeling it will be a most enlightening experience."

With a swish of her robes, she turned to Quentin. "Quentin, my dear, I must take my leave. But remember, your future is bright. Embrace your renewed passion, and let nothing hold you back."

Quentin bowed his head. "Thank you, Madam Rosalind. Your words mean the world to me."

As Madam Rosalind glided out of the room, Holmes watched her go, his face holding no expression. When he heard her footsteps become quieter, he said to Quentin Silverstone, "So, how precisely did Madam Rosalind bring about a change in you?"

Quentin began to recount his encounter with Madam Rosalind. "It all began about a month ago. That's when my performance began to slip. I kept forgetting my tricks and which props I should be using. The laughter from the audience, and my fellow performers only made matters worse. This went on for a few nights, my act becoming even more lacklustre. Madam Rosalind visited me here after one of my worst failures and said she could help. I thought I was past all help, but there was something about her that made me listen to her words. She explained how she could put me in a hypnotic state and get to the bottom of what was affecting my career, and once she'd done that, we could work on improving matters.

"She started that night and put me in a trance. Her voice was so hypnotic, I fell asleep within seconds! When I woke up, Madam Rosalind said my ancestors had spoken to her during my trance. They were worried about me and said I had lost my confidence. They said I had a lot of mental blocks that were holding me back from success. It all seemed far-fetched to me, but Madam Rosalind soon convinced me it was true. She said she would need to have more sessions with me, and one day, we would solve my lack of confidence."

Holmes interjected, "And how much did she charge for these visits?"

"Why, nothing at all, Mr Holmes. She said the spirits had led her to me and said it was her moral duty to help me. Which she was more than happy to do." Quentin smiled. "I started looking forward to her visits. She has the most calming of personalities, and her voice when she put me in a trance, oh, it was the voice of an angel. I must admit, I fell asleep every time, so I've no idea what conversations she was having with my ancestors."

"Did you see a change in your performance straight away?" Watson asked. "After Madam Rosalind's first visit?"

Quentin frowned. "I didn't. In fact, things got even worse. I was angry all the time. Angry at myself, at my colleagues, and especially angry at Mr Chamberlain for removing my wax figure. I asked Madam Rosalind why I wasn't feeling better. She explained that my inner doubts were blocking me, keeping me from the success I truly desired. And the more I fought it, the worse it would become. I trusted her, and knew that despite my regular outbursts, there was light at the end of the tunnel."

"And when did that light appear?" Holmes asked with a barely perceptible hint of irony.

"It was yesterday. Mr Barclay had told me a few days ago he was letting me go. I tried to stay optimistic, but when I saw Madam Rosalind waiting for me after my performance yesterday, I told her not to bother trying to help me anymore. But she took my hands and danced me around the room. She said the spirits had spoken to her during my performance and the block in my mind would be lifted during my next trance. She assured me it would be my last trance, and then, I would be cured. I had nothing to lose, so I agreed to one last session. And Madam Rosalind was right! When I woke up from my hypnotic state yesterday, I felt a change inside me. I felt confident, sure of myself. Well, you saw my performance this evening. I am cured. And it's all thanks to Madam Rosalind."

Watson seemed at a loss for words.

But Holmes had something to say, "Mr Silverstone, let me clarify something. When you were in a hypnotic state, could you hear Madam Rosalind at all?"

"No, not a word. But whatever she was saying to the spirits obviously worked. You're a lucky chap to have Madam Rosalind helping you with that mystery of yours. She'll have the spirits sorted out in no time at all! She's amazing." Quentin sighed softly and a wistful look came into his eyes.

"So, let me get this straight," Holmes began. "Madam Rosalind's visits to you were purely to help you overcome any mental blocks you had."

"That's right," Quentin confirmed.

"And she didn't receive any benefit herself, of any kind?" Holmes persisted. "She didn't have an ulterior motive?"

Quentin frowned. "None at all. She helped me because she has a kind heart. And because the spirits told her to."

Holmes' gaze swept around the room, taking in every detail. His eyes fell upon a red box half hidden beneath a dresser. He gestured towards it. "What do you keep in that box, Mr Silverstone?"

Quentin's expression grew serious. "That's where I keep my book of magic tricks. It's my most prized possession, and I never let anyone touch it. It's got details of my performances in it, including regular tricks and ideas for new ones."

"And when did you last look at your book?" Holmes asked.

Quentin considered the question. "Not for a while now. I usually make notes for new illusions after every performance, but since my act started to decline, I didn't have any new ideas to record."

Holmes said, "I wonder if we could look at your book? Not the inside pages, of course, but just to satisfy my curiosity about something. If you don't mind?"

"I don't mind at all." Quentin went over to the dresser. He pulled the box out, and with a few pushes on certain areas, a click sounded out and the box opened. Quentin peered inside it. A frown creased his brow as he reached in and pulled out the book.

"That's strange," he muttered, turning the book over in his hands. "I always place the cover face down, it's a superstition of mine. But just now, it was facing up. Someone has touched it and placed it the wrong way up. Who would do such a thing?"

Holmes stood up and said, "We will leave that mystery to you, at least for the time being. Thank you for talking to us, Mr Silverstone. You have helped us immensely."

With a nod of farewell, Holmes and Watson left the befuddled magician alone with his book of tricks.

Chapter 16

Holmes and Watson arrived back at 221B Baker Street, both deep in thoughts about the peculiar case they had found themselves embroiled in. As they ascended the stairs to their rooms, Mrs Hudson emerged from her quarters, a telegram in her hand.

"Mr Holmes, Dr Watson," she greeted them, "a telegram arrived for you just a short while ago."

"Thank you, Mrs Hudson," Holmes said, taking the telegram from her. He opened it and quickly scanned the contents.

"It's from Alfred Chamberlain," he informed Watson. "He's confirming that the séance with Madam Rosalind will be held tomorrow evening, after the museum has closed to the public. He formally requests our presence."

Watson gave his friend a considered look. "Holmes, I know how strongly you oppose such things. If you'd prefer, I could attend alone."

Holmes shook his head. "No, no, Watson. I appreciate the offer, but I must be there. I'm interested to see the performance that Madam Rosalind will put on. And I'm sure it will be quite a performance, intended to impress those who are present."

They entered the living room. The fire crackled in the hearth, casting a warm glow over the cluttered space.

Mrs Hudson followed them in. "I'll bring up some dinner for you, gentlemen. You must be famished after your day's adventures."

"That would be most appreciated, Mrs Hudson," Watson said with a smile.

As Mrs Hudson bustled out, Holmes settled into his armchair. Watson took his usual seat opposite him.

"So, what do you make of it all, Holmes?" Watson asked.

Holmes' eyes glinted in the firelight. "There are several threads to this case, Watson, and I'm not yet sure how they all tie together. But I have my suspicions."

"Do you think Marcus Bramwell could be behind the strange occurrences at the museum? He certainly seems to have a motive."

"Indeed, he does," Holmes agreed. "He would undoubtedly benefit from the downfall of Chamberlain's Waxworks. But there's more to it than that. I'm certain he holds other information that could help us. I'm determined to uncover what that is."

Mrs Hudson returned with a tray laden with steaming dishes. She put it on the table and began to lay out the plates.

"What about Thomas Hargreaves?" Watson asked. "Why would he lie to us about his feelings towards Chamberlain?"

Holmes drummed his fingers on the armrest. "That's a question I intend to ask him directly. Again, there's something he's not telling us. Something that could be useful to us."

Mrs Hudson informed them their meal was ready. She left them to it and walked out of the room.

Holmes and Watson sat in their usual seats at the dining table and filled their plates with delicious food.

They ate in contemplative silence for a few minutes, the only sounds the clink of cutlery and the occasional pop from the fire.

"And then there's Madam Rosalind," Holmes said at last. "Her involvement in this case is most curious."

Watson nodded. "It does seem rather convenient that she's holding a séance at the museum just as these hauntings are escalating as if she knew Mr Chamberlain was reaching the end of his tether with them."

"Precisely," Holmes said. "And her connection to Quentin Silverstone adds another layer of intrigue. Why did she contact him out of the blue like that? I don't believe her story about the spirits guiding her to the magician. Why should she care about such a man if there was no benefit to her? She is running a business, after all, and not a charity. She strikes me as a woman who will stop at nothing until she achieves whatever goal she has set for herself."

"And you think her goal is fame and fortune, as you mentioned to Mr Chamberlain earlier?"

"I do," Holmes confirmed. "I suspect Madam Rosalind may have contacted Quentin because she knew about his book of tricks. Perhaps she needed to add more illusions to her own arsenal of tricks. But, of course, asking Quentin outright wouldn't get her that information. You saw how guarded he was when we asked him to reveal how some tricks were done. So, I think she put him into a light trance whilst she contacted those so-called spirits. And while he was in such a relaxed state, or fast asleep as it turned out, she found that red box and unlocked it. Maybe she got Quentin to explain how to open it during one of his trance-like states. She could have made notes about certain tricks, ones she could use in her work. We may very well see some of those tricks tomorrow at the séance. Her mistake was placing the book the wrong way up when returning it to the box."

Watson said, "Quentin told us how someone could create those supposed supernatural conditions at the museum. Whilst he was in a trance, perhaps he told Madam Rosalind, too. And that's how she produced those spooky effects in Mr Chamberlain's building."

Holmes smiled. "That's exactly what I was thinking."

"So, what's our next move, Holmes?"

Holmes replied, "For now, we wait. Tomorrow evening, we'll attend this séance and see what Madam Rosalind has in store. But I have a feeling that the truth will be far more earthly than spiritual."

Chapter 17

The following afternoon, there was a visitor to 221B Baker Street. Fortunately, Holmes and Watson were both at home to receive her.

Their visitor was Mrs Eliza Morton, the cleaner at Chamberlain's Waxwork Museum. As Mrs Hudson ushered Eliza in, Holmes immediately noticed Mrs Morton's trembling hands and the worry etched on her face.

Holmes rose from his chair. "Mrs Morton. Good afternoon. Please, do take a seat. Mrs Hudson, some tea would be most appreciated."

"Of course, Mr Holmes," Mrs Hudson replied. "I'll bring up a fresh pot and some of that cake I just baked."

Mrs Hudson left the room and Holmes returned to his seated position. He smiled gently at Eliza and said, "Now, Mrs Morton, please tell us what brings you here. Forgive me for saying so, but you seem upset. Can you tell us why?"

Eliza let out a heavy sigh. "Oh, Mr Holmes, Dr Watson, it's the museum. The strange occurrences, they've become worse, much worse. Earlier this morning, some people reported being pushed by invisible hands. One of them stumbled to the floor and injured themselves. And that's not all. There have been voices, too. Whispers in empty rooms, laughter echoing down the halls. And threats. Vile threats hurled at people who walked past the waxworks figures. I could hear complaints coming from all directions. Some people were angry, but a lot of them sounded terrified and I heard them say they would never come back to the museum." She looked down at her hands, twisting them nervously.

Holmes said, "Please, go on, Mrs Morton. If it's not too distressing for you."

Eliza looked up. "Some visitors even claimed to have seen ghostly figures. Apparitions that vanished as quickly as they appeared. I think I might have seen something, too. Just out of the corner of my eye. But I'm sure it's just because everyone's talking about seeing such things. I can't be certain of what I saw, and my mind could be playing tricks on me. One thing I know for certain, is that there is an awful atmosphere amongst the rest of the staff. It's like everyone is on edge, waiting for something terrible to happen. I can't bear it, really I can't."

Mrs Hudson returned with the tea and cake, setting the tray down on the table. She poured each of them a cup before quietly leaving the room.

"Is there anything else, Mrs Morton?" Holmes asked.

Eliza hesitated, then nodded. "Yes, there is. Madam Rosalind arrived after lunchtime. I overheard her talking to Mr Chamberlain when I was doing some cleaning. He told her about the increased activity, and she said something that chilled me to the bone."

Watson asked, "What did she say?"

"She looked straight into Mr Chamberlain's eyes and said the spirits had somehow sensed she was coming to do a séance later. And because they know she will force them to leave the museum, they are causing as much mischief as they can before that happens."

Holmes' eyes narrowed. "And how did Mr Chamberlain react to this?"

Eliza shook her head, a look of unease crossing her face. "That's the strange part. I thought he might dismiss her comments, like he has done before whenever someone mentions spirits and the suchlike to him. But Mr Chamberlain agreed with her wholeheartedly. He said he was glad she was there, and he knew she would rid his museum of spirits. There was something about the way he stared into her eyes. It was unsettling, like he was being hypnotised by her. I didn't like it, Mr Holmes, not one little bit."

Holmes said, "Perhaps Mr Chamberlain was trying to keep Madam Rosalind happy to ensure the séance goes ahead."

Eliza pursed her lips, a look of disgust on her face. "I don't like the idea of a séance. I don't know why there has to be one. Mr Chamberlain said I could watch it, but I won't be there, oh no. I don't like things like that. And there's something about Madam Rosalind that gives me the shivers." She abruptly stopped talking, her lips pressed together as if holding back words.

Holmes gently encouraged her, "Please, Mrs Morton, speak your mind. Whatever it is, it might be important."

With some difficulty, Eliza continued, "After Madam Rosalind finished talking to Mr Chamberlain, he went back to his office. And then, Madam Rosalind turned around and stared right into my eyes, even though I was across the room and thought I hadn't been seen. She came over to me and said she had a message from my late husband, Charlie. She said he was in spirit form and had talked to her."

At the mention of her husband, Eliza's eyes glistened with unshed tears. Dr Watson immediately reached into his pocket and handed her a pressed handkerchief. Eliza accepted it gratefully, dabbing at her eyes.

In a gentle tone, Holmes asked, "What was the message, Mrs Morton?"

Eliza took a deep breath to steady herself. "Charlie's message was, 'Keep away from Sherlock Holmes. He can't be trusted.'"

A heavy silence fell over the room. Holmes and Watson exchanged a glance, both processing the implications of this supposed message from beyond the grave.

Holmes broke the silence, his tone still calm. "Mrs Morton, I assure you that I can be trusted. As can Dr Watson. We have no intention of causing any harm or distress to you or anyone else involved in this case."

Eliza looked up at him, her eyes searching his face. "I know that, Mr Holmes. I don't believe what Madam Rosalind said, not one little bit. Charlie would never say such a thing about you. He admired your work greatly. I'm sure she only said that to scare me. Someone must have told her my husband's name and that he had passed away. But to use that information to unsettle me! It's wicked, it is."

Watson spoke, his voice filled with concern. "Mrs Morton, do you think Madam Rosalind might be involved in these strange occurrences at the museum?"

Eliza hesitated, then nodded slowly. "I don't know for certain, Dr Watson, but I have a feeling she might be. The timing of her arrival today, and the increase in activity before this séance of hers, seems too coincidental."

Holmes nodded. "Your instincts may well be correct, Mrs Morton. Madam Rosalind's actions and words certainly raise suspicions. Watson and I will attend this séance tonight. It will provide an opportunity to observe Madam Rosalind closely and perhaps shed some light on her true intentions."

Watson agreed, "Yes, and we will also keep a close eye on Mr Chamberlain. His behaviour towards Madam Rosalind sounds most peculiar."

Holmes turned to Eliza. "Mrs Morton, I must ask you to be cautious. If Madam Rosalind suspects that you have shared your concerns with us, she may see you as a threat."

Eliza squared her shoulders, a determined look in her eyes. "I understand, Mr Holmes. I'll be careful. But I won't let her intimidate me. I want to help you in any way I can."

Holmes smiled, admiring her courage. "Your assistance is greatly appreciated, Mrs Morton. Please, if you notice anything else unusual, do not hesitate to contact us. Do take care of yourself, especially around Madam Rosalind. Will you stay to finish your tea and cake?"

Eliza stood up. "No, thank you, Mr Holmes. I haven't much of an appetite since Madam Rosalind spoke to me. I'd best be getting back to the museum. If I hear or see anything else, I'll come right back here."

With a final nod and a grateful smile, Eliza left the room, leaving Holmes and Watson to ponder the new information she had provided.

Chapter 18

As the evening drew near, Holmes and Watson made their way to Chamberlain's Waxwork Museum to attend the séance. When their hansom cab drew up outside the museum, they were amazed to see that the entrance was abuzz with activity as elegantly dressed guests arrived and went inside.

Holmes remarked to his companion that the affair appeared to be more of a societal event than the small gathering he was expecting.

Stepping inside, Holmes and Watson found themselves amidst a crowd of people adorned in their finest attire. The room hummed with excited chatter as the guests speculated about the upcoming event. Among the attendees, a few journalists stood out, their notebooks at the ready, hoping to capture a spectacular story for their papers.

Holmes and Watson made their way through the crowd, alert to the various conversations around them.

A well-dressed elderly woman remarked to her companion, "I attended one of Madam Rosalind's séances last month. It was simply extraordinary! She communicated with the spirits and brought such peace to those in attendance." Her eyes sparkled with excitement as she recounted the experience, her voice filled with reverence for the medium's abilities.

Her friend nodded in agreement. "I've heard similar stories. Madam Rosalind's gift is truly remarkable. I had a private reading with her, and the messages she conveyed from my dear departed mother brought me immense comfort. It was like Mother was right there in the room with us, speaking through her."

In a low voice, Watson said to Holmes, "It seems Madam Rosalind has quite a reputation among the upper echelons of society. Her supposed abilities have garnered her a devoted following."

Holmes inclined his head in agreement. "Yes, but we mustn't accept their accounts without reservation. Perhaps Madam Rosalind requested their presence, knowing she could rely on their unwavering support, regardless of the séance's outcome. She already has the cards stacked in her favour."

Watson smiled at his friend. "Not entirely, Holmes. We are true sceptics of all things paranormal. Madam Rosalind will never convince us that this museum is haunted."

As they continued to mingle, a sudden hush fell over the room. All eyes turned towards the entrance.

Madam Rosalind made her grand appearance. She was a vision in a stunning navy silk dress; the fabric adorned with delicate silver sequins that caught the light with every movement. On her arm, Mr Alfred Chamberlain stood tall, his eyes locked adoringly on Madam Rosalind's face.

Holmes' keen gaze observed the interaction between the two. He leaned closer to Watson and whispered, "Mr Chamberlain appears to be completely under Madam Rosalind's spell. This could prove problematic for our investigation."

Watson took in the scene. "You're right, Holmes. There's an unsettling dynamic at play here."

Madam Rosalind and Mr Chamberlain made their way through the crowd, acknowledging the guests with graceful nods and charming smiles.

Madam Rosalind cast a gracious smile on the people before her, her gaze resting for a moment on Holmes. Lifting her chin, she announced, "The séance is about to begin.

Please, follow me and I will lead you to the most haunted part of this building where the séance will take place."

A murmur of anticipation ran through the gathered people.

Under his breath, Watson said, "I hope it's not that reconstructed street. I'm in no mood to see Jack the Ripper pouncing out of the shadows."

Holmes smiled at his comments. "Let's see where Madam Rosalind takes us."

Madam Rosalind led the guests into the large room where waxwork figures of royalty and famous historic figures stood on raised platforms.

Watson leaned closer to Holmes and said, "I'm surprised the séance will take place here. I didn't think this was the most haunted area, at least not to me."

Holmes nodded, his brow furrowed in thought. "There's something 'off' about this room, Watson. Something I felt yesterday when we were here. But for the life of me, I can't quite put my finger on it."

A large table had been placed in the centre of the room, draped in a purple velvet cloth and surrounded by eight chairs. Three rows of additional chairs were arranged in a circle around the table, providing seating for those not invited to sit at the main table itself.

The journalists eagerly made their way to the front row, their pens poised and ready to capture every detail of the impending event.

Madam Rosalind gracefully took her seat at the head of the table, while Mr Chamberlain positioned himself opposite her. Holmes and Watson were about to settle into the outer row of chairs near the back of the room when Madam Rosalind's voice rang out across the room.

"Mr Holmes, Dr Watson, I must insist that you join me at this table. I would like you on either side of me. I politely ask that you don't bring your usual scepticism and non-belief about the spirit realms with you. Your negative feelings will affect my energy." A smug smile played on her lips as she said to the rest of the room, "I will convince the famous Sherlock Holmes and Dr Watson that spirits do, indeed, exist. By the end of this evening, I shall turn them from sceptics into believers."

Holmes and Watson had no choice but to comply with Madam Rosalind's request. They made their way to the table and took their seats on either side of her, their discomfort evident in their expressions.

Madam Rosalind, on the other hand, seemed to revel in their unease. She gave them a satisfied smile, her eyes glinting with a hint of triumph.

Once everyone was seated, Madam Rosalind said, "The séance shall now commence. From now on, the only voices you will hear will be mine and those of the visiting spirits."

Chapter 19

Madam Rosalind closed her eyes, her head tilted back slightly as if listening to a distant voice.

"Let us join hands," she intoned, her voice low and melodic. "We must create an unbroken circle, a conduit for the spirits to reach us."

Holmes and Watson exchanged a sceptical glance but did as instructed. They clasped hands with Madam Rosalind and the others seated at the table, forming a chain of linked fingers.

Madam Rosalind took a deep breath, the air seeming to crackle with anticipation. "Spirits of the beyond," she called out, her voice resonating through the room, "we implore you to make your presence known. Speak to us, guide us, and share your wisdom from the other side."

A gust of cold wind swept through the room, causing the candle flames to flicker and dance. The journalists in the front row leaned forward, their notepads open, ready to record every detail.

"I sense a presence," Madam Rosalind whispered, her brow furrowed in concentration. "A restless soul, trapped within these walls, yearning to be heard."

Some low gasps came from several areas.

Suddenly, a loud knock echoed through the room, causing several people to gasp. Madam Rosalind's eyes flew open, her gaze intense and focused.

"The spirits are among us," she declared, her voice trembling with emotion. "They wish to communicate."

Another knock, this time more insistent, reverberated through the space. The waxwork figures seemed to loom larger, their eyes gleaming in the candlelight.

Madam Rosalind began to speak, her words flowing in a stream of cryptic messages. "The past and the present collide, secrets buried deep within these walls. A betrayal, a hidden truth, a score to settle."

The room grew colder and strange shadows flickered across the walls, some of them eerily human-like.

Madam Rosalind's voice rose in pitch, her words becoming more urgent. "The spirits demand justice, a wrong to be righted. The truth must be revealed, or the haunting will continue."

Suddenly, a gust of wind extinguished the candles, plunging the room into darkness. Gasps and murmurs filled the air as the guests grappled with the sudden blackness. Ghostly groans and moans filled the air.

In the midst of the confusion, a piercing scream rang out, followed by the sound of shattering glass. Some people cried out in fear.

Holmes and Watson leapt to their feet.

"Remain calm!" Holmes called out, his voice cutting through the panic. "Watson, find a light source!"

As Watson fumbled in the darkness, a faint glow began to emanate from the centre of the table. Slowly, the light grew brighter, revealing Madam Rosalind, her eyes closed and her face contorted in a trance-like state.

The room fell silent, all eyes fixated on the eerie spectacle before them.

Watson reignited the candles and returned to his seated position. Holmes did the same, his steely glance focused on Madam Rosalind as he wondered what she was going to do next.

Madam Rosalind, her voice now a haunting whisper, spoke once more. "The spirits attached to these waxworks have sent me a message," she intoned, her eyes still closed in a trance-like state. "They are upset because of the fear and confusion they have caused. They only wished to make their presence known, to greet the visitors of the museum. They never wished to cause any harm." She nodded, as if receiving a new message. "Ah, yes, thank you. The spirits would like to give their appreciation to the owner of this museum, who set forth the process of creating them. They say he has done an excellent job and they are most impressed."

Holmes' gaze shifted to Chamberlain, noting the proud look that appeared on the man's face. It was a curious reaction, given the eerie circumstances that surrounded them.

Madam Rosalind said, "Spirits, thank you for talking to me. I appreciate your concerns, but I respectfully ask you to leave this building; to leave it in peace. Thank you, kind spirits, thank you."

A series of low groans came from the waxwork figures, followed by shadows racing across the room; shadows that vanished a few seconds later.

Holmes wondered how Madam Rosalind had created such illusions. He had to admit, they were extremely effective.

Suddenly, the atmosphere shifted, and a sense of unease permeated the air. Madam Rosalind's brow furrowed, and her voice took on a sharper edge. "An angry spirit is trying to get my attention. Spirit, yes, I can hear you. Spirit, please do not curse! Tell me what angers you so. Ah, I see. Yes, I do understand. We are of the same mind. Yes, I will tell them." She opened her eyes and said, "The spirit is upset with certain people in this room; people who doubt the existence of the spiritual world beyond the veil. The spirit has heard the way these two men talk about such matters, and it has ignited a fury in him. He wants these men to leave the museum and never set foot in it again."

Holmes could feel the weight of eyes upon him, but he didn't say a word. Watson squirmed in his seat, trying to avoid looking left or right at those who were glowering at him.

Madam Rosalind smiled, her gaze sweeping across the room. "The spirits have departed," she announced, her voice clear and strong. "The museum is now free from their presence."

A murmur of relief and amazement rippled through the assembled guests. Some of them broke into a round of applause. The journalists scribbled furiously in their notebooks.

As people began to leave the room, Madam Rosalind sank back in her chair, a look of satisfaction and exhaustion etched upon her face.

Mr Chamberlain rushed to Madam Rosalind's side, his face a picture of concern. "Madam Rosalind, are you all right?" he asked, his voice tinged with worry.

She smiled up at him. "Contacting the spirit world always takes its toll, Mr Chamberlain," she replied. "But I assure you, the spiritual activity that has plagued your museum will cease from this moment forward."

Chamberlain's face broke into a wide smile, his admiration for Madam Rosalind evident in his expression. "I cannot thank you enough, Madam Rosalind," he gushed, taking her hand in his. "I should have accepted your offer of assistance the moment you reached out to me. It was foolish of me to delay matters."

Madam Rosalind inclined her head graciously, accepting his praise. However, her gaze soon drifted past Chamberlain, settling on Holmes, who was still sitting at her side.

Chamberlain, noticing the shift in Madam Rosalind's attention, turned brusquely to face Holmes and Watson. "Gentlemen," he said, his tone curt and dismissive, "it appears that your services are no longer required. With all due respect, I must ask you to leave the museum immediately."

Holmes raised an eyebrow, his expression unreadable. Watson, however, looked taken aback by the sudden change in Chamberlain's demeanour.

"Please send your bill for any services rendered thus far," Chamberlain continued, waving a hand dismissively. "But consider this matter closed. Madam Rosalind has resolved the situation, and there is no further need for your involvement. And you heard what that angry spirit said to this dear woman. It's clear he was talking about you and Dr Watson as the ones who had vexed him. I can't take the chance of him returning and causing trouble."

Holmes' gaze locked with Madam Rosalind's for a brief moment, noticing the glimmer of triumph in her eyes.

Then, with a slight nod, he turned to Watson. "Come, Watson," he said quietly. "It appears our presence is no longer welcome."

Once outside the museum, Watson turned to Holmes, his face a mixture of confusion and frustration. "Holmes, what just happened in there?" he asked, gesturing back towards the museum. "Do you believe Madam Rosalind truly communicated with spirits, or was it all an elaborate hoax? I must say, she was very convincing. It was quite a show she put on."

"It was a show, my dear Watson, an extremely elaborate show. She wasn't communicating with the other world, but I wondered if she was communicating with us in some way."

Watson gave him a confused look. "I don't understand. Did I miss something?"

Holmes said, "At the beginning of the séance, Madam Rosalind mentioned a betrayal, a score that needed to be settled. She said there were secrets deep within the walls of the building. She never explained what those words meant, or if they were intended for anyone in particular."

Watson nodded. "I see. Do you think she has been betrayed by Mr Chamberlain or one of his employees in the past? Or do her words have something to do with this building and what may have happened here?"

"I'm note sure," Holmes replied. "Those words struck me as odd. I was going to speak to her about those comments, but alas, thanks to her clever invention of a vengeful spirit who has taken against us, that conversation won't take place. I must admit, I wasn't impressed with how quickly she dismissed the so-called spirits from the museum, or the reasons why she claimed they were causing mischief. Far too simple and not at all entertaining, in my opinion. I was expecting a lot more from Madam Rosalind, going by how popular she is. Yet, she achieved her purpose. I'm sure the newspapers will be full of her antics tomorrow. And Mr Chamberlain is certain the strange activities have now stopped."

Watson said, "What do you propose we do now?" he asked, falling into step beside Holmes as they walked away from the museum.

Holmes sighed. "There's nothing more we can do at the moment. We have been dismissed by Mr Chamberlain. But I have a feeling that this mystery is far from over."

Chapter 20

Over the next week, Holmes and Watson put the events of the séance behind them, focusing their attention on the new cases that arrived at their doorstep. One particularly intriguing case involved a missing heirloom, a family feud, and a web of deceit that kept the duo busy for several days. Another case, brought to them by a distressed young lady, revolved around a series of anonymous letters that threatened to expose a scandalous secret from her past.

One afternoon, upon the completion of their latest case, Holmes and Watson decided to take advantage of the fine weather and take a walk outside. They hadn't got very far, when they saw someone familiar heading towards them. It was Marcus Bramwell, smiling from ear to ear, and tipping his hat at every woman who passed him.

"He certainly looks pleased with himself," Watson noted. "I thought he would be annoyed about things turning around for Mr Chamberlain following that séance. After all, there's no chance of him buying the museum now."

"Yes, he does seem suspiciously chipper," Holmes agreed.

Mr Bramwell spotted them and called out, "Mr Holmes! Dr Watson! What a pleasure to see you. Isn't it a most splendid day?" He stopped in front of them, clearly wanting to engage them in conversation.

Holmes said, "Good afternoon, Mr Bramwell. You seem in fine spirits. May I ask, is there a reason for that?"

"Oh, absolutely!" His voice brimmed with delight. "I am positively thrilled about the recent turn of events at the Chamberlain Waxwork Museum."

Holmes and Watson exchanged puzzled glances.

"I beg your pardon, Mr Bramwell," Holmes said. "The last we heard, the museum was thriving after Madam Rosalind's supposed banishment of the spirits. Has something changed?"

Bramwell let out a hearty laugh, his eyes twinkling with amusement. "Oh, my dear Mr Holmes, there have been some rather interesting developments just this morning. While I don't have all the details, I do know that Her Majesty, Queen Victoria, was scheduled to visit the museum this morning. The establishment was closed to the general public for the occasion. But that's not the most intriguing part. Just after lunch, I was strolled past the museum. I noticed a sign indicating that the museum had been closed permanently with immediate effect."

"Closed? Just like that?" Holmes pressed.

Bramwell's eyes glinted with joy. "That's not all, gentlemen. I heard a rumour from a friend that Mr Chamberlain has been arrested by the police. Something about an incident during the Queen's visit, and there are whispers of 'treason' floating about. He is presently locked up behind bars at the local prison."

Watson asked, "But what exactly happened during the Queen's visit?"

"I've no idea," Bramwell replied. "And I don't much care. All I know is that the museum building will be up for sale soon, and I fully intend to make it mine. Good day to you both."

As Bramwell walked away, Holmes turned to Watson, his expression grave. "We must head to the prison immediately, Watson," he declared. "We need to find out what happened during the Queen's visit and why Chamberlain has been arrested."

Watson nodded in agreement. "Of course, Holmes. But treason? Against the Queen herself? I can scarcely believe it."

Holmes said, "I truly hope Madam Rosalind isn't behind this, but I wouldn't be surprised if she were. Despite being dismissed by him, I hope Mr Chamberlain will speak to us. I have a feeling he needs us now more than ever."

Chapter 21

The prison loomed before Holmes and Watson, its grey stone walls and barred windows a stark reminder of the grim fate that had befallen Mr Chamberlain. As they entered the dank, dimly lit building, the echoes of their footsteps mingled with the distant sounds of clanging metal doors and the muffled cries of inmates.

A guard, his face weathered and his eyes weary from years of service, led them through a maze of narrow corridors, past cells filled with despondent faces and hollow eyes. The prisoners, some resigned to their fate and others still clinging to a faint glimmer of hope, watched as the unlikely pair passed by, their presence a fleeting distraction from the monotony of incarceration.

At last, they reached the cell where Mr Chamberlain was being held. The once-proud owner of the waxwork museum sat hunched on a narrow cot, his face gaunt and his eyes ringed with dark circles, a shadow of the jovial man he had been mere days before. He looked up as Holmes and Watson approached, a flicker of relief crossing his features.

"Mr Holmes, Dr Watson," Chamberlain said. "I can't tell you how pleased I am to see you. I asked if I could send you a telegram requesting your presence, but was told no. But here you are. How did you know where to find me?"

Holmes answered, "Mr Bramwell told us about your predicament."

"Pah!" Chamberlain exclaimed. "I can imagine how happy that made him. But I'm grateful he did, because his words led you here. I am hoping with all my heart that you are here to help me. Although, I have no right to ask for your help, not after the way I treated you at the séance. You have my sincere apologies for the terrible way I spoke to you."

Holmes waved away the apology with a dismissive gesture of his hand. "You did what you thought was best at the time, Mr Chamberlain. We are here to offer our services, if you would like us to."

Chamberlain sagged in relief. "Thank you, Mr Holmes, Dr Watson. My situation is dire, very dire, indeed."

Dr Watson said, "Marcus Bramwell told us you had been arrested, and that 'treason' was the reason why. Surely, that's not the case."

Chamberlain gave them a grim-faced nod. "Alas, Dr Watson. It is true."

"Tell us everything," Holmes advised.

Chamberlain explained, "Following the newspaper article about Madam Rosalind's séance. Oh, did you see the papers?"

Holmes said, "I only saw the headline. 'Madam Rosalind Succeeds Where Sherlock Holmes Fails'. Please, continue."

Chamberlain cleared his throat, obviously embarrassed by the news headline. "Yes, right. After the séance, I received a message straight from the Palace. It was from Queen Victoria. She had seen the newspaper and wanted to see the museum for herself. She mentioned she had an interest in the paranormal and would love to know more about what had happened there during the séance."

"Did the Queen ask that Madam Rosalind be present at her visit?" Holmes asked.

Chamberlain shook his head. "I was glad about that as I never want to see Madam Rosalind ever again. I should have trusted you, Mr Holmes. You were right to be wary of her, and her so-called abilities. I allowed myself to be taken in by Madam Rosalind's charms, to believe that there was a special connection between us, something beyond the mundane world. I see now that I was merely a pawn in her game, a means to an end."

Watson said, "What happened, Mr Chamberlain? What made you realise that Madam Rosalind was not what she seemed?"

Chamberlain sighed heavily, his hand passing over his weary face as he recounted the painful memory. "A few days after the séance, I called at her house, hoping to invite her to dinner. I had thought, perhaps foolishly, that there was a genuine connection between us. But when I arrived, I saw the contempt in her eyes, and I heard the disdain in her voice. She told me, in no uncertain terms, that I was far too old for her, that I had misread the situation entirely. I was nothing more than a gullible old man to her.

"But that wasn't all. As I was leaving, dejected and humiliated, I noticed another room in her house, filled with people waiting for private readings. They were all eagerly anticipating their turn with the great Madam Rosalind." A note of bitterness crept into his voice. "And everywhere I looked, there were copies of newspapers, all praising Madam Rosalind's incredible abilities, her gift for communing with the spirits. It was then that I realised the true extent of her deception. It was just as you predicted, Mr Holmes, all Madam Rosalind is interested in is fame and fortune. She uses people to achieve those things, and when she has no further use for those people, she discards them without a second thought."

Holmes nodded. "I'm sorry you were so humiliated by her, Mr Chamberlain. She does have a way of easily manipulating others. But, please, tell us more about Queen Victoria's visit."

Chamberlain continued, "Arrangements were made for the Queen to visit the museum this morning. We closed it to the public and ensured the place was spotless. Thomas had just completed the waxwork of Her Majesty and we rushed to put it in place. The figure was the best work Thomas had ever undertaken. It was a work of art. I knew Her Majesty would be impressed. My plan was to show the figure first, and then tell the Queen more about the hauntings and the séance, pushing my feelings about Madam Rosalind to one side, of course.

"But things didn't work out that way. Queen Victoria arrived promptly at ten o'clock, accompanied by her ladies-in-waiting and a small contingent of guards. I greeted her at the entrance and escorted her directly to the room housing her new waxwork figure. I stood to one side to let her enter first. Only seconds later, I heard a gasp followed by an outrage cry. I dashed into the room and saw..." He paused to gather himself. "I saw that the beautiful waxwork figure of Queen Victoria had been sabotaged. Someone had deliberately caused it to melt, leaving a horrendous mess behind."

Dr Watson declared, "Good heavens! What happened then?"

"I tried to placate the Queen, told her someone had caused the damage on purpose to destroy my business. But she wouldn't listen. She demanded that I be arrested on the spot, and that the museum be shut down." He held his hands out helplessly. "And here I am. Ready to await my sentence. I keep thinking about that melted waxwork. It's deliberate sabotage, I'm sure of it. But who would do such a thing?"

Holmes said, "That is what we intend to find out, Mr Chamberlain. You have my word that Watson and I will do everything in our power to uncover the true culprit behind this heinous act. I suspect it could be the same person who has been behind these strange occurrences all along. Whoever it is, they have played an excellent game of deception, weaving a web of lies and misdirection. But I assure you, we shall bring the perpetrator to justice."

Chamberlain's eyes shone with gratitude. "Thank you, Mr Holmes. I don't know what I would do without your help. You have my full permission to access any part of the museum, if that would help. Please, do whatever you must to clear my name and restore the reputation of my beloved museum." He patted his pocket. "Unfortunately, I was rushed out of the museum so quickly that I didn't get the chance to collect my keys. There may be a member of staff still at the museum who could let you in, but I have a feeling everyone has left."

Holmes smiled and said, "I don't need keys. I have a way of opening locked doors. We must take our leave, Mr Chamberlain, but we will return soon, and we will return with good news."

Chapter 22

Holmes and Watson stepped out of the prison, their minds heavy with the weight of Chamberlain's plight. As they made their way towards the Waxwork Museum, Holmes' keen eyes spotted a familiar figure leaving the building and heading in the direction of the King's Arms pub.

"Watson, look there," Holmes said, pointing discreetly. "It's Thomas Hargreaves, and he seems to be in quite a hurry. I believe it's time we had another chat with Mr Hargreaves, especially in light of what has happened this morning."

The two men followed Hargreaves at a distance, careful not to draw attention to themselves. They entered the pub and found him sitting in a dimly lit corner, a pint of beer already in hand. Holmes and Watson approached his table and took a seat across from him.

Before either of them could speak, Hargreaves raised his glass and smirked. "Well, well, if it isn't the great Sherlock Holmes and his trusty sidekick. Come to drown your sorrows over the museum's closure?"

Holmes said, "On the contrary, Mr Hargreaves. We're here to discuss your role in this whole affair."

Hargreaves scoffed. "My role? I had nothing to do with it. In fact, I'm glad that wretched place is shut down."

Watson exchanged a glance with Holmes before speaking. "When we spoke to you before, you claimed to be happy with your job. Why the sudden change of heart?"

Hargreaves took a long swig of his beer, his eyes darkening. "Happy? That was a load of rubbish. I only said that because I needed the work. But Chamberlain and I didn't get along. He was always demanding more, never satisfied with my efforts. Do you know how many hours I spent slaving away in that workshop, creating his precious waxworks? And what thanks did I get? Nothing but criticism and contempt. Do you remember that waxwork figure I made of Queen Victoria? It was my best work ever. But it's been destroyed. And it's got something to do with Chamberlain. One of his enemies getting revenge, I expect, and my artwork has been mutilated in the process. I didn't deserve that, not at all."

Holmes listened intently, allowing Hargreaves to vent his frustrations. When the sculptor paused to take another sip of beer, Holmes interjected. "Did your resentment drive you to cause the strange occurrences at the museum? The unexplained noises, the moving figures?"

Hargreaves let out a bitter laugh. "I wish I'd been that clever. No, Mr Holmes, I had nothing to do with those happenings. Though I can't say I'm sorry they occurred. Chamberlain deserved every bit of trouble that came his way."

Watson leaned in, his brow furrowed. "What about Madam Rosalind? Do you think she could have been behind it all?"

Hargreaves shook his head. "I doubt it. She's a bit of a charlatan, if you ask me. All that talk of spirits and whatnot. But..." He hesitated, his glance darting around the pub.

Holmes' gaze sharpened. "But what, Mr Hargreaves? If you have information, it's crucial that you share it with us."

Hargreaves sighed, lowering his voice. "Well, I did see her setting up some strange equipment before that séance evening. Wires, pulleys, that sort of thing. Thought it was odd at the time, but I didn't say anything. Figured it was none of my business."

Watson nodded. "We were there at the séance. We saw the illusions she created."

Holmes said, "Mr Hargreaves, during our initial meeting at the museum, you presented yourself as content in your work. Why did you not share your true feelings then?"

"If I had spoken ill of Chamberlain then, he might have overheard. The man has ears everywhere."

Watson frowned, puzzled. "But we were in your workshop, Mr Hargreaves. Surely, you could have spoken freely there?"

Hargreaves leaned forward, his voice lowering to a conspiratorial whisper. "You don't know the half of it. That museum is full of secrets, including passageways that Chamberlain uses to move about unseen. He could have been lurking behind any wall, listening to our every word. I often get the feeling I'm being watched, even when I'm alone in my workshop."

Holmes said, "Secret passageways? I had no idea. This changes things considerably."

Hargreaves nodded, a grim satisfaction on his face. "Oh, yes. Chamberlain is a sly one. Uses those hidden corridors to keep tabs on everyone, making sure we're all toeing the line."

Watson frowned. "But why would he need such a thing? Surely, as the owner, he could go where he pleased?"

"It's not about access, Dr Watson," Hargreaves explained. "It's about control. Chamberlain likes to know everything that goes on in his precious museum, without anyone being the wiser."

Holmes leaned back in his chair. "Mr Hargreaves, this information could be vital to our investigation. Is there any way you could show us these passageways?"

Hargreaves hesitated for a moment, then reached into his pocket and pulled out a set of keys. He slid them across the table to Holmes. "Here, take these. They'll get you into the museum and Chamberlain's office. I won't be needing them anymore, not now that I'm done with that place."

Holmes picked up the keys, examining them closely. "And in his office, we'll find the plans for the building? The ones that reveal the secret passageways?"

Hargreaves nodded. "That's right. Chamberlain keeps them locked up tight, but with those keys, you should be able to get your hands on them."

"How do you know about these passageways, Mr Hargreaves?" Holmes asked.

Hargreaves smirked. "Everyone who works there knows about them. I can't remember who told me, but it's common knowledge amongst the staff. Of course, Chamberlain isn't aware of this. He thinks he's got one over on us, but he hasn't."

Watson looked at Holmes. "This could be the break we've been looking for, Holmes. If Madam Rosalind or someone else has been using these passageways to create the illusion of hauntings..."

"Then we may be closer to unravelling this mystery than we thought," Holmes finished, a glint of determination in his eye. He turned back to Hargreaves. "Thank you, Mr Hargreaves. Your information has been most helpful."

Hargreaves waved a dismissive hand. "Don't mention it. Just promise me one thing, Mr Holmes. When you catch the person responsible for all this, make sure they pay for what they've done. Chamberlain may be a difficult man, but he doesn't deserve to rot in prison for someone else's crimes."

Holmes nodded solemnly. "You have my word, Mr Hargreaves. Justice will be served, one way or another."

With that, Holmes and Watson bid farewell to the disgruntled sculptor and made their way out of the pub. As they stepped into the cool London air, Holmes turned to his companion, a glint of anticipation in his eye.

"Come, Watson. We have a set of plans to examine and a network of secret passageways to explore. We are getting closer to discovering the person who's responsible for all this trouble."

Chapter 23

Holmes and Watson walked briskly towards Chamberlain's Waxwork Museum. Upon reaching the building, they were greeted by a large sign on the door, proclaiming in bold letters: "CLOSED PERMANENTLY."

Holmes pulled out the set of keys Hargreaves had given them. With a deft turn of the key, the lock on the main door clicked open, and the two men stepped inside the museum. The silence that greeted them was eerie, the usual bustle of visitors replaced by an oppressive stillness.

As they made their way through the exhibits, they came upon the melted figure of Queen Victoria. Watson shook his head, a mixture of disbelief and sympathy on his face.

"The poor Queen," he murmured. "To see herself depicted in such a manner... it must have been quite a shock."

Holmes examined the distorted features of the waxwork. "It's clear that this was no accident. Someone deliberately sabotaged this figure, knowing full well the reaction it would provoke."

They continued on, their footsteps echoing in the empty halls, until they reached Chamberlain's office. Holmes immediately set to work, rifling through drawers and files with practised efficiency. Watson went to the other side of the room to see if he could find anything useful there.

"Aha!" Holmes exclaimed, holding up a set of blueprints. "Here we are, Watson. The plans for the museum. Let's have a good look at them." He opened them out on the table.

Watson hurried over, peering over Holmes' shoulder at the intricate lines and symbols. "Good Lord, Holmes. Those hidden passageways are everywhere. Running behind the walls, connecting the exhibits..."

Holmes traced a finger along one of the passages. "And look here, Watson. A passageway running alongside the room housing King Henry VIII and other royal figures. The very room where I felt something was amiss, remember?"

Watson peered closer. "Of course! That room is smaller than the one preceding it. That must be because the passageway was taking up some of the space. Well spotted, Holmes. I never would have noticed such a thing. That explains all the strange activity in that area. Someone must have caused the incidents from within that hidden area. But how?"

Holmes folded up the plans and tucked them into his coat pocket. "We will soon have the answer to that question. Let us proceed to that place and find a way into the passageway. With some luck and keen observation, we might locate a clue."

Watson nodded, steeling himself for the task ahead. "Lead on then, Holmes. Let's see what secrets these walls have to hide." As soon as he said those last words, his eyes widened. "That's what Madam Rosalind said during her séance, or something similar. That there were secrets deep within the walls of the museum."

Holmes said, "I was about to say the same thing to you, my dear Watson. If she is the culprit, let's see if Madam Rosalind has left any evidence behind."

With that, the two men exited the office and made their way back through the museum. As they approached the room housing the Tudor monarch, Holmes paused, his eyes scanning the walls with intense concentration. He moved over to the wall where the passageway was, according to the blueprints, and ran his hands gently over the patterned wallpaper.

"There," he said, pointing to a barely visible seam in the wallpaper. "That must be the entrance to the passageway. Now, how do I open this door?"

Holmes' nimble fingers probed the edges of the door, searching for a mechanism. After a moment, he pressed firmly on a slightly raised portion of the wall, and with a soft click, the door swung open, revealing a narrow, dimly lit passageway.

"Ingenious," Holmes murmured, stepping inside. "A spring-loaded mechanism, triggered by pressure on a specific point."

Watson followed close behind. They noticed a gas lamp hanging on a nail, its soft light casting eerie shadows on the walls. Holmes reached up and carefully lifted the lamp from its perch, holding it aloft to illuminate their path.

Holmes said, "Someone has left this lamp burning, which suggests there has been a recent visitor to this hallway. Perhaps it's the same person who caused damage to the Queen's waxwork figure."

As they walked, they soon noticed small holes at eye height along the passageway, spaced at regular intervals. Watson peered through one of the holes and gasped. "Holmes, look. You get an excellent view of the room from here."

Holmes peered through another hole, his brow furrowed in concentration. "Yes, and from this vantage point, it's perfect for observing the reactions of unsuspecting visitors. And because of the intricate pattern of the wallpaper on the other side, it would be easy to remain unspotted. Let's examine this area thoroughly. The culprit may have left something behind."

Holmes ran his hand slowly over the wall, searching for evidence.

Watson did the same, and moments later, he said, "Holmes, look at this. There's a nail sticking out here, and on it, is a scrap of fabric."

"Well done, my friend. Please put that in your pocket. That could be the evidence we're looking for. But, on the other hand, it could be nothing significant. Let's keep looking."

"Rightio." Watson took a folded handkerchief from his pocket and carefully placed the fabric inside it. He put the handkerchief back in his pocket, adding a little tap of satisfaction.

They continued searching the area.

Holmes got to his knees. He placed the lamp at his side and ran his hands over the lower part of the wall. All of a sudden, he let out a cry of jubilation.

"What have you found?" Watson asked, kneeling next to him.

Holmes placed his fingers smoothly against the wall. He said, "This area is slightly raised. I am hoping there is a concealed compartment here. Let me see if I can find a way to open it. Maybe it's the same spring mechanism that's on the door."

A click sounded out, and a large drawer slid smoothly open.

Inside the drawer was a variety of items; wires, pulleys and something else.

Holmes picked an item up and examined it more closely. He gave Watson a grim look. "Looks like we've found our culprit."

Chapter 24

Holmes and Watson sat in their cosy living room at 221B Baker Street, the morning sun streaming through the windows. The room was filled with the aroma of freshly brewed tea and the faint scent of pipe tobacco. Holmes reclined in his armchair, deep in thought. Watson, ever the early riser, sat at the desk, pen in hand, jotting down notes from their latest case.

A soft knock at the door drew their attention. "Come in, Mrs Hudson," Holmes called out.

The door opened, and Mrs Hudson entered, followed by a nervous-looking Mrs Eliza Morton. "Mrs Morton to see you, Mr Holmes," Mrs Hudson announced, a warm smile on her face.

Holmes rose from his chair, a welcoming smile on his lips. "Ah, Mrs Morton, thank you for coming. Please, do take a seat." He gestured towards the settee, his voice gentle and reassuring.

Eliza nodded, her hands clasped tightly in front of her. She made her way to the settee and sat down. "Thank you for seeing me, Mr Holmes, Dr Watson. I hope I'm not interrupting anything important, but your telegram said you wanted to see me as soon as possible. I've never had a telegram before." She gave them a small smile.

Watson put down his pen and moved over to his usual armchair. He said, "I hope the telegram didn't cause you any distress. We invited you here to tell you about our latest case, the one involving the wax museum."

Eliza said, "Have you found out who did it, Dr Watson? I'm ever so worried about Mr Chamberlain, what with him being in prison and all. It's just not right, him being locked up like that."

Holmes nodded, his expression sympathetic. "I understand your concern, Mrs Morton. It's a troubling situation, to be sure."

"And that waxwork of Her Majesty, Queen Victoria," Eliza continued, her voice trembling slightly. "Who would do such a wicked thing, melting it like that? It's just horrible, it is."

Holmes replied, "Indeed, it is a most distressing act of vandalism. But I assure you, Mrs Morton, Dr Watson and I have been working tirelessly to unravel the mystery of the hauntings at the museum. And I am pleased to say that we have solved the case."

Eliza's eyes widened. "You have, Mr Holmes? Oh, that's wonderful news! I knew you'd get to the bottom of it, I did. Is it Madam Rosalind, then? I've had my suspicions about her from the start, what with all her talk of spirits and such."

Holmes shook his head. "No, Mrs Morton, much as it pains me to admit it, Madam Rosalind is not the culprit behind the hauntings. While she certainly staged some of the effects at the séance, likely learned from her association with Quentin Silverstone, she is not responsible for the larger mystery."

Eliza frowned, confusion etched on her face. "Quentin Silverstone? I've never heard of him. Who is he?"

A heavy silence fell. Holmes leaned back in his chair, his eyes fixed on Eliza, who stared at the clock on the mantelpiece.

Finally, Holmes spoke, his voice gentle yet firm. "Mrs Morton, you must know who Quentin Silverstone is. You have been working as a cleaner at the theatre where he performs for the past three years, and you often stop to talk to him in his dressing room when he's resting between performances."

Eliza's eyes widened, her hands clasped tightly in her lap. She opened her mouth as if to speak, but no words came out.

Holmes continued, "After making an interesting discovery at the museum yesterday afternoon, Dr Watson and I called on Quentin last evening. He spoke very fondly of you, Mrs Morton. He mentioned how interested you were in his magic tricks and how he even shared the secrets behind some of his simpler illusions with you. He didn't know you worked at the waxworks museum and was extremely surprised when we told him."

Eliza's cheeks flushed, and she looked down at her hands, her fingers twisting together. The silence stretched on, broken only by the soft ticking of the clock.

"And that's not all," Holmes said, his voice still gentle but with an undercurrent of steel. "You also work as a cleaner at Marcus Bramwell's establishment, don't you? And you're on friendly terms with him as well."

At the mention of Bramwell's name, Eliza slowly smiled. She looked up and said, "Marcus is a wonderful man. He always has time for me, always greets me by name and asks how I am. Not like some places where I'm invisible, where no one even sees me, let alone knows my name. But not Marcus, he always notices me." She stopped talking, a faraway look in her eyes. "He sees me as I am. I'm not invisible to him, not at all."

Holmes continued, "Is that why you created the disturbances at the museum, Mrs Morton? The ones that led to rumours about it being haunted?"

Eliza's eyes widened, her hands gripping the fabric of her skirt. She fell silent again, her lips pressed together in a thin line.

"You knew how Marcus felt betrayed by Alfred Chamberlain," Holmes said. "He had spoken to you about that during one of your chats, hadn't he? And so, you caused the disturbances with the aim of getting the museum to close. Then, Mr Bramwell could buy it."

Eliza's gaze remained fixed on her lap, her shoulders hunched as if under a great weight.

Dr Watson spoke, "We weren't sure why you would create the disturbances, Mrs Morton. At first, we thought you might have a grudge against Mr Chamberlain. Perhaps he had treated you harshly or was critical of your work. But then, Holmes wondered if there was another reason; a score to settle, so to speak. But a score on someone else's behalf which led us to Mr Bramwell. We paid him a visit yesterday, and he told us about your chats."

Eliza looked up, a smile on her face. "He did? He talked about me? He's such a lovely man, don't you think so, Dr Watson? And so very handsome, too."

Dr Watson merely smiled, but gave no response.

Holmes looked at Eliza and said, "You must have been angry with Madam Rosalind and her séance, claiming that the so-called spirits had left. You could have waited a while before starting up the disturbances again. But instead, you resorted to something so shocking, something you knew would cause the museum to be closed immediately."

Eliza averted her gaze.

"You were the one who caused the damage to Queen Victoria's waxwork, weren't you, Mrs Morton?" Holmes' voice was gentle, but there was no mistaking the underlying accusation. "Watson, would you be so kind as to show Mrs Morton what we found inside that hidden passageway at the museum?"

Watson reached towards a box sitting on a table at the side. He opened it and pulled out a scrap of cloth, holding it up for Eliza to see. "We found this snagged on a nail inside one of the hidden passageways at the museum. It appears to be part of a cleaning cloth."

Eliza's gaze fixed on the scrap of fabric. Her hands trembled slightly in her lap.

"And that's not all," Watson continued, reaching into the box once more. "Holmes and I discovered a hidden compartment in the lower part of that passageway. When we looked inside, we found this notebook along with some wires and a pulley system." He pulled out a small, leather-bound notebook, its cover worn and tattered.

Holmes said, "The notebook contains detailed descriptions of tricks, complete with drawings and instructions. Tricks that a magician might use to create illusions. Or someone who wanted to create eerie effects in a museum. We have checked the handwriting in the notebook. It matches the handwriting on your employee records, which we found in Mr Chamberlain's office."

A single tear rolled down Eliza's cheek, leaving a glistening trail on her skin. She bowed her head, her shoulders shaking with silent sobs.

Watson's expression softened, his brow furrowed with concern. "Why did you do it, Mrs Morton?" he asked.

Eliza sobbed quietly.

Holmes said softly, "You're in love with Marcus Bramwell, aren't you, Mrs Morton? You wanted to prove your love to him, to show him how much you cared."

More tears spilled down Eliza's cheeks. Her voice was barely audible as she spoke. "You're right, Mr Holmes. I do love Marcus, with all my heart."

Holmes nodded, his expression sympathetic. "You loved seeing how happy he was after hearing about the rumours of hauntings at the museum and how it was affecting Mr Chamberlain's business. It filled your heart with pride, knowing that you had made him so happy."

Eliza looked up, her eyes shining with tears. "Yes, it did. I wanted nothing more than to see him smile, to know that I had brought him joy."

"And the ultimate goal," Holmes continued, "was to close the museum, so that Marcus could buy it. You planned to tell him what you had done for him one day, to show him the depth of your love."

A sob escaped Eliza's lips, and she buried her face in her hands. Her shoulders shook as she wept.

Holmes and Watson exchanged a glance, their expressions a mix of sympathy and concern. Holmes knew that Eliza's actions, though misguided, had been driven by love. But he also knew that the consequences of her choices would be severe.

Eliza stopped crying. She looked up at Holmes and Watson. "I had to keep going with the illusions," she said, her voice trembling. "Seeing how happy they made Marcus, it was like a drug. I couldn't stop, even when I knew it was wrong."

Holmes said, "You didn't mean to hurt anyone, did you, Mrs Morton?"

Eliza shook her head vehemently. "No, of course not! I never wanted to cause any harm. And I certainly didn't mean to fool you and Dr Watson. I have the greatest respect for you both, truly I do."

Watson said, "But you did lie to us, Mrs Morton. About the things that had happened in the museum, about what people had said and things that had happened. To make us believe things were even worse. And, it threw the blame completely off you."

A flush of shame crept up Eliza's neck, staining her cheeks. "Yes, I did lie. And I'm so sorry for that. I never thought Mr Chamberlain would engage you. When I saw you there in the museum, I was so shocked, so afraid of being found out."

Holmes said, "We never had you down as a suspect, which is our fault and we should have known better. But, I must admit, you were extremely convincing, Mrs Morton. Can I ask, did Madam Rosalind actually give you a message from your late husband?"

Fresh tears came to Eliza's eyes. "She didn't. I'm so ashamed of bringing my Charlie into this mess. I don't recognise the woman I've become; a woman who so easily lies. But I couldn't stop myself. Oh, I know there could never be anything serious between Marcus and me; he has far younger woman fawning over him all the time. But it's the way he looks at me. No one ever looks at me like that. Not since my husband died."

Holmes smiled. "Everyone likes to be noticed, Mrs Morton. And people make mistakes where it comes to matters of the heart. Many a crime has been committed because of love."

"Including mine," Eliza said sadly. "What will happen now, Mr Holmes? I can't let Mr Chamberlain stay in prison."

Holmes said, "We will take you down to the police station, Mrs Morton. There, you can confess to your actions. I'm afraid you'll have to face the consequences."

Eliza's face crumpled, tears spilling down her cheeks. "I'm so scared, Mr Holmes. I don't know what will happen to me."

To her surprise, Holmes reached out and placed a hand on her shoulder, his touch gentle and reassuring. "I will stay by your side, Mrs Morton. I will make sure that you are treated fairly."

Eliza looked up at him, her eyes wide with disbelief. "You would do that for me? After everything I've done?"

Holmes' expression softened. "Much stronger crimes have been committed because of love, Mrs Morton. I understand the power it can hold over a person. And maybe, once Queen Victoria hears about your reasons for damaging her waxwork, she may offer some compassion towards you. After all, she is no stranger to love."

Eliza's shoulders shook with silent sobs, her head bowed in gratitude. "Thank you," she whispered, her voice choked with emotion. "Thank you both so much. I hope that one day, you can find it in your hearts to forgive me. I hope Mr Chamberlain will, too."

Chapter 25

Later that day, Holmes and Watson returned to their home and settled down in their armchairs.

"Well!" Watson exclaimed. "You pulled in a lot of favours with the police today, Holmes. I do hope that leads to Mrs Morton receiving a softer sentence. That poor woman, falling for a man like Marcus Bramwell. I didn't dare tell her how dismissive he'd been about her when we spoke to him. How he laughed at how much she fawned over him. He's a truly obnoxious man. Not worth the likes of Mrs Morton whatsoever."

"I agree, Watson," Holmes said. "But people like Marcus Bramwell often end up receiving the treatment they dole out."

Dr Watson smiled, "Speaking of which, do you intend to talk to Madam Rosalind about those things she said at the séance?"

"About scores to be settled, and secrets deep within the walls? No, I've decided against it. Those claims could apply to any old building, and looking back, it was a generic thing for her to say. She probably says that at all places she visits. Also, I don't wish to give her the satisfaction of giving any credit to her words. I am content with never seeing that woman again."

"However," Dr Watson said, "I can sense there's something else you wish to say.

Holmes smiled. "You know me so well, my friend. Yes, I am content with never seeing that woman again. However, I have a feeling our paths will cross again soon. But for now, let's put all thoughts of Madam Rosalind to one side. Let us take a well-deserved rest, as I am sure we will soon be investigating a new mystery."

"One more thing before we put this behind us," Watson said. "Would you ever consider having a waxwork figure of yourself made? To display in some museum?"

Holmes laughed. "Not after this case! Anyway, I'd rather be immortalised in the written word, rather than wax. Mrs Morton was right about you, my dear friend, and how you have a way with words. And your stories, well, they will keep us alive for many years to come."

Book 3 - Sherlock Holmes and The Hasty Holiday

Chapter 1

It was early afternoon, and inside 221B Baker Street, Sherlock Holmes and Dr John Watson relaxed in their respective armchairs, enjoying a brief respite from the bustling streets of London. Holmes, his eyes closed in contemplation, gently plucked at the strings of his violin, while Watson perused the pages of the latest medical journal, occasionally making notes in the margins.

Their tranquil moment was interrupted by a sharp knock at the door. Mrs Hudson, their landlady, poked her head into the room. "Mr Holmes, there's a Mrs Agnes Fairfax here to see you. She seems quite distressed."

Holmes's eyes snapped open, and he set aside his violin. "Send her in, Mrs Hudson."

A moment later, a woman in her early thirties entered the room. She was dressed in a fashionable, though slightly travel-worn, ensemble, and her face bore the unmistakable signs of worry and fatigue.

"Mr Holmes, Dr Watson," she began, her voice trembling slightly, "I apologise for the intrusion, but I desperately need your help."

Watson rose from his chair, offering the woman a seat. "Please, Mrs Fairfax, sit down and tell us what troubles you."

As she settled into the proffered chair, Mrs Fairfax took a deep breath to compose herself. "It's my younger sister, Dorothy Davenport. She's gone missing." She paused, as if struggling to find the next words. "Well, not missing, I don't suppose. But she has left London suddenly in peculiar circumstances, and I fear something dreadful may have happened to her."

Holmes said, "Please, Mrs Fairfax, start from the beginning. When did you last see your sister?"

Mrs Fairfax explained, "Dorothy and I have a standing arrangement to meet for lunch on the first Saturday of every month, which is today, of course. I live in Birmingham with my husband and children, while Dorothy resides here in London. She works as a social secretary for Lord and Lady Cavendish. These monthly meetings for lunch are a cherished tradition for us both."

Watson nodded sympathetically. "And she failed to arrive for your scheduled lunch today?"

Mrs Fairfax continued, "She did, but I already knew she wasn't going to be there. Two days ago, I received a telegram from Dorothy, sent from a village in Devon. She said she'd won a competition for a two-week holiday there and wouldn't be able to make our monthly meeting."

Holmes's eyebrows rose slightly. "And this struck you as unusual?"

"Highly unusual, Mr Holmes. Dorothy is not one for spontaneous trips or entering competitions, as far as I am aware. She's always been the sensible, reliable sort. I sent a return message to make sure she was okay, and to ask why she hadn't told me of her holiday earlier. She answered my telegram with a very brief note saying she was fine and I was not to worry. No explanation was given about the sudden trip away. Well, my imagination ran riot, and I imagined Dorothy had been kidnapped, or she had been lured to that village in Devon because some terrible fate awaited her. I was all for travelling down to Devon, despite the long journey, but my husband said Dorothy was most likely taking a break from the stresses of her job. But I couldn't shake the feeling that something was wrong, so I contacted the police." She stopped talking and her mouth set in a firm line.

"And what did the police tell you?" Watson prompted gently.

With a hint of annoyance in her voice, Mrs Fairfax replied, "They treated me like a hysterical woman who had nothing better to do with her time than worry about her sister. They agreed with what my husband said, and that Dorothy was most likely having a restful holiday and the last thing she needed, was a visit from the police to check up on her."

Holmes frowned. "I assume you emphasised how concerned you were, Mrs Fairfax?"

"I most certainly did, Mr Holmes." Her grip on her handbag tightened. "But they didn't take me seriously, not at all. And that's why I came here. I only wished I'd have come here sooner. Goodness knows what may have happened to Dorothy because of my delay."

Holmes said gently, "Tell me, Mrs Fairfax, does your sister have any reason to fear for her safety? Has she mentioned any troubling incidents or individuals in her life recently?"

Mrs Fairfax shook her head. "No, nothing of the sort. Dorothy is well-liked by all who know her. She's kind, considerate, and utterly devoted to her work with the Cavendishes. I can't imagine anyone wishing her harm."

Watson frowned thoughtfully. "And you're certain she sent the telegram herself? Could someone else have sent it in her name?"

"Oh! I never thought of that. I suppose it's possible," Mrs Fairfax admitted, "but who would do such a thing? And why?"

Holmes said, "Mrs Fairfax, I understand your concern for your sister's well-being. While it is entirely possible that she did, indeed, win a holiday and took advantage of the opportunity for a rest, your instincts should not be dismissed. Watson and I will look into the matter and see if we can uncover any information regarding your sister's whereabouts and the circumstances surrounding her sudden departure."

Relief washed over Mrs Fairfax's face. "Thank you, Mr Holmes. I cannot tell you how much this means to me. I just want to know that Dorothy is safe and well."

Watson offered the woman a reassuring smile. "We will do our utmost to locate your sister, Mrs Fairfax. In the meantime, if you can provide us with any additional information—her address here in London, her place of employment, and the names of any close friends or acquaintances—it would be most helpful."

Holmes added, "And may we take those telegrams your sister sent you? Has she given the address of where she is staying in Devon?"

Mrs Fairfax nodded. "She has, and it is a blessing to know that. Unless it's a fake address." Tears sprang to her eyes. "I cannot stop thinking the worst about her, no matter how hard I try."

Dr Watson handed her a handkerchief and said, "I understand your concern, really I do. We will deal with this matter with utmost urgency. You have my word."

Holmes added his agreement, smiling kindly at the distraught woman.

Mrs Fairfax dabbed at her eyes and composed herself. She handed the telegrams to Holmes and then gave the requested information about Dorothy to Dr Watson.

Once they had everything they needed, Holmes said, "Where might we contact you, Mrs Fairfax?"

Mrs Fairfax replied, "I wish I could stay in London longer, but I have to return to Birmingham to look after my children. I suspect my husband is already at his wits' end after looking after the little ones in my absence. Could you contact me by telegram, please? I'll give you the address of my nearest telegram office. I shall call in there often to look for any messages from you." She smiled sadly. "I suppose I could wait for telegrams to be delivered to my house as normal, but I am so worried..." Fresh tears came to her eyes.

Holmes held up his hand. "There is no need to explain your worries, Mrs Fairfax. I will ensure that regular telegrams are sent to you. We will make some enquiries locally today and see what information we can uncover about your sister's disappearance. We will also journey to Devon and meet her in person."

"You will?" Mrs Fairfax asked.

"We will," Holmes confirmed. He smiled gently. "Now, is there anything else you wish us to know? Or anything you need from us?"

Mrs Fairfax stood. "I can't think of anything else." She smiled at them. "Thank you so much, Mr Holmes, Dr Watson. I already feel a little better by knowing you are helping me."

Dr Watson escorted Mrs Agnes Fairfax out of the room and down the stairs. Holmes heard his reassuring words to her drifting up the steps.

Once Mrs Fairfax had left the building, Dr Watson returned to the living room and said, "Well, Holmes, what do you make of this?"

Holmes replied, "I believe we have a most intriguing case on our hands. While Mrs Fairfax's concerns may prove unfounded, there is something about this sudden disappearance that doesn't sit right."

Watson nodded in agreement. Concern filled his face. "Let us hope that this mystery has a happy resolution for all involved."

Chapter 2

Holmes glanced out of the window and saw Mrs Fairfax walking along the street, dabbing at her eyes. He said, "Watson, we must waste no time. Our first stop shall be the boarding house where Miss Davenport resides. Perhaps there, we may uncover some clues as to her sudden disappearance."

Watson nodded in agreement, already reaching for his hat and coat.

The two men set off through the bustling streets of London, their strides purposeful and their minds focused on the task at hand. It wasn't long before they arrived at the boarding house where Dorothy Davenport lived, a well-maintained building with a modest but respectable exterior.

Holmes rapped sharply on the door, and moments later, it swung open to reveal a woman in her late fifties. Her greying hair was pulled back into a neat bun, and her keen eyes regarded the visitors with a mixture of suspicion and curiosity.

"Good afternoon, madam," Holmes greeted, tipping his hat. "I am Sherlock Holmes, and this is my associate, Dr John Watson. Are you Mrs Olive King, the proprietress of this establishment?"

The woman's gaze narrowed slightly, but she nodded. "I am. And what brings you gentlemen to my door?"

"We were hoping to speak with you about one of your lodgers, a Miss Dorothy Davenport," Holmes explained.

Mrs King's suspicion seemed to deepen at the mention of Dorothy's name. "And what, pray tell, is your interest in Miss Davenport?"

Watson stepped forward, his kind face and gentle demeanour serving to put the landlady slightly more at ease. "We've been engaged by Miss Davenport's sister, Mrs Agnes Fairfax, who is deeply concerned about her well-being."

After a moment's hesitation, Mrs King stepped aside, allowing the two men to enter. "Very well. Come into the parlour, and we can discuss this further."

Once settled in the modest but well-appointed room, Holmes began, "Mrs King, we understand that Miss Davenport recently departed on a sudden holiday. Her sister found this behaviour quite out of character and has asked us to look into the matter."

Mrs King sighed, her hands folded primly in her lap. "I must admit, I was surprised myself when Miss Davenport informed me of her plans. It was most unlike her to make such a decision on a whim."

Watson nodded. "And did she give any indication as to where she was going or how long she intended to be away?"

"She mentioned having won a holiday to Devon, to a village called Clovelly, I believe. Said she'd be gone for two weeks." Mrs King paused, a thoughtful expression crossing her face. "But you know, even though it was unexpected, I wasn't overly concerned. Miss Davenport is a sensible woman. I have no doubt she'll return safely when her holiday is through."

Holmes asked, "And did you notice anything unusual about her behaviour in the days leading up to her departure? Any changes in routine or demeanour?"

Mrs King considered the question for a moment. "No, not really. She seemed her usual self."

Holmes took a moment's pause to ask his next question. "Did Miss Davenport have any unusual visitors recently? Or any letters that may have caused her some concern?"

"The only letter she received was the one informing her about that holiday, not that I saw it," Mrs King replied. "As for any unusual visitors, no, she didn't. She seldom receives any visitors at all."

Holmes rose from his seat, "Mrs King, I think it would be most helpful if we could take a look at Miss Davenport's room. It may hold some clues as to her state of mind before her departure."

Mrs King's eyes widened at Holmes' request, her expression shifting from one of polite concern to outright indignation. "I beg your pardon, Mr Holmes," she said, her voice rising slightly, "but I absolutely cannot allow you or Dr Watson to enter Miss Davenport's room. It is strictly against the rules of this establishment for males to enter the rooms of my tenants."

Holmes said, "Mrs King, I assure you that our intentions are purely investigative. We have no desire to compromise the reputation of your boarding house or to cause any discomfort to your other lodgers."

But the landlady was having none of it. She rose from her seat, her posture rigid and her face set in a stern expression. "Mr Holmes, I have run this boarding house for many years, and I have done so by maintaining a strict code of conduct. No men, under any circumstances, are permitted to enter the private rooms of my lodgers, and that is that. I must insist that you respect my rules."

Watson, sensing the rising tension, attempted to intervene. "Mrs King, we do apologise for any offence. We certainly don't wish to cause any trouble."

Mrs King turned her steely gaze upon the doctor. "Dr Watson, while I appreciate your apology, I'm afraid my decision is final. I must ask you and Mr Holmes to leave now. I have nothing further to say on the matter, and I no longer wish to discuss Miss Davenport's private life with you."

Holmes, realising that further persuasion would be futile, said, "Very well, Mrs King. We shall take our leave. Thank you for your time."

With that, the two men made their way out of the boarding house, the door closing firmly behind them. Once on the path outside, Holmes turned to Watson, a thoughtful expression on his face.

"It seems we've reached an impasse, Watson," he said, his eyes narrowing slightly. "Mrs King is clearly a formidable woman, and her dedication to her rules is admirable, if somewhat inconvenient for our purposes."

Watson nodded, his brow furrowed. "Indeed, Holmes. But where does that leave us? If we can't access Miss Davenport's room, how are we to proceed with our investigation?"

Holmes replied, "Fear not, my dear Watson. I have a solution in mind. We shall need to enlist the help of someone who can navigate the inner workings of the boarding house without any objections from Mrs King."

"Who did you have in mind, Holmes?"

Holmes smiled. "I know just the person. And so do you."

Chapter 3

Sherlock Holmes and Dr John Watson returned to 221B Baker Street. Upon entering the building, Holmes immediately sought out Mrs Hudson, their loyal and ever-helpful landlady. He found her in the kitchen, preparing a pot of tea for her tenants.

"Ah, Mrs Hudson," Holmes said, his voice tinged with urgency. "I wonder if I might have a word with you about a most pressing matter. We need your help with our present investigation."

Mrs Hudson looked up from her task. "Of course, Mr Holmes. What seems to be the trouble?"

Holmes proceeded to explain the details of the case, recounting their visit to Mrs King's boarding house and the stern rebuff they had received when requesting access to Miss Davenport's room.

"You see, Mrs Hudson," Holmes continued, "it is imperative that we gain entry to Miss Davenport's quarters.

There may be vital clues within that could shed light on her abrupt departure and the reasons behind it. At this stage, we don't know if the supposed holiday is real, or if there is something more sinister at play."

Mrs Hudson listened intently, her brow furrowed in thought. "And you believe that Mrs King would be more amenable to granting me access, despite what she said to you about not wanting to discuss Dorothy's private life any further?"

Holmes nodded, a glimmer of hope in his eyes. "Precisely. Mrs King may be more inclined to trust a fellow woman in this delicate matter."

Mrs Hudson smiled. "Well, Mr Holmes, I would be delighted to assist you in your investigation. I've known Olive for many years, and despite her gruff exterior, I'm certain she'll see the wisdom in allowing me to take a peek into Miss Davenport's room."

Watson, who had been listening intently to the conversation, reached into his pocket and retrieved one of his small, leather-bound notebooks. He handed it to Mrs Hudson with a grateful smile.

"Here, Mrs Hudson," he said, "please take this notebook. If you should come across anything of interest in

Miss Davenport's room, you can jot down your observations. Your keen eye for detail may prove invaluable."

Mrs Hudson accepted the notebook with a nod. "I shall do my very best, Dr Watson. You can count on me to be thorough in my examination."

With that, Mrs Hudson bustled out of the kitchen, a determined spring in her step. Holmes and Watson watched her go, a sense of relief washing over them.

"I do believe we've made the right choice in enlisting Mrs Hudson's aid," Holmes said. "And while we wait for her return, I suggest we discuss Dorothy's case further."

"Excellent idea. I'll pour some tea and bring it up."

Minutes later, Holmes and Watson were ensconced in their familiar armchairs, the crackling fire in the hearth casting a warm glow upon their pensive faces.

Watson said, "So Holmes, what are your thoughts regarding Miss Davenport's abrupt departure?"

Holmes answered, "There are several theories that come to mind. The first, and perhaps most obvious, is that Miss Davenport has won a holiday and simply neglected to inform her sister of her prize when she was first notified of it. However, given the close relationship between the two, as described by Mrs Fairfax, this seems unlikely."

Watson nodded. "What other explanations have you considered, Holmes?"

"The second possibility is that Miss Davenport has been lured away under false pretences. Perhaps someone has used the guise of a holiday competition to entice her to Devon, with odious intentions in mind. A possibility that has already occurred to Mrs Fairfax and is causing her a great deal of concern."

Watson sighed. "Yes, I agree with your thoughts on that point. But who would wish to harm Miss Davenport? From what we have gathered so far, she is a kind and gentle soul, beloved by all who know her."

"That, my dear Watson, is the crux of the matter. We must delve deeper into Miss Davenport's life and relationships to uncover any potential motives for her disappearance. Perhaps there is a jilted suitor, or a jealous rival, who may have cause to wish her ill."

Watson frowned. "It did strike me as odd that Miss Davenport left so suddenly. Mrs King told us Dorothy had received a letter confirming she had won a holiday. And yet, instead of taking the time to prepare for such a break, it appears Dorothy left in quite a rush. Surely if one wins a stay at a cottage, one could choose when they wish to go."

Holmes held up one finger. "Unless someone wanted Miss Davenport there at a certain time for some reason. Or, this is something else we need to consider, someone could have wanted Miss Davenport to leave London quickly and not return for two weeks, and somehow made that happen."

"Why would they want her out of London?" Watson asked.

"That is what we are going to find out," Holmes replied. He stood and strode over to the window. "I do wish Mrs Hudson would hasten back. We can't proceed with the next part of our investigation until she does."

Dr Watson joined him at the window. "She'll be back in due course; she won't let us down. Holmes, should we book our tickets to Devon soon? We told Mrs Fairfax we would visit Dorothy there."

Holmes looked at Watson. "Let's hold on a little longer and gather more information. I'm not entirely convinced Miss Davenport is in Devon, yet." He turned his attention back to the streets below, muttering impatiently under his breath for Mrs Hudson to return.

Chapter 4

Another hour passed by as Holmes and Watson awaited the return of their landlady. Holmes attempted to keep himself busy by learning a new melody on his violin, and Dr Watson read the newspaper. They kept looking towards the door, expecting to see the welcome face of Mrs Hudson.

At last, the familiar sound of her footsteps echoed up the stairs, and she entered the sitting room, a triumphant smile upon her face and the notebook clutched in her hand.

"Ah, Mrs Hudson!" Holmes exclaimed, setting aside his violin and rising to greet her. "I trust your visit to the boarding house was fruitful?"

Mrs Hudson nodded, settling herself into a chair and opening her notebook. "It was, Mr Holmes. I have gathered quite a bit of information about the boarding house and its residents."

Watson placed the newspaper on the table. "Do tell us, Mrs Hudson. What did you discover?"

Mrs Hudson began to recount her findings, her voice filled with enthusiasm. "I managed to speak to some of the lodgers and they were all quite surprised by Miss Davenport's sudden holiday, as it seemed quite out of character for her. None of the women I talked to had seen the letter about the holiday."

Holmes nodded, his brow furrowed in thought. "And what of Miss Davenport's room? Did you have the opportunity to examine it?"

"I did," Mrs Hudson replied, looking through her notebook. "It's a small attic room, with solid walls and only one door in and out. The room is quite charming and cosy, in my opinion. The walls are painted a soft shade of powder blue, with a delicate floral wallpaper bordering the ceiling. Quite lovely. There's a sturdy wooden bed frame against one wall, adorned with a handmade quilt in shades of lavender and cream. I've got a similar one in green."

Watson smiled, picturing the cosy space in his mind's eye. "It sounds like a pleasant retreat, Mrs Hudson."

Mrs Hudson nodded. "It is, Dr Watson. There's a bedside table, with an oil lamp and a small vase of wildflowers. Opposite the bed, there's a simple writing desk tucked beneath the dormer window, with a quill pen, an inkwell, and a stack of books. The books are a mix of novels and reference books. Some of the novels are recently published stories. I saw 'The Time Machine' by H.G. Wells and 'The Jungle Book' by Rudyard Kipling."

Watson nodded. "A well-read young woman, it seems."

Mrs Hudson continued, describing the personal touches that adorned the room. "There are sketches and watercolour paintings on the walls, mainly of London's parks and gardens. Lovely, they are. A framed photograph of her sister and family is on the windowsill. There is only one armchair in the room. It looked worn, but comfy."

Holmes smiled. "Mrs Hudson, you have been most thorough in your findings. I am most impressed and think you may have picked up on more details than I would have."

Mrs Hudson chuckled. "Oh, I wouldn't say that, Mr Holmes. I just notice things like the wallpaper and furniture."

"And what of storage, Mrs Hudson? Did you note anything of interest?" Watson asked.

"There is a wardrobe in one corner and a small dresser in the other." She looked up from her notes, a rather stern look in her eyes. "If you are going to ask me if I looked in those items, then I am going to say no, I didn't. A woman's belongings deserve respect, no matter if she is in the room or not."

Feeling like he'd been chastised, Holmes nodded and said gently, "I understand, but do we know if Miss Davenport took some clothes before she left?"

"She did," Mrs Hudson confirmed. "One woman I spoke to, Sally, helped Miss Davenport down the stairs with her packed suitcase a few days ago and she said it was heavy enough to contain sufficient clothes for a two-week holiday. I did have a quick look for the letter you mentioned, the one about the holiday, but I didn't find anything out in the open in Dorothy's bedroom. But according to Sally, Dorothy said the letter was firmly tucked in her handbag."

"I see," Holmes replied. "Did you observe any evidence of a hasty departure? Anything out of place or suggesting that Miss Davenport left in a hurry?"

Mrs Hudson paused for a moment, her brow furrowed in thought as she mentally retraced her steps through the room. "No, Mr Holmes," she replied, shaking her head. "Everything seemed to be in its proper place. The bed was neatly made, and there were no signs of disarray or rushed packing."

"It seems that we are left with more questions than answers," Holmes mused. "The lack of any sign of a hurried exit or proof of a holiday won suggests that there may be more to this case than meets the eye."

Mrs Hudson closed the notebook and said, "I must say, I rather enjoyed playing the role of detective for a while. It was quite thrilling to be a part of your investigation, even in a small way. I hope I have been of use."

Holmes smiled. "Your assistance has been invaluable, Mrs Hudson," he said, his tone sincere. "Your keen observations and attention to detail have provided us with valuable insights into Miss Davenport's character and circumstances."

Mrs Hudson beamed with pride, her cheeks flushing slightly at the praise. "Well, I am always at your disposal, Mr Holmes," she said. "If you and Dr Watson ever require my help again, you need only ask."

Watson smiled. "I have no doubt that we shall call upon your services again, Mrs Hudson," he said, his voice laced with fondness. "Why don't you keep that notebook in case you need to use it again in a future investigation?"

Mrs Hudson held the notebook closer. "Thank you. I'll do that. Now, gentlemen, I will return to the kitchen and make a start on preparing dinner. I assume you will be in for the rest of the day."

"I'm afraid not," Holmes answered as he rose to his feet. "We have another call to make before this day is over."

"We do?" Watson asked.

"We do, and we need to leave immediately," Holmes replied.

"Rightio," Watson said. "I'll get my coat."

Chapter 5

Holmes and Watson took a hansom cab to their next destination, the home of Lord and Lady Cavendish. Watson asked Holmes what information they hoped to discover there.

Holmes answered, "I wonder if Miss Davenport's disappearance is connected to her role as a social secretary for Lord and Lady Cavendish."

"Ah, I see. It's a possibility, Holmes," Watson said. "Miss Davenport's position would have granted her access to the inner workings of the Cavendish household and their social circles. From what I have read in the papers, the social events organised by Lord and Lady Cavendish are lavish affairs with no expense spared. Are you suggesting that someone is now covering for Miss Davenport during her absence? Someone who intends to commit a crime? And could it be this person who orchestrated Miss Davenport's unexpected departure?"

Holmes smiled at his friend. "It would be the perfect cover for someone with nefarious intentions, to infiltrate the Cavendish household, once they had taken Miss Davenport out of the picture, and carry out their plans undetected in their role as a temporary secretary."

Watson asked, "But who would have the means and motive to carry out such a scheme?"

Holmes answered, "That is what we must discover. I hope someone is at home to receive us. We should have sent a telegram requesting a meeting with Lord and Lady Cavendish, but time is of the essence."

The hansom cab soon arrived at the grand residence of Lord and Lady Cavendish. The house, situated in one of London's most exclusive neighbourhoods, stood tall and proud. The immaculately manicured gardens and the gleaming brass fixtures on the front door spoke of luxury and refinement.

Holmes knocked on the front door. It was opened by a well-dressed butler who gave them an enquiring look.

Holmes bowed his head. "I sincerely apologise for our unannounced visit, but may we speak with Lord and Lady Cavendish, if they are at home? I am Sherlock Holmes, and this is Dr John Watson."

The butler said, "May I ask what this is in connection with?"

"It's a matter concerning Miss Dorothy Davenport."

At the mention of Dorothy's name, the butler's look softened. He opened the door wider and invited them in. He told them Lord Cavendish was at home and was sure he would talk with them.

The butler led them through the marble-floored foyer and into an impressive drawing room. The room was adorned with fine art, antique furniture, and plush velvet curtains that framed the large windows overlooking the meticulously landscaped gardens. The butler offered them refreshments, which they politely declined, before informing them that Lord Cavendish would be with them shortly.

As they waited, Holmes looked around the room, taking in every detail, while Watson marvelled at the grandeur of their surroundings. The sound of footsteps approaching drew their attention, and they rose to greet Lord Cavendish as he entered the room.

"Mr Holmes, Dr Watson," Lord Cavendish said warmly, extending his hand in greeting. "What a pleasure to meet you. I must admit, I am rather surprised by your visit."

Holmes shook the Lord's hand firmly. "Thank you for seeing us, Lord Cavendish. We are here on a matter of some urgency, regarding your social secretary, Miss Dorothy Davenport, and her sudden departure from London."

Lord Cavendish's brow furrowed slightly as he gestured for them to take a seat. "Yes, I was quite surprised when Miss Davenport informed me of her holiday plans at such short notice. She's always been such a dedicated and hardworking member of our staff, but I suppose even the most diligent among us needs a break from time to time." He settled into a plush armchair opposite them.

"The thing is, Lord Cavendish," Watson said, glancing at Holmes before continuing. "Miss Davenport's sister, Mrs Agnes Fairfax, came to us with concerns about her sudden departure. She said it was quite out of character for Miss Davenport to take off so suddenly, and without informing her family beforehand of her intentions."

Lord Cavendish nodded thoughtfully. "I can understand Mrs Fairfax's concern, but I assure you, Miss Davenport was in good spirits when she informed me of her plans. She said she'd won a holiday in a competition and was looking forward to a rest before returning to work with renewed energy."

Holmes said, "Lord Cavendish, has Miss Davenport's absence caused any disruption to your social calendar? I imagine her role is quite crucial in the planning and execution of your events."

Lord Cavendish shook his head. "Not at all, Mr Holmes," he said, a note of pride in his voice. "Miss Davenport is an exceptionally organised individual. Before her departure, she ensured that all of our upcoming events were meticulously planned and arranged. From the guest lists to the RSVPs and the catering, everything is in place and will run like clockwork, even in her absence."

Holmes nodded. "I see. And have you appointed a temporary replacement for Miss Davenport?"

Lord Cavendish shook his head once more. "There was no need. Miss Davenport's planning is so thorough that we are more than capable of handling the events she has arranged without the need for additional staff."

"Lord Cavendish, if you would indulge me for a moment, I would like to know more about Miss Davenport as a person," Holmes said. "What is she like, both in her professional capacity and on a more personal level?"

Lord Cavendish smiled warmly, his eyes reflecting a genuine fondness for his social secretary. "Miss Davenport is an exceptional individual, Mr Holmes. In her professional life, she is the epitome of efficiency and organisation. Her attention to detail is unparalleled, and she handles even the most complex social events with grace and poise." The nobleman paused for a moment as if collecting his thoughts, before continuing. "On a personal level, Miss Davenport is well-liked by all who have the pleasure of knowing her. She is unfailingly polite and courteous, treating everyone she encounters with the utmost respect, regardless of their station in life. Her kind and gentle nature has endeared her to many, both within our household and beyond."

Watson asked, "In your opinion, does Miss Davenport have any enemies? Anyone who might wish her harm or seek to disrupt her life in some way?"

Lord Cavendish shook his head firmly. "No, Dr Watson, I cannot imagine anyone harbouring ill will towards Miss Davenport. She is a true gem, and her presence brings nothing but joy and light to those around her. If she has any enemies, I am not aware of them."

Holmes rose from his seat and extended his hand to Lord Cavendish. "Thank you for your time and insight. Your words have been most helpful in our investigation."

Lord Cavendish shook Holmes' hand warmly, a smile on his face. "It is my pleasure, Mr Holmes. If there is anything else I can do to assist you, please do not hesitate to ask. In my opinion, Mrs Fairfax has no need to worry about her sister. I am certain Miss Davenport will return from her holiday rested and happy in due course."

With a final nod of thanks, Holmes and Watson took their leave, stepping out into the bright sunlight of the London street.

"Watson," Holmes said, "I believe it is time for us to journey to Devon. We must speak with Miss Davenport directly to clear up this confusion surrounding her holiday, if only to put her sister's mind at rest. Speaking of Mrs Fairfax, I must send her a telegram before we head to Devon, and let her know how our investigation is proceeding."

Watson looked back at the impressive home behind them. "Holmes, I have a strange feeling about Miss Davenport."

"Go on," Holmes prompted.

Watson looked back at him. "What if we are looking at this case from the wrong angle? What if there wasn't a competition at all and Miss Davenport took herself to Devon for some reason?" Holmes' smile increased. "My dear Watson, if I didn't know any better, I would wager you are a mind-reader. I was just pondering the same thing. Yes, if Miss Davenport arranged her own sudden departure, it begs the question, why?"

"Indeed," Watson said. "Why would she need to be away from London at this time? Away from her lodgings, her family, and her place of work. Is she up to something? Or is she running away from something or someone?"

"All great questions, and ones we will find answers to." Holmes hailed a cab." Watson, it's too late to get a train to Devon tonight, but let's make our way to the station and purchase tickets for the earliest departure tomorrow. I would like to speak to Miss Dorothy Davenport as soon as possible. Considering how long the journey will take us, we should find somewhere to stay overnight once we arrive in Devon."

Watson said, "And if we don't find Miss Davenport in Devon, what will we do then?"

Holmes flashed him a smile. "Then, my dear friend, we will pursue a different avenue of investigation. I'm not sure what, but I'm certain something will come to us if the need arises."

Chapter 6

Early the next morning, and with their overnight bags packed, Holmes and Watson got ready to bid farewell to Mrs Hudson and set off on their journey to Devon.

Mrs Hudson insisted on packing some provisions for their journey in case Holmes and Watson didn't like the refreshments provided on the train. She said, "Best to be prepared, I always say," as she handed Dr Watson a small basket filled with carefully wrapped sandwiches, pastries and fruit in wax paper.

Holmes smiled at their landlady. "Mrs Hudson, how would we ever manage without you? Your thoughtfulness and generosity fills my heart with gratitude."

Mrs Hudson waved his words away and told her tenants to take good care of themselves on their journey.

Holmes and Watson left their home and hurried along the streets towards King's Cross Station. When they arrived, the bustling terminal was alive with activity, as travellers from all walks of life hurried to and fro, their voices mingling in a cacophony of excitement and anticipation. The air was thick with the scent of coal smoke and the hissing of steam engines. The trains waited like resting dragons on the lines, curls of smoke drifting from their funnels.

Holmes and Watson boarded their train and located the first-class carriage they had booked the night before. Their luggage was stowed overhead.

A short while later, the whistle blew, and the train lurched forward.

Dr Watson settled back in his upholstered seat and sighed contentedly. "I love travelling on trains. There's something, oh, I don't know, something magical about them, don't you think, Holmes?"

Holmes nodded. "There is. And this journey will give us time to discuss Miss Davenport's case and what questions we need to ask her. Should we find her, of course."

Dr Watson reached into his pocket and pulled out his notebook. He opened it and said, "I have already recorded my thoughts on the matter. It took me a while to get to sleep last night, so I decided to make use of my restless state."

"I am interested to hear your thoughts," Holmes said leaning forward. "Please, proceed."

As the train pulled out of the station, Dr Watson and Holmes discussed the matter of Dorothy Davenport. They soon agreed to a course of action, and then the matter was put to one side.

Dr Watson opened out the newspaper he had bought on the way to the station and began to read it.

Holmes settled back more in his comfy seat and looked out of the window at the passing scenery of London, taking in its familiar sights. Before too long, the scenery changed and the countryside began to unfold before his eyes. Rolling hills, verdant fields, and picturesque villages dotted the landscape, their beauty enhanced by the golden hues of the rising sun.

The rhythmic chugging of the engine filled the air as the train took them further away from London.

The journey was a long one; the train winding its way through the picturesque countryside of England. The two men kept themselves occupied with a variety of things to pass the time. Watson occasionally read aloud an article of interest from the newspaper, while Holmes alternated between gazing pensively out of the window and jotting down notes in his notebook. They engaged in lively discussions, their conversation ranging from the particulars of the case to the latest advancements in science and medicine. The miles slipped away beneath the rhythmic clacking of the train's wheels, bringing them ever closer to their destination and the mystery that awaited them in the village of Clovelly.

Much to Holmes' annoyance, there were several delays along the way and their journey took far longer than they had anticipated. When the train finally pulled into the town nearest to Clovelly, night had well and truly fallen. The platform was dimly lit by flickering gas lamps, casting eerie shadows across the weathered brickwork.

Holmes and Watson disembarked, their bags in hand, and made their way to the station exit. There, they found a friendly local man with a horse and cart. Holmes asked if there was a nearby inn where they could spend the night.

The friendly chap said he knew just the place and invited Holmes and Watson to take a seat in his cart.

The cart wound its way through the streets of the town, the full moon shining brightly above them.

Soon, they arrived at the inn, a warm and inviting establishment with a cheerful fire crackling in the hearth. The innkeeper, a jovial man with rosy cheeks and a twinkle in his eyes, greeted them warmly and showed them to their rooms.

After a hearty dinner of local fare, Holmes and Watson retired to their respective chambers, ready to locate the elusive Miss Davenport the following day.

Chapter 7

The next morning, after a hearty breakfast at the inn, Holmes and Watson arranged for a horse-drawn carriage to take them to the cottage where Dorothy Davenport was staying in Clovelly.

As they travelled along the winding country roads, Holmes and Watson marvelled at the stunning scenery. Rolling hills, lush green fields, and charming cottages dotted the landscape, each one more picturesque than the last.

Finally, the carriage arrived at a charming cottage with roses growing around the door. The scent of the blooms was intoxicating, and the sight of the sea in the distance was breathtaking. Holmes asked the driver if he could wait for them, as he wasn't sure how long their visit would take. The driver was happy to do so and leaned back in his seat, enjoying the warmth of the morning sunshine.

Holmes and Watson walked towards the cottage. They noticed a young woman in the front garden. She was resting on a wooden chair next to a table. She seemed lost in thought, her gaze fixed on the distant horizon.

"Miss Davenport, I presume?" Holmes called out, his voice carrying across the garden.

The woman turned, startled by the sudden interruption. "Yes, that's me," she replied, rising from her chair. "And who might you be?"

Holmes and Watson introduced themselves, explaining the purpose of their visit. "Your sister, Mrs Agnes Fairfax, has engaged our services," Holmes explained. "She is quite concerned about your sudden departure and asked us to look into the matter."

Dorothy sighed, a rueful smile on her face. "I'm not at all surprised," she said, gesturing for the two men to join her at the table. "Agnes has always been a worrier, and I know my sudden trip must have seemed quite out of character. I normally plan such events months in advance, sometimes years. So, yes, I can understand why she engaged your services. Although, I fear you may have had a wasted journey. But seeing as you're here now, would you like a cup of tea? There's plenty in the pot."

Holmes and Watson took their seats at the table, and Dorothy poured them each a cup of steaming tea. The aroma of the freshly brewed beverage mingled with the sweet scent of the roses, creating a delightful ambience in the cottage garden.

"Now, Miss Davenport," Holmes began, his keen eyes studying her expression, "would you be so kind as to tell us more about this prize you've won?"

Dorothy smiled, a hint of confusion in her hazel eyes. "To be perfectly honest, Mr Holmes, I was rather surprised to receive the news myself. I couldn't recall entering any competitions recently, but then I wondered if it might have been part of a charity event I'd organised for Lord and Lady Cavendish. I do make small donations from time to time, you see, and I have bought raffle tickets on some occasions, but I never check to see if I've won anything. I always assumed I'd be notified if I had won anything. When the letter arrived confirming I'd won a holiday here, I automatically presumed it was something connected with my work."

Watson took a sip of his tea and then said, "And did you confirm the legitimacy of the prize?"

"Oh, yes," Dorothy replied. "The letter had come straight from the owners of this cottage. I contacted them by telegram to confirm the details and was told that the person who had rented the cottage as a prize wished to remain anonymous. One thing did puzzle me, though. The letter said I was to claim my prize immediately or else I would lose the holiday. Which seemed strange to me. Surely, if you win a holiday, you should be free to choose when to take that holiday, within reason, of course."

"Yes!" Dr Watson exclaimed. "That's exactly what I said to Holmes."

Dorothy continued, "Bearing the restricted date in mind, I had to take my leave more abruptly than I wished to. Fortunately, Lord and Lady Cavendish were agreeable to my unexpected leave, and I made sure everything was in place for all upcoming social events. But even so, a worrying thought niggled me about the time restriction placed upon my prize. Even though I had received a reassuring telegram from the cottage owners, I had to take my safety into account."

"Of course," Dr Watson said. "A most sensible attitude considering you didn't know the identity of the person who is behind this prize."

Dorothy nodded in agreement. "Luckily, I have a friend who lives in Clovelly, Mary. We grew up as neighbours in Birmingham, and when she moved away, we kept in touch. Mary moved to Clovelly a few years ago with her new husband. Her letters were full of the beauty and the charm of this place. She extended an open invitation to me and said I could stay with her and her husband whenever I felt the need to escape London. So, when I received the letter about the holiday, I contacted Mary and told her about it. She thought it was a most peculiar situation, but said it was the perfect opportunity for me to finally visit her. And, if the cottage holiday was a jape of some kind, then at least I would have somewhere safe to stay when I arrived."

Dr Watson said, "And did you contact Mary upon your arrival in Clovelly?"

Dorothy laughed. "She was waiting for me when I arrived by horse and cart, her husband at her side. They insisted on staying with me for a few hours in this cottage to make sure everything was above board. The key was where the cottage owners said it would be, and the owners had kindly provided food and drinks for me. Once Mary was satisfied the cottage was a safe place for me to stay, we paid a visit to the cottage owners, who live a few streets away. They showed me the correspondence they had received from the anonymous person behind the prize. Again, everything seemed above board, albeit of a secretive nature."

Holmes asked, "In what form was the correspondence between this anonymous person and the cottage owner?"

"It was all by telegrams," Dorothy explained. "The ones coming from the unknown person were sent from a central London office."

Holmes said, "And you are satisfied everything is in order, in the legal sense?"

"Oh, yes, I am. And so is Mary." Dorothy glanced towards the sea. "I am enjoying the respite. It's been quite lovely to take a break from the hustle and bustle of London. If I ever find out who organised this holiday, I shall thank them most sincerely."

"Miss Davenport," Holmes began, "have you considered the possibility that there might be something more sinister at play here? That perhaps someone wanted you out of the way for a specific reason?"

Dorothy's eyes widened, a flicker of unease passing over her delicate features. "Sinister? I... I hadn't really thought about it like that. What do you mean, Mr Holmes?"

Holmes explained, "Well, let us consider the facts. You are a woman of routine, Miss Davenport, not prone to sudden, unplanned trips. And yet, here you are, the recipient of a mysterious prize that whisked you away from London at a moment's notice. It's all rather convenient, wouldn't you say?"

Watson nodded, setting down his teacup. "I agree. Miss Davenport, is there anyone at your boarding house or in your work with Lord and Lady Cavendish who might have cause to want you out of the way, and at this particular time?"

Dorothy frowned. "I can't imagine why anyone would want me gone, Dr Watson."

Holmes said, "And yet, the timing of this surprise holiday is most curious. It's possible that someone saw an opportunity to remove you from the equation, for reasons that remain, as yet, unclear."

Dorothy's face paled. "But who would do such a thing? And why? I can't believe that anyone would go to such lengths to get rid of me."

Watson placed a reassuring hand on Dorothy's arm. "We don't know for certain that there is anything dubious at play here, Miss Davenport. But it is our job to investigate all avenues."

Holmes nodded, his expression grave. "And that is precisely what we intend to do. It might be wise for you to return to London with us. It concerns me that the person who rented this cottage wished to remain anonymous. Or, if you wish to continue with your holiday, perhaps you could stay with your friend until we find out who is behind this gift of yours. Your safety is paramount."

Dorothy said, "Given your concerns, I will stay with Mary. But please, keep me informed of any developments, Mr Holmes. I need to know what's going on."

"You have my word, Miss Davenport," Holmes replied, rising from his chair. "We will return to London and continue with our investigations there. We will get to the truth of this matter, no matter where it leads us. In the meantime, try to enjoy your stay in this charming village. We will be in touch. Before we go, is there anything else you wish to tell us? Have you any social events coming up that you will now miss because of your stay here?"

Dorothy considered the question. "The only event I'm missing is my book club. The meeting is booked for this Friday evening at six p.m. We meet every month."

Holmes paused. "Tell me more about this book club, Miss Davenport. Where is it held, and who attends?"

Dorothy's face lit up as she spoke. She told Holmes about the book club, where it was held, and the three other women who attend it.

Dr Watson recorded the information in his notebook.

She said, "It's not just a place to discuss our love of reading, it's always a place to talk about our personal lives, too."

"Such as?" Holmes asked.

"Oh, you know, the usual things," Dorothy explained. "I talk about my family and how quickly my nephews are growing. Sometimes, I talk about the events I had organised and the people who attended them."

"I see," Holmes said. "And had you also spoken about your friend, Mary, who lives here?"

Dorothy laughed. "Yes, I often talked about her and how I would love to take a holiday here."

Holmes looked closer at Miss Davenport. "May I ask, did you talk about any upcoming events that you have organised for Lord and Lady Cavendish?"

Dorothy's cheeks coloured. "Well, yes, even though I know I shouldn't. I only mentioned the briefest of details, though, such as where and when the event would be held." She frowned. "Is this important, Mr Holmes?"

"It could be," Holmes answered. "Thank you for your time, Miss Davenport. We'll be sure to keep you informed of any developments in our investigation. I will send a telegram to your sister to confirm we have seen you in good health."

"Thank you," Dorothy said.

As they bid farewell to Dorothy and made their way back to the waiting horse and carriage, Holmes turned to Watson with a determined expression. "We must return to London immediately, Watson. I have a feeling that Miss Davenport's book club may hold the key to this mystery."

Watson nodded. "Do you suspect one of the members might be involved in her sudden holiday?"

"It's too early to say for certain," Holmes replied. "But I do feel one of them could be behind Miss Davenport's hasty holiday."

Chapter 8

The following day, after an exhausted sleep following their long return journey from Devon, Holmes suggested to Watson that they call upon the members of Miss Davenport's book club, starting with Miss Lillian Goodwin.

Watson nodded, setting down his morning cup of tea. "Agreed, Holmes. Perhaps she can shed some light on any tensions or rivalries within the group that might have led to Miss Davenport's removal."

With their plan set, the two men finished their breakfast and set out for the Goodwin residence, a grand townhouse located in one of London's more affluent neighbourhoods. Upon their arrival, they were greeted by a stern-faced butler, who ushered them into a well-appointed drawing room to await Miss Goodwin.

Lillian Goodwin swept into the room a few moments later, her elegant gown rustling as she moved. She regarded

Holmes and Watson with a curious expression, her eyebrows raised in surprise.

"Mr Holmes, Dr Watson," she said, extending her hand in greeting. "To what do I owe the pleasure of this unexpected visit?"

Holmes bowed slightly. "We apologise for the intrusion, Miss Goodwin, but we are here on a matter of some urgency. It concerns your friend and fellow book club member, Miss Dorothy Davenport."

Lillian's eyes widened, a flicker of something unreadable crossing her features before she composed herself. "Dorothy? Is she all right? Has something happened?"

Watson stepped forward, his voice gentle. "Miss Davenport has won a holiday to Devon, quite unexpectedly. She left without informing her sister, who was extremely worried about her sudden departure, and asked Mr Holmes and myself to look into the matter. We were hoping you might have some insight into the situation."

Lillian's lips curved into a smile that didn't quite reach her eyes. "A holiday? How lovely for her. I had no idea she had left town. I suppose that means she won't be at our book club this Friday. What a shame."

Holmes' gaze intensified. "And yet, you don't seem entirely surprised by this development, Miss Goodwin.

Might there be some tension within your book club that could have led to Miss Davenport's sudden absence?"

Lillian's smile faltered, her fingers twisting the fabric of her gown. "Tension? No, of course not. We're all the best of friends in the book club. It's true that Dorothy and I don't always see eye to eye on the books we read, but that's hardly cause for concern."

Watson's brow furrowed. "Could you elaborate on that, Miss Goodwin? What sort of disagreements have you had with Miss Davenport?"

Lillian sighed, a hint of exasperation creeping into her voice. "Oh, it's nothing serious, really. Dorothy has a tendency to dismiss the romance novels that I suggest as reading material for the group. She looks down on them and claims the novels are 'unrealistic nonsense.' She prefers those dreadful adventure stories, always going on about how they're more intellectually stimulating. It can be quite grating at times."

Holmes said, "And with Miss Davenport gone, I suppose you'll be free to choose the next book for your club without opposition?"

Lillian's eyes flashed with something akin to triumph. "As a matter of fact, yes. I already have the perfect novel in mind, a delightful romance set in the Italian countryside.

I'm sure the other ladies will be thrilled to read something a bit lighter for a change. I love reading romances. I always have. They inspire me to look for the romance in my life. I hope one day to find my one true love; someone who will make me his beloved wife. That special man who I'll spend the rest of my days with." She glanced wistfully towards the window as if expecting to see her knight in shining armour standing there with love shining in his eyes just for her.

Watson's expression grew serious. "Miss Goodwin, I must ask. Did you have anything to do with Miss Davenport's sudden holiday? Perhaps as a way to ensure your book choice would prevail?"

Lillian's face flushed with indignation. "Certainly not, Dr Watson! I may not always agree with Dorothy's taste in literature, but I would never stoop so low as to orchestrate her removal from the book club. The very idea is absurd!"

Dr Watson said, "I apologise. I did not mean to upset you, but we have certain questions that we need to ask."

Lillian gave him a stern look and said coldly, "Are there any other 'certain' questions you need to ask? I have a busy day ahead of me, and many social engagements to attend."

Holmes said, "One more question, if I may. How do you get on with the other members in the book group? Miss Harris and Miss Brown?"

"Like I told you mere minutes ago, Mr Holmes, we are the best of friends." Lillian ran her hands smoothly down her silk gown. "Is there anything else?"

Holmes said, "We have no further questions, Miss Goodwin. We appreciate your time and candour. If you think of anything else that might be relevant to our investigation, please don't hesitate to contact us."

As they took their leave from the building, Watson said to Holmes. "Do you believe her? Could Miss Goodwin have had a hand in Miss Davenport's disappearance? I imagine Lillian is receiving a wealthy allowance, which would give her the funds to rent that cottage in Clovelly."

Holmes shook his head, his eyes distant. "I'm not certain, Watson. But one thing is clear – there is more to this book club than meets the eye. Let's call on Miss Esther Harris next and see what she has to say."

Chapter 9

Holmes and Watson stepped into the bustling office where Esther Harris worked as a bookkeeper in her father's accountancy firm. After speaking to Esther's father and giving him the reason for their visit, Holmes and Watson were shown to Miss Harris' desk.

"Esther," Mr Harris said as they approached the young woman. "You have some visitors. Mr Holmes and Dr Watson. Don't be alarmed. They merely wish to talk to you about Dorothy."

Esther's eyes widened in alarm. "Dorothy? Is she okay?"

"Perfectly fine," Holmes answered, smiling at Miss Harris. "As your father said, we have a few questions for you, if we may take up some of your time?"

Mr Harris pointed towards a meeting room and suggested they talk in there. Holmes thanked him and then followed Esther as she led the way.

Esther took her visitors into the room and closed the door behind them.

She said, "Please, have a seat. What would you like to know about Dorothy?" She sat opposite them, concern in her eyes.

Holmes explained about Dorothy's sudden departure from London because of the holiday she had apparently won.

Esther shook her head. "I can't take it in. Taking off like that is certainly out of character for Dorothy. She never does anything on the spur of the moment. Where has she gone on this holiday?"

Holmes replied, "Clovelly in Devon."

Esther smiled. "Ah, now I understand. Dorothy often talks about going to Clovelly for a break. She has a friend who lives there who is always telling her how lovely it is. I suppose that if Dorothy had the chance to go there, she would have made all the arrangements in double-quick time. She's organised enough to do so. Good for her. I hope she's having a relaxing time."

Holmes asked, "And what is your relationship with Miss Davenport, if I may ask?"

Esther said, "Dorothy and I have been friends for years. We set up the book club together about a year ago. She's always been so kind and supportive, even when we disagree on the books we read."

Watson raised an eyebrow. "Disagree? How so?"

Esther chuckled. "Oh, you know how it is with book clubs. Everyone has their own tastes and preferences. Dorothy tends to favour adventure stories, while I lean more towards historical fiction. But we've always managed to find common ground and we respect each other's opinions."

Holmes nodded. "And what of the other members of your book club? Do you know them well?"

Esther's smile faltered slightly. "I know Lillian, of course. She's been a member for as long as I have. And then there's Violet Brown, but I'm afraid I don't know her very well. She's a recent addition to the group."

"Miss Violet Brown?" Dr Watson said. "We were hoping to speak with her, but Miss Davenport couldn't provide us with her address. Do you happen to know where she lives?"

Esther replied, "I'm afraid I don't. Violet only joined our book club about four months ago. She met Dorothy at a charity event where Violet was working as a waitress."

Dr Watson asked, "And how did Miss Brown become a member of your club?"

"Well, according to Violet, she and Dorothy got chatting at the end of the event, and the book club came up in conversation. Violet mentioned she was a keen reader, so Dorothy invited her to the group."

Watson frowned. "That seems rather generous of Miss Davenport, to invite a stranger to join your group."

Esther nodded. "That's what I thought, too. In fact, Dorothy later confided in me that she couldn't really remember talking to Violet at all, or even meeting her. But Dorothy felt it would be rude to ask her to leave the group as Violet had already been to one meeting and seemed to get along with everyone."

Holmes asked Esther, "And what do you make of Miss Violet Brown?"

Esther hesitated, her fingers fidgeting with the edge of her sleeve. "To be honest, there's something about her that doesn't quite ring true. At the second book club meeting, she told us she no longer works as a waitress, but now works as a governess, but she's been very vague about the family she works for and where they live. It seemed a strange progression to me; to be a waitress one month, and then a governess the next. And it's not just that, it's just a feeling I get, like she's not being her true self."

Holmes smiled. "Intuition can be a powerful tool, Miss Harris. Often, our subconscious picks up on subtle cues that our conscious mind might miss."

Esther said, "I suppose so. I think Dorothy might have felt the same way, even though she didn't share her feelings with me. At the meetings, after we had talked about the book, we would chat about our everyday lives. Violet would always ask Dorothy lots of questions about her work. You know, like when and where was the next social event being held? Who would be there? That sort of thing. I could see how uncomfortable Dorothy felt about Violet's constant questioning. Dorothy had talked about her work before Violet was a member of the group, as had I, but we never went into much detail, not as much detail as Violet was demanding of Dorothy of late."

"Did Violet show the same level of interest in your work?" Holmes asked.

Esther smiled. "Not at all. She didn't show any interest in Lillian's life either. It was almost as if we were insignificant to her. She was only interested in Dorothy, or rather, Dorothy's work."

"That is very useful information, Miss Harris," Holmes said. "Thank you for sharing that with us. Is there anything else you wish us to know about the book club, or Violet Brown?"

Esther shook her head. "Not that I can think of. Mr Holmes, do you think Dorothy took that sudden holiday to get away from Violet? Maybe Dorothy made up the excuse about winning it in a competition because she was becoming frightened of Violet somehow."

Holmes frowned. "Ah, now that's something I haven't considered yet. That's an interesting observation, Miss Harris. I am beginning to think that Miss Violet Brown has got something to do with Dorothy leaving London, although the reasoning behind that is not clear to me."

"Yet," Esther added confidently. "I know you'll find out what's going on, Mr Holmes. My father always says there will never be a mystery that you and Dr Watson can't solve. And I agree." She smiled from one man to the other.

"Thank you," Holmes replied with a smile. "Your confidence in our abilities is pleasing to hear."

With that, Holmes and Watson took their leave, ready to take the next step in their investigation, and hopefully, one step closer to solving it.

Chapter 10

Holmes and Watson headed to the building where the book club meetings were held. It was a modern four-storey townhouse, part of a row of buildings that included both businesses and shops. As they entered the reception area, they were greeted by a helpful man behind the desk.

"Good afternoon, gentlemen," the receptionist said with a friendly smile. "How may I assist you today?"

Holmes said, "We're here to inquire about the book club that meets in this building. I believe a Miss Dorothy Davenport is a member?"

The receptionist nodded, his expression turning thoughtful. "Ah, yes, Miss Davenport's book club. They meet here every month, always in the same room."

Holmes asked, "And which room would that be?"

"It's the one at the very top of the building," the receptionist replied. "Miss Davenport has been booking it for their meetings for quite a while now. In fact, she's already reserved it monthly for the rest of this year."

Holmes nodded. "I see. And is that room used for any other purposes?"

The receptionist shook his head. "No, sir. It's mainly a storage area, but the book club ladies are the only ones who use it regularly. Apparently, it's in a convenient location for all of them, given where their homes are."

"Interesting," Holmes mused. "Would it be possible for us to take a look at the room?"

The receptionist hesitated for a moment, then nodded. "I don't see why not."

Holmes and Watson climbed the stairs to the top floor, their footsteps echoing in the narrow stairwell. When they reached the landing, they faced a plain wooden door with a simple brass handle.

Holmes tried the handle, and the door swung open easily. The room beyond was of medium size and dimly lit, with a few dusty bookcases standing flush against the walls and a scattering of mismatched chairs arranged around a low table.

Watson moved to one of the bookshelves, running his finger along the spines of the books. "These don't look like they've been touched in years," he remarked.

Holmes nodded, his glance sweeping the room. "Yes. It seems this room is used for little else besides the book club meetings. Despite the shabbiness of the room, it offers a cosy feel and I can imagine the ladies speaking freely about their chosen books here, and also, their personal lives."

Holmes moved to the window, peering out at the street below. The view was unremarkable, just a narrow alleyway and the backs of the neighbouring buildings.

He turned to face Watson. "Let's say that someone in the book club wanted Miss Davenport out of the picture before their next meeting, which takes place this Friday. But why would one of them want Dorothy out of the way?"

Watson said, "Miss Lillian Goodwin has made it clear that she clashes with Dorothy over their book choices. And with Dorothy away, Miss Goodwin will now get to put her choice forward this month. But is that really a reason for this holiday win charade?"

"As you said earlier, Miss Goodwin likely has the funds to undertake such a project, and maybe she did it out of spite. Now, let's turn our thoughts to Esther Harris. I can't see any reason why she would want Dorothy out of the way. And yet, she was very keen to cast suspicions upon Violet Brown; a woman we have not met. Why is that?

Is Esther planning something that she will later blame on Violet? She has already sown the seeds of doubt about Miss Brown's character in our minds."

Watson sighed. "It's a lot to take in, Holmes. How do we proceed now?"

Holmes turned around slowly. "The answer lies in this room. Once we find out why it is so important, then we will discover who is behind this mystery. Watson, we must search this room thoroughly. Move every piece of furniture. Look under tables, behind paintings, lift the rugs. I am certain that will find something of great interest here."

"Rightio." Watson took off his jacket, not wanting to get dust on it. "I'll take this side of the room, if that's okay with you."

Holmes nodded.

The duo started their search of the room, leaving no rug unturned and no bookcase unmoved.

It was Watson who found what they were looking for. He called Holmes over and pointed to an area behind one of the bookcases he had moved.

Holmes rushed over. He broke into a wide smile when he saw what his friend had discovered. "Well done, Watson! This is exactly what I suspected might be in this room.

Now, we need to explore this area a little further. Are you ready?"

"Always," Watson said with a smile.

Chapter 11

Late afternoon, three days later, Holmes and Watson returned to the street where the book club meeting was held, but instead of entering that building, they made their way to the adjacent structure, which housed an arts space. As they stepped inside, they were greeted by the sight of Lord Cavendish, who looked extremely worried.

Lord Cavendish approached Holmes and Watson, his face etched with worry. "Mr Holmes, please explain why you wished to meet me here. Your message was very vague. Has this got something to do with the charity event I'm holding here tonight?"

Holmes said, "I believe it's got everything to do with your charity event, Lord Cavendish. I fear someone will attempt to steal the valuable artwork that will be displayed later on."

"But that's not possible," Lord Cavendish said. "We always have the highest security in place at such events. I can't imagine someone walking in off the street and stealing something."

Holmes said, "Lord Cavendish, when will the artwork for the event arrive?"

The Lord checked his pocket watch. "Within the next hour. Usually, Miss Davenport would be here to ensure everything runs smoothly, but in light of her absence, I will be the one doing that. Not that there's much work involved, as Miss Davenport has given me a plan of where each piece will go."

Holmes nodded. "And once the artwork is in place, will you leave the building?"

"I will," Lord Cavendish answered. "The event doesn't begin until eight p.m. I will return shortly before that to receive my guests, and my good wife will be with me."

"So, there will be a few hours where this building will be empty, and that will take place after the artwork has been put in place. Am I right?" Holmes asked.

"Yes, that's right. I say, you don't think someone will try to break in during those hours, do you? This is a busy street, Mr Holmes, people will notice if someone is trying to get in. Surely."

Holmes held up a finger. "Ah, they won't be breaking in from outside, Lord Cavendish. They will enter the building from an upstairs room. Please, let me explain. The building next door is where Miss Davenport and her friends hold their monthly book club meetings. They use the top room. A few days ago, Watson and I examined that room, and after moving one of the bookcases out of the way, we discovered a door which leads directly to the top room of this building. The door had been locked, but someone had recently forced the lock, making it easy to enter the room above.

"Watson and I went through that door and into this building. For a while, we couldn't work out why someone would want access to it. Then I remembered the events Miss Davenport organises for you. After making some enquiries, we found out about the event taking place tonight. Am I right in assuming the items on display will be valuable?"

Lord Cavendish nodded, his face pale. "Extremely valuable. We are hoping to raise a lot of money from them. But if they were to be stolen whilst in my care, my reputation would be ruined. Mr Holmes, has this proposed theft got something to do with Miss Davenport's sudden holiday?"

"It most certainly has," Holmes replied. "Someone has come up with a devious plan, a very devious plan indeed. One of the ladies in the book club is behind this. Miss

Davenport must have told them about this event coming up, quite innocently, I believe, and I suspect she spoke about how precious the artwork is. That person wanted Dorothy out of the way, so that she wouldn't be at the book club meeting this month, which is taking place in a few hours. The person in question will use the adjoining door in the top room and will enter this building to commit the theft. She arranged for Miss Davenport to take a sudden holiday away from London, to a place Dorothy had often spoken about visiting, which made the alleged win even more attractive to her."

Lord Cavendish exclaimed, "Good grief! I can't believe someone would have the nerve to commit such a crime! Mr Holmes, do you know the identity of this woman? The one who is planning the theft?"

"I had my suspicions, and they were confirmed when I received some news earlier about Miss Lillian Goodwin and Miss Esther Harris, two members of the book club. Unfortunately, both women had been taken ill earlier today. It seems they were poisoned by chocolates that were delivered to their homes this morning. Thankfully, they received medical assistance and are now on the road to recovery." He shook his head. "I am annoyed with myself for not warning the ladies that something like this might happen. I have let them down most badly."

Watson spoke up, "Holmes, you weren't to know. You mustn't judge yourself too harshly."

"But I do, Watson. Things could have turned out much worse." Holmes sighed before continuing, "The person behind this devious plan is Miss Violet Brown. Well, that is the name she has given to the others. Violet first saw Miss Davenport at a charity event where Violet was working as a waitress. She realised Dorothy had access to people of wealthy means. Violet ingratiated herself into the book club and proceeded to bombard Dorothy with questions about upcoming events, hoping to pick the perfect one to commit a robbery. This event must have caught her attention, and Violet began to put her plan into place, starting with getting Dorothy out of the way."

"But why send her on holiday? That seems extreme," Lord Cavendish said.

"That's what I thought," Holmes answered. "But maybe Dorothy was already becoming suspicious about Violet's endless questions and was about to voice her concerns to the others. Perhaps she was about to ask Violet to leave the group. That would ruin Violet's plans and it's possible she panicked and arranged the win to get Dorothy away as soon as possible."

Lord Cavendish nodded slowly, trying to take it all in. "And you assume this Miss Brown broke the lock on that door upstairs so that she could get into this building when the time was right?"

"I do," Holmes confirmed. "Perhaps her first plan was to steal the keys to this place from Dorothy and enter through the front door as though she worked here. But after our examination of the room the other day, I spoke to the man on reception about the members of the book club. He said Miss Violet Brown was always the last one to leave, only by a few minutes, but that would have given her enough time to scope out the room to see if there was access anywhere. She must have been delighted to discover the door behind the bookcase. It has made her planned theft a lot easier."

Lord Cavendish shook his head in disbelief. "And you really think a theft will take place today?"

"All the evidence points to that," Holmes said.

"So, what should I do? Cancel the event?"

"No, don't do that. The event should go ahead as planned. The thief needs to be caught in the act. We have to let Miss Brown proceed with her plan, and when she has the stolen items in her possession, an arrest can be made. She might not be working on her own, of course. She might turn up with extra people tonight. Perhaps she plans to tell the man on reception they are new members of the book club so as not to arouse suspicion."

"Seems she's thought of everything," Lord Cavendish mumbled, his brow furrowed in thought.

Holmes said, "I have already contacted the police about this matter, and a small group of officers will be in attendance with Dr Watson and myself this afternoon. We will conceal ourselves behind some of the furniture in the upstairs room, and await Miss Brown's appearance. We will let her commit the theft, and the officers will arrest her as she returns to the room."

Lord Cavendish didn't look entirely convinced. "Mr Holmes, I respect your opinion, but it seems so very hard to believe. Is there any chance you could be wrong?"

Dr Watson took a sharp intake of breath.

Holmes lifted his chin a fraction. "Lord Cavendish, I can assure you that I am not wrong. A theft will take place today."

Chapter 12

Once the artwork had been delivered and put in place, and Lord Cavendish had left the building, Holmes, Watson, and a small contingent of police officers including Inspector Lestrade, concealed themselves behind an array of stored furniture in the top room. They kept silent as they waited for the thieves to make their move. The room was dimly lit, the shadows cast by the furniture providing ample cover for the waiting party.

Time seemed to crawl by, each second feeling like an eternity. Watson shifted uncomfortably, his leg cramping from the prolonged crouching position. Holmes, on the other hand, remained perfectly still, his keen eyes fixed on the door that connected the room to the upstairs chamber where the book club meetings took place.

Sometime later, the silence that had settled over the room was abruptly shattered by the grating sound of hinges as the door gradually swung open, the shadows of three figures spreading across the floor. Low voices, barely above a whisper, drifted into the room, carrying with them an air of smug superiority. One voice, unmistakably feminine, stood out from the others, her words dripping with disdain and contempt.

"Can you believe these wealthy toffs?" the woman scoffed, her tone laced with a mixture of amusement and derision. "They've got nothing better to do than spend their hard-earned money on fancy artwork. Well, I'm more than happy to take it off their hands and put it to better use."

The woman's words were met with a chorus of harsh, grating laughter from her two male companions, their voices echoing in the confined space of the room.

"Too right, Violet," one of the men said. "They won't even know what hit 'em until it's far too late."

"We'll be long gone before they even realise their precious paintings are missing," the other man added. "By the time they discover the theft, we'll be halfway across the city, enjoying the fruits of our labour. And we'll make enough to pay for that holiday you organised. I don't know why you had to splash out like that, Vi."

The woman tutted. "I had to get her out of the way and away from the others. I could tell she was getting ready to kick me out of the club." She sniggered. "I wish I could see her face when she finds out about this theft. She'll know it's all her fault for going on and on about all the posh people she works for, and how much money they have. Serves her right."

The trio moved further into the room, their footsteps echoing on the hardwood floor. They were completely oblivious to the presence of Holmes, Watson, and the police officers hidden behind the furniture.

As the thieves made their way out of the room and down the stairs, Holmes signalled to the waiting officers to remain in position, his hand raised in a silent command. They needed to catch the culprits red-handed, with the stolen artwork in their possession, to ensure that justice would be served.

It wasn't long before the thieves returned, their voices once again filling the room, the sound of their self-congratulatory chatter shattering the tense silence.

"That was almost too easy," Violet crowed, her tone dripping with self-satisfaction.

"We'll be set for life with this haul," one of the men said. "No more scraping by, no more living hand to mouth. This is our ticket to the good life, and we've earned every penny of it."

At that very moment, Inspector Lestrade and his officers emerged from their carefully chosen hiding places.

"Police!" Lestrade shouted, his authoritative voice ringing out through the air, echoing off the walls of the gallery. "Drop the bags and put your hands in the air, now!"

The thieves froze instantly, their eyes growing wide with fear as they realised they had been caught completely off guard, the stolen artwork still clutched tightly in their trembling hands.

As the police officers moved in swiftly to apprehend the criminals, Holmes and Watson stepped forward.

Holmes fixed his piercing gaze on the woman, his voice calm and measured. "Miss Violet Brown, I presume?" he asked, his tone almost conversational, as if he were greeting an old acquaintance.

Violet's eyes narrowed, her lips curling into a sneer as she regarded the famous detective with undisguised contempt. "Sherlock Holmes," she spat, her voice dripping with venom, each word laced with a bitter hatred. "I should have known you'd stick your nose into this. Why can't you leave people like us alone? I should have sent you on holiday, too, got you out of the way. I'll know for next time."

"Next time?" Holmes raised one eyebrow. "Are you sure there will be a next time?"

Violet Brown's only reply was a smug smile.

As the police officers handcuffed the thieves and led them away, Watson said to Holmes, "Another case solved, old friend," he said joyfully, clapping Holmes on the shoulder.

Chapter 13

A week had passed since the dramatic events at the art gallery, and the city was still abuzz with talk of the foiled heist and the brilliant detective work of Sherlock Holmes and Dr John Watson. The newspapers had been filled with accounts of the daring arrest, each article more sensational than the last, and the public's fascination with the case showed no signs of abating.

On a crisp, sunny morning, Mrs Hudson ushered two visitors into the cosy confines of 221B Baker Street. Dorothy Davenport and her sister, Mrs Agnes Fairfax, were shown into the sitting room, where Holmes and Watson were enjoying a leisurely breakfast, the remnants of toast and marmalade scattered across the table. They stood as the women entered.

"Mr Holmes, Dr Watson," Dorothy began. "We simply had to come and express our gratitude in person. Your actions in apprehending Violet Brown and her accomplices were nothing short of heroic."

Mrs Fairfax nodded in agreement, her eyes shining with admiration. "We cannot thank you enough for your tireless efforts on our behalf. When I first came to you with my concerns about Dorothy's sudden disappearance, I never imagined it would lead to those criminals being arrested."

Holmes waved away their praise with a dismissive gesture. "Think nothing of it, ladies," he said, his voice warm and reassuring. "It is our duty and our pleasure to see justice served."

Dorothy lowered her gaze, her cheeks flushing with embarrassment. "I must admit, Mr Holmes, I feel terribly ashamed of how easily I was taken in by Violet. I shared so much information with her, never suspecting that she might use it for such devious purposes. My desire to visit Clovelly, the details of the upcoming art exhibition, even the estimated value of the paintings. I spoke of these things so freely, never imagining the consequences."

Watson said, "You mustn't blame yourself, Miss Davenport. Violet Brown is a master manipulator, skilled in the art of deception. Even the most discerning among us might have fallen victim to her charms."

Dorothy nodded. "Thank you for your understanding, Dr Watson. Because of what I'd done, I offered my resignation to Lord Cavendish. I felt I had failed in my duties, that I had put his lordship's reputation at risk through my own foolishness. But Lord Cavendish refused to accept my resignation. He said I was too important an employee for him to lose, and that we should put the past behind us."

Mrs Fairfax reached out and took her sister's hand, squeezing it gently in a gesture of support. "He recognises your worth, Dorothy, and he knows that you would never knowingly put his interests at risk."

Holmes said, "It may interest you to know, ladies, that Violet Brown and her associates have a long history of such thefts. Her husband and her brother have been her willing accomplices in a string of crimes that have spanned the length and breadth of the country. Until now, they have managed to evade capture, always staying one step ahead of the law."

Mrs Fairfax's eyes widened in surprise. "Truly, Mr Holmes? I had no idea that their criminal activities were so extensive."

Holmes continued, "And I must say, Mrs Fairfax, that if it were not for your concern over your sister's sudden departure, Violet Brown and her gang would have undoubtedly succeeded in yet another audacious theft. Your instincts were correct, and your actions set in motion the chain of events that led to their ultimate downfall."

Mrs Fairfax turned to her sister and said kindly, "You see, Dorothy, I was right to worry about you. I'll never stop worrying about you, no matter how far apart we live."

Dorothy smiled. "And I will always worry about you, my dear sister." She turned to Mr Holmes and Dr Watson. "Thank you again for all you've done. We will wish you farewell. My sister and I have a lot to catch up on."

As the door closed behind the departing sisters, Holmes and Watson settled back into their chairs, the room seeming somehow quieter in the wake of their guests' departure. For a moment, the only sound was the gentle crackling of the fire in the grate and the distant rumble of carriage wheels on the cobblestones outside.

"Well, Watson," Holmes said at last, breaking the contemplative silence, "I must say, this case has been a most interesting one. The machinations of the human mind never cease to amaze me, and Violet Brown's scheme was as devious as it was daring."

Watson nodded in agreement. "To think that she had been planning this theft for months, ingratiating herself with Miss Davenport and the other members of the book club, all the while gathering information that she could use to her advantage. It is a chilling reminder of the lengths to which some people will go in pursuit of their own selfish ends."

For a moment, the two men sat in companionable silence, each lost in their own thoughts. Then, Watson spoke again, his tone lighter, almost playful. "You know, Holmes, perhaps we should consider taking a holiday ourselves. Somewhere peaceful, perhaps by the sea."

Holmes chuckled, his eyes sparkling with amusement. "My dear Watson, I do believe you are becoming quite the romantic in your old age. A holiday by the sea, indeed! I can just imagine it now. You, lounging on the beach with a good book, while I am left to my own devices, searching for some mystery to solve amidst the tranquil countryside."

Watson laughed, shaking his head ruefully. "You are probably right, Holmes. Knowing you, you would likely stumble upon some nefarious plot or another. Perhaps it is best that we remain here in London, where the criminals are at least somewhat predictable."

Holmes smiled, leaning back in his chair with a contented sigh. "Ah, Watson, you know me too well. London is indeed where I belong, with its endless supply of puzzles and intrigues. But who knows? Perhaps one day, we shall find ourselves taking a holiday by the sea, chasing down some elusive criminal mastermind amidst the beaches and rocky cliffs."

Watson raised his teacup in a mock toast. "To future adventures, then, Holmes. Whether in London or further afield, I have no doubt that there will always be mysteries to solve and wrongs to right, as long as we are together."

Holmes raised his own cup in response, his expression one of genuine affection. "To future adventures, indeed, my dear Watson."

Book 4 - Sherlock Holmes and The Baker Street Thefts

Chapter 1

It was early afternoon, and inside 221B Baker Street, Sherlock Holmes was reading a mystery novel and occasionally shaking his head at the unlikely plot twists within the story. His companion, Dr John Watson, sat across from him, a newspaper on his lap. Dr Watson's eyes were closed and a light series of snores came from him.

The tranquil scene was suddenly shattered by the sound of hurried footsteps on the stairs, followed by a frantic knock at the door.

"Come in, Mrs Hudson," Holmes called out, recognising her knock.

Dr Watson snorted, opened his eyes and blinked. "What? What was that? What's going on?"

The door burst open, revealing their landlady, Mrs Hudson, her face flushed with agitation. "Mr Holmes, Dr Watson! Thank goodness you're both here."

Watson turned to look at their landlady. "Whatever is the matter, Mrs Hudson?"

"There are thefts taking place! Right here on Baker Street!" she exclaimed. "I've just heard about them from my neighbour, and I fear our home may be targeted next. Whatever shall we do?"

Holmes closed the book he was reading and placed it on the table next to him. "Thefts? Pray tell us more, Mrs Hudson. Please, sit down."

Mrs Hudson took a seat across from the two men. "My neighbour, Vera Wilkins, was telling me all about it. Apparently, there have been several incidents of valuable items going missing from various households on our very street."

"What sort of items?" Watson inquired.

"It seems to be jewellery," Mrs Hudson replied. "This morning, she saw the Thompsons on their doorstep discussing a missing brooch. They live further up the road, and on the opposite side. Anyway, Vera was walking past them on her way to the shops. Mrs Thompson was upset about something and her voice was quite loud. Well, Vera couldn't help but hear what they were saying, could she?"

Holmes smiled. "I suppose not. And what did Mr and Mrs Thompson have to say about this missing brooch?"

"Mr Thompson seemed to think it might have simply been misplaced," Mrs Hudson explained, "but Mrs Thompson was adamant it was on her dressing table because she always kept it there, but when she looked for it that morning, intending to wear it, it was gone. Mrs Thompson had searched her bedroom, but it was nowhere to be found."

Watson reached for his pocketbook and made a note about the incident.

"And then there's Mrs Henderson," Mrs Hudson continued, "who noticed a pearl necklace missing from her jewellery box a few days before."

"And how do you know about that?" Holmes asked.

Mrs Hudson replied, "Mrs Henderson told me. I was walking through the park yesterday as it was such a lovely day, and I saw Mrs Henderson sitting on a bench. She didn't look like her normal happy self at all. So, I asked if something was wrong. She told me about the missing necklace. She said she always keeps it in the jewellery box when she's not wearing it. But it's no longer there. She thinks she might have put it somewhere else for some reason, but now can't remember where she put it. She thinks she's losing her memory. Poor woman. I tried to be positive and said, these things turn up in unexpected places sometimes."

"That's true," Watson said. "I hope she finds that necklace soon."

Mrs Hudson's eyes narrowed. "The thing is, Dr Watson, I think it's been stolen, and I think Mrs Thompson's brooch has been stolen, too." She paused. "Someone else has noticed a missing piece of jewellery on this street, Mrs Baxter. She's lost some diamond earrings. And this happened last week, according to Vera, who is friends with Mrs Baxter's sister. Three missing items, all from people who live on this street. And they all occurred within the last few weeks. These are not coincidences. Not at all. And I know your feelings on coincidences, Mr Holmes."

"Indeed," Holmes replied. "I don't believe in them. Mrs Hudson. I agree these incidents are not coincidences, but evidence of something else taking place. Those missing items are small and easily transportable. This suggests a thief who is adept at moving swiftly and undetected."

"Precisely my thoughts, Mr Holmes," Mrs Hudson agreed. "I don't have many valuables, but the ones I have are very precious to me. And I know you two have items of value, too. With the thefts occurring so close to home, I'm worried that we may be the next targets."

"We shall take every precaution to ensure that does not happen," Holmes assured her. "Watson and I will look into this matter, and we will do so immediately."

Mrs Hudson sighed with relief. "I'm so glad to hear that, Mr Holmes, so very glad."

Holmes turned to Watson, a determined glint in his eye. "Watson, we shall pay a visit to the Thompsons and inquire about this missing brooch. It seems the most recent incident, and therefore, the one with the freshest trail to follow. Mrs Hudson, could you give me the house numbers of where Mrs Thompson and the other ladies live, please?"

"Of course." Mrs Hudson gave Holmes the required information.

As the two men prepared to depart, Mrs Hudson rose from her seat, a grateful smile on her face. "Thank you, gentlemen. I feel much better knowing you're on the case."

Holmes offered her a reassuring nod. "Have no fear, Mrs Hudson. We shall uncover the truth behind these thefts and ensure the perpetrator is brought to justice."

With that, the famous detective and his trusted companion set off, ready to make their investigations.

Chapter 2

Minutes later, Sherlock Holmes and Dr Watson approached the ornate front door of the building where Mr and Mrs Thompson lived.

Holmes rapped on the door, and a few seconds passed before it swung open, revealing a young woman in a crisp maid's uniform.

"Good afternoon, sirs," she greeted, her tone polite but guarded. "How may I be of assistance?"

Holmes offered a warm smile. "Good day, miss. I am Sherlock Holmes, and this is my colleague, Dr John Watson. We're here to speak with Mrs Thompson regarding a rather delicate matter."

The maid's expression softened slightly, and she nodded. "Of course, Mr Holmes. Do come in." She ushered them inside, leading them through the foyer and into an elegantly appointed sitting room. "If you'll excuse me for a moment, I'll inform Mrs Thompson of your arrival."

As the maid departed, Watson leaned in closer to Holmes. "What are your initial observations, Holmes?"

Holmes scanned the room, taking in every detail. "The household appears well-kept, with no obvious signs of disarray or disturbance. I didn't see any signs of a forced entry on the main door or the front-facing windows. However, we mustn't draw any premature conclusions until we've spoken with Mrs Thompson herself."

Moments later, the maid returned, followed by a woman in her late fifties. Mrs Thompson was impeccably dressed, her greying hair styled in an elegant coiffure, and her demeanour exuded a sense of refinement and poise.

"Mr Holmes, Dr Watson," she greeted, her voice tinged with a hint of concern. "I understand you wished to speak with me about a delicate matter."

Holmes inclined his head respectfully. "We do, Mrs Thompson. We've been made aware of a recent incident involving a missing brooch belonging to yourself, and we were hoping you could provide us with more details."

Mrs Thompson's expression grew grave, and she motioned for them to take a seat. "Ah, yes, the brooch. A most distressing situation, I must say. It was a family heirloom, passed down through generations, and of immense sentimental value. I had placed it on my dressing table, as I always do after wearing it. I wished to wear it this morning, but when I looked for the brooch, it was gone."

Watson smiled gently, "Forgive me for asking, but are you certain it wasn't simply misplaced? These things do happen."

Mrs Thompson shook her head firmly. "I am meticulous in my habits, and I can assure you that the brooch was precisely where I always left it. I wear it most days and like to have it to hand when needed."

Holmes nodded. "And have you noticed any other items missing from your home, or any signs of a potential break-in?"

"Not that I'm aware of, Mr Holmes," Mrs Thompson replied. "The house appears undisturbed, and nothing else seems to be missing. It's as if the brooch simply vanished into thin air."

Holmes said, "Mrs Thompson, we've been informed that there have been other incidents of missing valuables on this very street. Are you aware of this?"

Mrs Thompson frowned. "No, I am not aware of that. Have these items vanished as mysteriously as mine?"

"It appears so," Holmes confirmed.

"May I ask, who has reported these incidents?" Mrs Thompson said.

"They haven't been reported as such," Holmes replied. "But the information has come to us via contacts. It seems Mrs Henderson has lost a pearl necklace, and Mrs Baxter has lost a pair of diamond earrings."

Mrs Thompson gasped. "No! But I am friends with those ladies. We meet almost every day for lunch. They never told me about their missing jewellery."

"Perhaps they thought the items had been misplaced and they would find them soon," Holmes offered.

Mrs Thompson nodded slowly. "Ah, yes, that could be the case. My husband thinks I've misplaced my brooch. We had quite the animated discussion on the doorstep this morning about it. I'm surprised the neighbours didn't hear us." Comprehension dawned on her face and she broke into a smile. "One of the neighbours did hear us, though, didn't she? I noticed Mrs Wilkins going by, and how her steps slowed when she passed our home. And Mrs Wilkins is a good friend of your lovely landlady. Now, I understand how you know about my brooch."

Holmes bowed his head a little. "Yes, people are prone to discuss their neighbour's lives. This information was passed to us with honest intentions, and not as malicious gossip, I assure you."

Mrs Thompson waved a hand dismissively. "I can see that, Mr Holmes. And I'm glad the information was passed to you. Can I assume you will look into this matter on my behalf?"

"Of course," Holmes replied. "We will investigate this mystery thoroughly, and we will find the person behind it. You have my word. Furthermore, we will do our utmost to reunite you with your brooch.

Mrs Thompson clasped her hands together, her eyes shining with relief. "Oh, Mr Holmes, I cannot begin to express my gratitude. This brooch means the world to me, and the thought of losing it forever is simply unbearable."

Holmes rose from his seat, offering Mrs Thompson a reassuring smile. "We shall leave no stone unturned in our investigation. If any further information comes to your mind about this mystery, no matter how insignificant it may seem, I implore you to share it with us."

Mrs Thompson nodded, her expression resolute. "Of course, Mr Holmes. Anything to aid in the recovery of my beloved brooch."

"One more thing before we go. May we speak with your maid, the one who answered the door? She may have noticed someone unusual hanging around recently. Perhaps someone who was showing an interest in your home, and those of your neighbours."

Mrs Thompson said, "Matilda? Oh, of course. Yes, please do speak to her. She'll be in the kitchen at this time of the day."

"Thank you, we will seek her out. How long has Matilda worked for you?" Holmes asked.

Mrs Thompson smiled. "Ten years. She's like part of the family. I don't know what I'd do without her."

Chapter 3

Sherlock Holmes and Dr Watson left the sitting room and headed to the kitchen, where Matilda was placing some freshly cooked scones on a cooling rack.

Holmes cleared his throat. "Please excuse our intrusion, but may we speak to you, Matilda? We won't take up much of your time."

For a second, Matilda looked startled to see them, but then she smiled and said, "Of course. Won't you sit down?" She gestured towards the small table in the corner. "Can I get you anything to eat or drink?"

"Not for me." Holmes said as he sat down.

"Me neither, but thank you," Dr Watson said, taking a seat next to Holmes. He reached into his pocket and retrieved his notebook and pen.

Matilda moved away from the cooling rack and sat opposite them, expectation in her eyes.

Holmes said, "We have been asked to look into the disappearance of Mrs Thompson's brooch. Are you aware it has gone missing?"

Matilda nodded. "Yes, Mrs Thompson is ever so upset about it. I helped her look for it. We've searched this house from top to bottom, we have." She paused and studied Holmes more closely. "But you don't think it's been lost, do you, Mr Holmes? I know you're a detective. You wouldn't look into a brooch that's been lost. Do you think it's been stolen?"

Holmes answered, "The question is, do you think it's been stolen?"

She gave them a slow nod. "I do, but I'm not sure how. I'm friends with some of the other maids on this street, and they've told me that items belonging to their employees have also gone missing. It's too much of a coincidence to be, well, an actual coincidence, isn't it? There's something funny going on."

"Who do your friends work for?" Dr Watson asked.

"Betsy works for Mrs Henderson, and Enid works for Mrs Baxter." She cast a glance towards the kitchen door. "Mrs Thompson is friends with those other ladies, and they meet up nearly every day."

Holmes said, "Yes, Mrs Thompson was kind enough to share that information with us. Tell me, is the house empty during the day?"

"It is. Mrs Thompson usually goes out at eleven in the morning. She returns about two or three in the afternoon. She hasn't been out today because she's so upset about her brooch. I really don't like to see her like that." Matilda fell silent and stared at the table.

"And what about you, Matilda?" Holmes asked. "Do you leave the house during the day?"

Matilda looked up. "Yes, I do. I have chores that take me out of the house, like shopping, collecting cleaning, delivering messages on behalf of Mr and Mrs Thompson, that sort of thing. I make sure Mrs Thompson has everything she needs before she leaves at eleven, and after that I'll leave and get on with my chores. I make sure I'm back about one o'clock so that I can make a start on afternoon refreshments for when Mrs Thompson returns."

Dr Watson made some notes in his book. He looked up and said, "So, the house is normally empty between eleven and one? Is that right?"

"It is." Matilda's eyes widened. "Oh! Is that when you think the brooch was stolen?"

"It is a window of opportunity," Holmes replied.

Matilda frowned. "But how would they get in? I always make sure everything is locked up properly. And I haven't seen any damaged locks or broken windows."

"How someone gained entry is something we'll find out in due course," Holmes said. "Have you noticed anything out of the ordinary around the house in recent days? Any strange occurrences or visitors that might be connected to the theft?"

"Not that I can recall," Matilda replied, shaking her head. "The comings and goings have been much the same as always."

Holmes pressed on, "Who are the regular visitors to this household?"

Matilda paused, gathering her thoughts. "Well, there's Mrs Thompson's circle of friends, of course. Ladies like Mrs Henderson and Mrs Baxter, whom she mentioned to you earlier. They often stop by for tea or to discuss the latest society gossip. But mostly, they prefer to meet at cafés or restaurants."

Watson interjected, "And do any of these ladies have a particular interest in jewellery or valuable items?"

"Not that I'm aware of," Matilda said with a frown. "They're all well-to-do ladies, of course, but I've never known any of them to be overly interested in such things."

Holmes nodded, his expression thoughtful. "And what about deliveries or tradespeople? Are there any regular visitors of that nature?"

"Yes, Mr Holmes," Matilda replied. "We have the usual deliveries of food and household goods. And there's the chimney sweep, who comes by every few months to clean the flues."

Watson asked, "And have there been any new faces around the household recently? Any visitors or tradespeople out of the ordinary?"

Matilda nodded and opened her mouth to respond, but before she could utter a word, a sharp knock echoed from the back door. Her eyes widened, and a flicker of fear crossed her features as she glanced towards the frosted glass pane where a man's silhouette was visible.

Chapter 4

With a steadying breath, Matilda stood up and crossed the kitchen. She opened the door, revealing a person clad in the attire of a milkman.

"Jimmy," Matilda greeted stiffly, her tone devoid of warmth.

The man grinned, his glance roving over her in a manner that made her shift uncomfortably. "Well now, don't you look pretty today, Matilda." He stepped briskly into the kitchen without an invitation. "Lovely day, ain't it? Got any plans for the rest of the afternoon?"

Matilda retreated a few paces. "Just my usual duties, Jimmy. Nothing out of the ordinary."

"Is that so?" Jimmy's gaze drifted towards Holmes and Watson, his brow furrowing as he regarded the two men with obvious disapproval. He made no attempt at a greeting, turning his attention back to Matilda. "And what about the missus? She got any fancy parties or soirees lined up?"

Matilda's discomfort was palpable, her glance flickering towards the detectives as if silently pleading for intervention. "I couldn't rightly say, Jimmy. You know how it is."

Jimmy chuckled, a low, rumbling sound that seemed to make Matilda shrink further into herself. "Aye, I reckon I do." He gestured towards the locked drawer near the stove. "Well, go on then, love. Let's have the money."

Matilda crossed to the drawer and retrieved an envelope, which she handed to Jimmy. He pocketed it without a glance, his gaze once again sweeping over her in a manner that made Holmes' jaw tighten.

"You know, Matilda," Jimmy began, "a pretty little thing like you shouldn't be cooped up in this place all day. Why don't you come out with me tonight? We'll have a bit of fun, just you and me."

Matilda's hands twisted in the fabric of her apron, her eyes downcast. "That's kind of you, Jimmy, but I really must decline. I have too much work to do here."

Jimmy's smile faded, replaced by a look of petulant annoyance. "Work, work, work. Is that all you ever think about?" He closed the distance between them with a few long strides. "You need to learn to live a little, love."

Matilda retreated until her back was against the wall, her eyes wide with apprehension. "I...I can't, Jimmy. Please, I need to get back to my duties."

Holmes rose and stepped forward, his sharp gaze fixed on Jimmy. "I believe the lady has made her position quite clear," he said, his voice calm but firm. "It would be best if you respected her wishes and took your leave."

Jimmy's eyes narrowed as he regarded Holmes, a flicker of annoyance crossing his features. For a moment, it seemed as though he might argue, but something in the detective's unwavering stare made him think better of it. With a final, dismissive snort, he turned and strode out of the kitchen; the door slamming shut behind him.

In the silence that followed, Matilda seemed to sag against the wall, her relief evident.

Holmes turned to her, his expression softening. "Are you all right?"

Matilda nodded, her hands still trembling slightly as she smoothed her apron. "Yes, thank you, Mr Holmes. I'm sorry you had to witness that."

Watson said, "Does this happen often? That man's behaviour was entirely inappropriate."

Matilda explained, "Jimmy started delivering milk here about a month ago. The previous milkman used to collect his money once a week, but Jimmy insists on collecting it daily."

Holmes' eyes narrowed thoughtfully. "And has he always been so familiar with you?"

Matilda's cheeks flushed, and she nodded. "I'm afraid so. He's over-friendly with everyone, always wanting to know everyone's business. There's something about him that makes me uneasy. Some of the other maids have mentioned it to me, too. They say he's always asking questions, trying to find out more about the families we work for."

Watson's expression darkened. "That's most concerning. A man in his position should not be prying into the affairs of others."

Holmes nodded in agreement with Dr Watson. "Matilda, could you tell me when Jimmy typically does his rounds?"

Matilda replied, "He's usually delivers the milk around five a.m., Mr Holmes. Thankfully, he leaves the bottles outside on the doorstep, so I don't have to face him at that hour. He delivers to everyone on the street, not just the Thompsons. He collects his money anywhere between three and four in the afternoon."

Holmes exchanged a meaningful glance with Watson before turning back to Matilda. "Thank you, Matilda.

You've been most helpful. If Jimmy gives you any more trouble, please don't hesitate to let us know."

Matilda smiled gratefully. "I will, Mr Holmes. Thank you."

With a nod, Holmes and Watson took their leave, stepping out into the bright sunlight of the afternoon. As they walked Holmes' brow was furrowed in thought, his mind already piecing together the fragments of information they had gathered.

"What do you make of it, Holmes?" Watson asked, keeping pace with his friend's long strides.

Holmes hummed thoughtfully. "There's something not quite right about this Jimmy character, Watson. His behaviour towards Matilda was most inappropriate, and the fact that he's been asking questions about the families on the street is certainly cause for concern."

Watson nodded in agreement. "Do you think he could be involved in the thefts?"

Holmes replied, "We can't rule it out. A man in his position would have easy access to the homes on the street, and his insistence on collecting payment daily could be a cover for something more sinister. If he is the thief, he could have easily taken a spare set of keys, had he spotted any."

"What shall we do now?" Watson asked.

"Let's call upon the other ladies who have experienced the loss of items. We shall soon see if there is a pattern to this mystery."

Chapter 5

Holmes and Watson made their way to the home of Mrs Henderson, the woman who had lost her pearl necklace.

Mrs Henderson was of similar age to Mrs Thompson and had an air of quiet elegance. She welcomed them into her sitting room and offered refreshments, which Holmes and Watson politely declined.

"Mr Holmes, Dr Watson," Mrs Henderson said as she settled into an armchair, "what brings you here today?"

Holmes explained, "We're investigating a series of suspected thefts that have occurred in the area. Mrs Thompson has reported a missing brooch, and we have reason to believe that others on this street may have experienced similar losses."

Mrs Henderson's hand flew to her throat, her eyes widening. "Goodness! Mr Holmes, only recently, I noticed my pearl necklace had gone missing. I thought I had simply misplaced it, but now that you mention suspected thefts..." She trailed off, a look of concern crossing her features.

Watson leaned forward, his voice gentle. "When did you last see the necklace, Mrs Henderson?"

"A week ago. I wore it to a dinner party and remember putting it back in my jewellery box that evening. But when I went to wear it again a few days ago, it was gone."

Holmes asked, "And have you noticed any signs of a break-in? Any disturbances or out-of-place items in your home?"

Mrs Henderson shook her head. "No, nothing at all. Everything has been quite normal, apart from the missing necklace."

Watson recorded the details in his notebook. "And when is your house typically empty?"

"Well, I often go out to visit friends or run errands in the late morning and early afternoon. My husband is at work during the day. My children have all grown and left the family home."

Holmes nodded thoughtfully. "Thank you, Mrs Henderson. This information is most helpful. Your maid, the one who showed us in, may we talk to her, please?"

"Why, of course," Mrs Henderson replied. "She'll be polishing the silver in the dining room. It's just along the hallway at the end. You can't miss it."

"Thank you." Holmes rose. "Is her name Betsy?"

Mrs Henderson's eyebrows rose. "She is. My word, Mr Holmes, how did you know that?"

Holmes smiled. "Mrs Thompson's maid told us. Does Betsy leave the house during the day at all?"

"Yes, but she always waits until I've left, in case I need anything. She's most attentive to my needs. Is there anything else you wish to know, Mr Holmes?"

"Not at the moment, thank you." He smiled. "We will try our best to return your precious pearls to you."

Mrs Henderson let out a sigh of relief. "Thank you, thank you so much."

Holmes and Watson entered the dining room a few moments later, and found Betsy diligently polishing the silver. Her movements were precise and methodical, but there was a tension in her shoulders that betrayed her unease.

Holmes approached her, his voice gentle but firm. "Betsy, we'd like to ask you a few questions, if that's okay?"

Betsy's hands stilled, and she looked up at the two men. "Of course, Mr Holmes. Is it about Mrs Henderson's missing necklace?"

Holmes nodded. "It is. What do you know about its disappearance?"

Betsy gave him a grim look. "I think it's been stolen. I don't know where or how someone got in, but I know Mrs Henderson hasn't misplaced it. She's got an amazing memory and she would never forget something like that. It makes me angry to see her so upset about that lovely necklace of hers, it really does." She resumed her polishing work, her anger transferred to the silver goblet in her hands.

Dr Watson smiled gently at the young woman and said, "We are making enquiries into its disappearance. We understand there's a new milkman, Jimmy, who's been making his rounds in the neighbourhood. Have you had any interactions with him?"

Betsy replied, "Yes, sir. He's been delivering milk here for the past month."

Holmes' eyes narrowed slightly. "And how would you describe your interactions with him?"

The maid's polishing actions grew more agitated. "He's a bit odd, if I'm being honest. Always asking questions. About me, about Mrs Henderson and her husband. It's not right, the way he pries."

Watson frowned, his concern clear. "What sort of questions does he ask?"

"He wants to know about Mrs Henderson's schedule, when she's home and when she's out. He asks about Mr Henderson's work. I've tried to keep my answers short, but he's a persistent one."

Holmes said, "And have you noticed anything unusual about his behaviour? Any patterns or inconsistencies?"

Betsy thought for a moment, her brow furrowed. "Well, there was one thing. Last week, he came by to collect his money much earlier than usual. He normally gets here late in the afternoon, but he turned up at midday. I was late setting off for the market that day. A few minutes later, and I would have left the house and missed him. When I asked him why he was early, he just laughed it off, said he had a busy day ahead."

Holmes said, "Thank you, Betsy. This information is most helpful. If you remember anything else, please don't hesitate to let us know."

Betsy nodded. "I will, Mr Holmes."

Holmes and Watson left the home of Mrs Henderson and walked along Baker Street.

Watson said, "It seems our milkman is becoming more suspicious by the moment."

Holmes replied, "Indeed, Watson. His questions are far too pointed to be mere curiosity. And the change in his money collection schedule is noteworthy. We shall have to keep a close eye on him."

They called upon the remaining friend of Mrs Thompson's, Mrs Baxter. She confirmed a pair of diamond earrings had gone missing from her home over a week ago, and despite a thorough search, she hadn't found them. Like her friends, she advised there had been no signs of forced entry to the property.

Holmes and Watson also spoke to the maid in the house, Enid, who had the same opinion about Jimmy as the others had. Enid told them Mrs Baxter usually left the house between eleven a.m. and returned later in the afternoon, And, yes, she used that time to complete errands for Mrs Baxter which involved leaving the house.

After saying goodbye to Enid, Holmes and Watson made their way along Baker Street, calling upon several other neighbours to see if anyone else was missing valuable items.

To their surprise, no one had. At least, not to their knowledge, they told Holmes and Watson.

As they walked back towards 221B Baker Street, Holmes said, "The only residents who have confirmed the loss of an item are Mrs Thompson, Mrs Henderson, and Mrs Baxter. Three friends who leave the house usually at the same time every day. Their maids are absent from the house as well, albeit for a shorter time frame. I wonder if that is why they have become targets. The thief knew they were going to be out at a certain time, and it would be safe to enter their properties during those hours. Perhaps the thief left the other properties on this street alone because there was no guarantee as to when those homes would be empty."

Watson nodded. "So, it seems the suspicion is falling upon the milkman. I must say, Holmes, I disliked that man most intensely. His manner, the way he looked at Matilda, and how he talked to her. Also, did you notice how he dismissed us with one glance?"

"I did notice. There was a flicker of resentment in his eyes, too, as if the mere sight of us was repulsive to him. Watson, let's have a coffee at that new café on the corner and discuss this further."

A short while later, Holmes and Watson sat at a small table in a quaint café on Baker Street, their minds still preoccupied with the peculiar case. The aroma of freshly brewed coffee and the gentle clatter of cups and saucers filled the air as they discussed their findings.

"It seems our milkman, Jimmy, is the most likely suspect," Holmes mused, stirring his coffee thoughtfully. "The thefts began shortly after he started his rounds in the area, and they occur during the hours when he has finished his deliveries for the day."

Watson nodded. "But how does he gain entry into the houses unnoticed? Surely, someone would have seen or heard something if he were breaking in."

Holmes replied, "I suspect Jimmy uses his morning rounds to scope out the houses, looking for weak points of entry. Perhaps he notices a loose window or a faulty lock during his deliveries."

"That's a possibility," Watson agreed. "But even so, it would be risky for him to attempt a break-in during daylight hours."

"I agree," Holmes said, his eyes glinting with a sudden realisation. "But what if he doesn't need to break in at all? Consider this, Watson: when Jimmy collects his payment from the households, perhaps on occasions he is likely left alone in the kitchen for a few minutes. That would give him ample opportunity to steal a spare key or make an imprint of one for later use."

Watson's eyes widened. "Of course! And if he's skilled at picking locks, he could easily gain entry without leaving any signs of a forced break-in. So, what's our next move, Holmes?"

Holmes smiled. "I believe it's time for me to go undercover, Watson. I shall join Jimmy on his early morning rounds and observe his behaviour. Perhaps I can catch him scouting out his next target or gain some insight into his methods."

Watson sat back, a look of concern crossing his face. "Are you sure that's wise, Holmes? If Jimmy is our thief, he may become suspicious if he notices you following him."

"Fear not, my dear Watson," Holmes said, his voice brimming with confidence. "I shall be the very picture of discretion. Jimmy will never suspect that he has the great Sherlock Holmes on his tail."

With that, the two men finished their coffee and set about making preparations for Holmes' undercover mission.

Chapter 6

Holmes rose at four a.m. the next day and set about preparing for his undercover mission. He carefully donned the attire of a railway maintenance worker, ensuring that every detail was in place. He rubbed dirt and grime onto his clothes and skin, giving himself the appearance of someone who had just finished a long night's work at the station.

With his disguise complete, Holmes slipped out of 221B Baker Street and made his way to a shadowy spot at the far end of the road. From this vantage point, he had a clear view of the street, allowing him to observe the comings and goings of the early morning deliveries.

Before long, the clopping of hooves echoed through the quiet streets. Jimmy appeared on his horse-drawn cart, laden with the day's supply of milk. Holmes watched intently as Jimmy began his rounds, delivering milk to the doorsteps of the houses along Baker Street.

As Jimmy went about his work, Holmes noticed that the milkman seemed to take an unusual interest in the buildings he passed. His attention lingered on the windows and doors, as if he were studying the layout and security of each residence.

Seizing the opportunity, Holmes emerged from the shadows and approached Jimmy with a friendly greeting, careful to change the sound of his voice. "Morning, mate. You're up and early, aren't you? I thought I was the only one out at this time."

Jimmy looked up, surprised by the sudden appearance of the dirt-covered man. "Aye, that I am. Gotta get the milk delivered before the toffs wake up, don't I?" A nasty look came over his face. "These posh folk, they don't know the meaning of a hard day's work, do they? Not like us."

Holmes nodded, playing along with the conversation. "Aye, they've got more money than sense, some of 'em."

Jimmy laughed heartily. "Too right, mate! I'll tell you something. I charge these toffs a lot more than I do in the poorer streets, and they don't even bat an eye. They've got that much money, I reckon it's only right that some of it comes my way."

"I don't blame you," Holmes said with an admiring smile at Jimmy.

"Oh, yeah," Jimmy boasted, puffing out his chest. "It's easy money, mate. These rich folk, they don't even notice a few extra pennies here and there. And if they do, they're too proper to kick up a fuss about it."

Holmes tipped his cap to Jimmy. "Good luck yo you, I say. Well, I best be on my way. I'm off home for a kip, and then I'll be back at work. Take care, mate."

Jimmy waved goodbye, a self-satisfied grin on his face. "Aye, you too."

With that, Holmes turned and headed away from Baker Street. Jimmy's boastful attitude and keen interest in the houses he serviced only strengthened Holmes' suspicions about his involvement in the recent thefts.

Chapter 7

After taking a circular route back to Baker Street, and making sure Jimmy was far away, Holmes quietly entered his lodgings, taking care not to wake his slumbering friend, Dr John Watson. He quickly changed out of his railway worker's disguise and into his usual attire, washing away the grime and dirt from his face and hands.

By the time Watson emerged from his room, Holmes was already seated in his armchair, his fingers steepled beneath his chin in contemplation. Watson, still groggy from sleep, poured himself a cup of tea and settled into the chair opposite his friend.

"I trust your early morning excursion was fruitful, Holmes?" Watson inquired, taking a sip of the hot liquid.

Holmes nodded. "It was. My conversation with Jimmy was most enlightening. It's clear he harbours a deep resentment towards the wealthy residents of Baker Street."

Watson raised an eyebrow. "Resentment? In what way?"

"He spoke of how easy it is to make a profit from the 'rich folk,' as he called them," Holmes explained. "He boasted about charging more for his services in this area than he would in poorer neighbourhoods."

"I see," Watson mused, setting his cup down. "And you believe this resentment could be a motive for the thefts?"

"It's certainly a possibility," Holmes agreed. "I've been giving this matter some thought. And I propose we lay a trap for our milkman. We must catch him in the act if we are to prove his guilt."

"And how do you suggest we go about that?" Watson asked, intrigued by his friend's plan.

"We will need Mrs Thompson's assistance. However, I believe it would be prudent to meet with her away from Baker Street. If Jimmy is our thief, he may be watching our every move."

Watson agreed, "A wise precaution, Holmes. Where do you propose we meet Mrs Thompson?"

"The art gallery a few miles from here should suffice," Holmes answered. "It's far enough away to avoid arousing suspicion, yet still easily accessible."

"When shall we contact her about this proposed meeting?" Watson asked.

"I won't contact Mrs Thompson during daylight hours in case Jimmy is nearby. I will wait until midnight, and using the cover of darkness, I will deliver a written message to Mrs Thompson, requesting her presence at the gallery tomorrow at eleven-thirty a.m."

Watson chuckled, shaking his head in admiration. "You do have a flair for the dramatic, Holmes."

"Merely a necessary precaution, my dear Watson," Holmes replied with a smile. "We must take every measure to ensure the success of our plan."

As the day progressed, Holmes and Watson went about their usual routines, careful not to draw any undue attention to themselves. They discussed the details of their plan, refining and adjusting as needed, until they were both satisfied with the course of action.

When the clock on the mantelpiece finally chimed out the midnight hour, Holmes slipped out of 221B Baker Street, a folded piece of paper tucked discreetly in his pocket. Staying in the shadows, he made his way to Mrs Thompson's residence.

With a quick glance to ensure he was unobserved, Holmes approached the front door and deftly slipped the message through the letterbox.

His task complete, Holmes melted back into the shadows, making his way home.

Chapter 8

Holmes rose early the next morning, hoping Mrs Thompson had found his note, and better still, had replied to it.

He quickly dressed and headed downstairs to check for any messages. As he approached the doorway, he noticed a small slip of paper tucked neatly into the letterbox. He quickly retrieved it.

"Ah, excellent," he murmured to himself as he read the words. "She's agreed to meet us at the gallery."

Dr Watson, still groggy from sleep, walked down the stairs, his hair tousled and his dressing gown hastily tied. "What's that, Holmes?" he asked, stifling a yawn.

"A message from Mrs Thompson," Holmes replied, holding up the note. "She's confirmed our meeting later this morning. I suggest we get there a little earlier in case our thief is hanging about outside our home. They would soon know something was up if we came out of our building at the same time as Mrs Thompson came out of hers, especially if set off in the same direction"

"Splendid idea," Watson said, his eyes brightening. "I suppose I should get dressed."

After a hearty breakfast, the two men hailed a cab and headed to the art gallery. The journey wasn't too long, and soon they found themselves standing before the impressive edifice, its stone exterior gleaming in the morning light.

They wandered around the gallery for a while, marvelling at the impressive work on display.

Mrs Thompson arrived just before eleven-thirty at the agreed meeting point within the gallery. She greeted the two men with a warm smile, though a hint of worry lingered in her eyes.

"Mr Holmes, Dr Watson," she said, extending her gloved hand. "It's good to see you again so soon."

Holmes took her hand and bowed slightly. "I trust you are well?"

"As well as can be expected, given the circumstances," she replied, her smile faltering slightly.

Watson gestured towards a nearby bench. "Shall we sit? We have much to discuss."

The three of them settled onto the bench, the hustle and bustle of the gallery's visitors fading into the background.

Holmes began, "Mrs Thompson, we believe that Jimmy, your milkman, may be responsible for the recent thefts in Baker Street."

Mrs Thompson's eyes widened as Holmes revealed his suspicions about Jimmy. She said, "I've only met the man once. Even though our meeting was brief, I didn't take to him at all. There was something about the way he looked at me. Not hateful, I think, but certainly with disdain. And you think Jimmy is the culprit?"

Holmes said, "We do. Mrs Thompson, when was the last time you wore your missing brooch?"

She furrowed her brow, her mind racing back to the events of the past few days. "It was two days before it went missing."

"And did Jimmy have the chance to see you wearing the brooch?" Holmes asked.

"Why yes! I was wearing it when I went into the kitchen to have a word with Matilda about something. It was after I'd returned home from meeting my friends, and Jimmy was there. He had come to collect the milk money. He was chatting with Matilda, although now that I think about it, he was doing all the chatting and Matilda was doing all the listening. I didn't want to discuss private business in front of him, so I told Matilda I would speak to her later and I left the kitchen."

Dr Watson said, "It's quite possible that he noticed your brooch then, Mrs Thompson. A valuable piece would certainly catch the eye of a thief."

Holmes said, "Mrs Thompson, if Jimmy is our thief, I believe we could lay a trap for him. But we will need your help."

"My help?" she asked. "What can I do?"

"We need you to wear another precious item, something that will catch Jimmy's attention when he's in the kitchen collecting his money in the afternoon," Holmes explained. "Make sure he sees it, and then leave it in your room, somewhere easy to find. Depart the house as normal the following day and stay out until your usual hour."

Mrs Thompson's face paled at the thought. "You want me to use myself as bait?"

Dr Watson said, "We understand your apprehension, Mrs Thompson, but it may be the only way to catch this thief red-handed. However, we don't want to place you in any danger. And if you don't feel comfortable doing this, please say so."

Mrs Thompson took a deep breath, her hands clasped tightly in her lap. "I suppose I can do it. I have a necklace that belonged to my mother. It's quite valuable, and yes, you're right, it would catch Jimmy's eye."

Holmes reached into his pocket and pulled out an envelope. He said, "We don't want you to use your items if case they get damaged. Inside this envelope is a fake diamond necklace. It came into our possession during a case we dealt with last year. Its value is worthless, but to the untrained eye and from a distance, it looks like the real thing. Please don't open the envelope until you get home." He lowered his voice a little. "Don't look now, but we are being observed by a security guard who is giving us suspicious looks. If you pull out the necklace now, it may look like we are passing you stolen goods."

Watson let out an almost inaudible chuckle.

Mrs Thompson took the envelope. "Thank you. I feel better about not using my own jewellery. I will go ahead with your plan this afternoon. I can't believe that man has the nerve to steal from me, and my neighbours. The sooner you catch him, the better."

Holmes nodded in agreement. "We appreciate your help, Mrs Thompson. Like I said, if you wear the item today when Jimmy collects his money, then, if he is the thief, it's likely he will enter your home tomorrow sometime between eleven a.m. and one p.m. when your house is empty. Watson and I will take up hiding positions on Baker Street and keep watch. Should Jimmy attempt to enter your home, we will be there to apprehend him."

Mrs Thompson smiled at Holmes and Watson. "I want to see this thief brought to justice. Should I tell Matilda about this plan? She'll be surprised to see me wearing an unfamiliar necklace."

Holmes pondered the matter for a moment. He said, "I think it's best we keep Matilda out of the picture for now. She might become nervous in front of Jimmy when you appear wearing the item, and then he would know something is amiss. Mrs Thompson, could you say the necklace was an impromptu gift from your husband? And that you wanted to see how it looked before placing it in your jewellery box?"

Mrs Thompson replied, "That's an excellent idea. I'll proceed on that basis. And to ensure Matilda is out for hours tomorrow, I'll give her some extra deliveries to make."

Holmes said, "Thank you, Mrs Thompson. With your help, we shall put an end to these thefts and ensure that Baker Street is safe once more."

Chapter 9

The following day, Holmes and Watson left their lodgings at ten a.m. and set out to take up their respective positions. The two men walked briskly, their faces set with determination as they prepared to catch the thief who had been plaguing the residents of the street.

"You remember the plan, Watson?" Holmes asked, his keen eyes scanning the street for any signs of suspicious activity.

"Of course, Holmes," Watson replied, patting the stack of newspapers tucked under his arm. "I'll be at the café, pretending to read while keeping a watchful eye on Mrs Thompson's house. If Jimmy shows up, I'll be ready."

Holmes nodded. "Excellent. But do keep in mind that Jimmy may be in disguise. He's a devious one, that milkman."

Watson chuckled, adjusting his hat. "I've no doubt about that, Holmes. But I suspect, even in disguise, Jimmy is the kind of man who would have an arrogant swagger. A man like that can't help but show his true colours."

"Indeed," Holmes agreed, his eyes twinkling with amusement. "Well, I shall be at the rear of Mrs Thompson's house, keeping watch from there. If Jimmy attempts to gain entry there, I'll be ready to apprehend him."

With a final nod, the two men parted ways, each focused on their assigned tasks. Watson crossed the street and entered the café, settling himself at a table near the window with his newspapers spread out before him. He ordered a cup of tea and a scone, doing his best to appear as a regular patron engrossed in the day's news.

Meanwhile, Holmes made his way to the back of Mrs Thompson's house, his sharp gaze taking in every detail of the surrounding area. As he approached it, he spotted a familiar figure tending to some flower pots in the backyard of his house, which was directly opposite Mrs Thompson's.

"Ernest!" Holmes called out, waving to his neighbour and friend. "Good morning, my dear fellow. I was hoping to catch you in."

Ernest, a kindly older gentleman with a twinkle in his eye, looked up and smiled broadly. "Sherlock Holmes!

What a pleasant surprise. I don't usually see you around the back of Baker Street. What brings you here?"

Holmes stepped closer, lowering his voice. "I'm afraid I'm here on a rather serious matter. I'm conducting a surveillance operation, attempting to catch a thief who has been targeting the homes on Baker Street. And I need your help with this case."

Ernest's eyes widened. "A thief? Well, that simply won't do. How can I be of assistance?"

Holmes smiled. "I was hoping I might use your backyard as a vantage point. I need a clear view of the rear of Mrs Thompson's house. I can conceal myself in the shadow cast by the sun across your yard; a shadow that will elongate as the day passes on."

"Of course, of course!" Ernest exclaimed, already opening the garden gate to allow Holmes to enter. "But why stop at the backyard? Come inside, my boy. You can use the bedroom window upstairs. It has a much better view of the backstreet, and the net curtain will keep you well hidden."

Holmes' eyebrows rose, impressed by Ernest's suggestion. "That's a splendid idea. Thank you."

As they entered the house, Ernest suddenly snapped his fingers. "Oh, and I have just the thing to help you with your surveillance!" He hurried over to a nearby shelf and retrieved a pair of binoculars. "I use these for my bird watching, you see. But I have a feeling they'll serve you well today."

Holmes accepted the binoculars with a grateful smile. "Perfect! Thank you."

The two men went upstairs, and Ernest showed Holmes to the bedroom window. Holmes positioned himself carefully, adjusting the binoculars to get a clear view of the back street and Mrs Thompson's house.

"I'll be downstairs if you need anything," Ernest said, giving his friend a supportive pat on the shoulder. "Best of luck catching that scoundrel."

"Thank you, Ernest," Holmes replied. "With any luck, we'll have our thief in custody before the day is through."

As Ernest left the room, Holmes settled in for what he hoped would be a productive surveillance operation. With Watson watching the front of the house and himself keeping an eye on the rear, they had all the bases covered. Now, it was simply a matter of waiting for Jimmy to make his move.

Chapter 10

Holmes focused his keen gaze on the backstreet behind Baker Street, watching the comings and goings of various people.

He noticed a young woman carrying a basket of laundry, a boy delivering newspapers, and an elderly gentleman walking his dog. He had no idea people used the backstreet so much.

A soft knock at the door drew Holmes' attention away from the window. Ernest entered the room, carrying a tray with a steaming cup of tea and a slice of cake.

"Thought you might need a little something to keep your energy up," he said with a smile.

"That's very kind of you," Holmes replied, accepting the tea and cake with a grateful nod.

Ernest set the tray down on a nearby table and glanced out the window. "Any sign of the scoundrel yet?"

Holmes shook his head. "Not yet. But I have a feeling he'll show his face soon enough."

"Is there anything I can do to help?" Ernest asked, his eyes twinkling with excitement at the prospect of being involved in one of Sherlock Holmes' cases.

Holmes took a sip of his tea and said, "Actually, I'm keeping an eye out for the milkman. He's a suspect in our current case."

Ernest's face darkened. "Oh, I know exactly who you mean. That Jimmy fellow, right? Can't stand the man, myself. Always talking down to me like I'm some sort of fool. Several of the neighbours have complained about him too. In fact, I've already lodged a complaint with the dairy he works for. Wouldn't be surprised if he's been sacked already."

Holmes frowned, a hint of concern crossing his features. "If he's been sacked, he may not show up today. Which means he has got away with his previous thefts."

Ernest shook his head. "Don't you worry about that. Bad pennies always turn up somewhere. If he's guilty, you'll catch him."

Holmes smiled, reassured by his friend's confidence. He turned his attention back to the street below, just in time to see Matilda, Mrs Thompson's maid, leaving the house through the back door. He watched as she carefully locked the door behind her. She pulled the hood of her cloak over her head and set off down the street, her stride purposeful.

The minutes ticked by as Holmes maintained his vigil, his attention never leaving the backstreet. He watched as the shadows lengthened and the activity in the street began to dwindle. But still, there was no sign of Jimmy.

Ernest, who had been sitting quietly in a chair near the window, broke the silence. "Sherlock, do you think he might have caught wind of your investigation? Maybe he's decided to lay low for a while."

Holmes considered this for a moment. "It's possible. But I have a feeling he's too arrogant to believe he could be caught. No, I think he'll show his face, eventually. We just need to be patient."

Chapter 11

One hour later, and with his attention still focused intently on the backstreet, Holmes was surprised to see Matilda returning to Mrs Thompson's house much earlier than expected. He checked his pocket watch. It was midday. She shouldn't be back until at least one o'clock. Mrs Thompson said she'd give Matilda extra duties to make sure the house was empty for long enough for a theft to occur. Why had she come back so early? And was she about to sabotage the carefully laid plan he had put in place?

As he watched Matilda approach the house, Holmes' suspicions began to grow. Could it be that Matilda, and not Jimmy, was behind the recent string of thefts?

It was true that Matilda had easy access to the valuable items within. Perhaps, Holmes mused, she had returned early to steal the diamond necklace he'd given to Mrs Thompson. Once the necklace was in her possession,

Matilda could easily take it to the nearest pawnbroker and then return to the house at her usual time of one o'clock in the afternoon, as if nothing had happened.

But what about the thefts from Mrs Henderson and Mrs Baxter's homes? Holmes' mind raced as he considered the possibilities. Could Matilda have somehow obtained spare keys to those residences as well? Perhaps she had visited those friends of hers who worked there as maids and managed to pilfer a spare set of keys during her visits.

As Holmes pondered these thoughts, his gaze never wavered from the Mrs Thompson's house. He watched as Matilda emerged five minutes later, her movements quick and furtive. He looked closer. There was something different about the way she was walking and the tilt of her head. Suddenly, a realisation struck him like a bolt of lightning. The person he had assumed to be Matilda was not the maid at all, but it was someone disguised as her.

Holmes' heart raced as he processed this new information.

He turned to Ernest and said, "I have spotted the culprit! I must go!"

With that, Holmes hurried out of the room, raced down the steps and out of Ernest's house, his heart pounding with the thrill of the chase. His keen eyes locked onto the figure disguised as Matilda, who was now hurrying down the street with a sense of urgency that betrayed their guilt.

"Stop right there!" Holmes called out, his voice ringing through the narrow alleyway.

The imposter glanced over their shoulder, their eyes widening in surprise and fear as they saw the detective in hot pursuit. Without a moment's hesitation, they broke into a run, their skirts billowing behind them as they fled.

Holmes gave chase, his long strides quickly closing the distance between them.

The imposter darted around the corner, disappearing from view for a moment. Holmes followed.

The chase led them past the café where Dr John Watson sat, gazing out of the window, a newspaper in his hands. The sound of running footsteps and Holmes' shouts caught his attention. He saw his friend, and the disguised figure sprinting by.

Without hesitation, Watson threw down his newspaper and leapt to his feet, abandoning his half-finished cup of tea on the table. He dashed out of the café and joined the pursuit.

The imposter, realising they now had two pursuers, redoubled their efforts to escape. They wove through the crowded streets, pushing past startled pedestrians and narrowly avoiding collisions with horse-drawn carriages.

Holmes and Watson, undeterred by the obstacles in their path, maintained their relentless pursuit.

As they raced down a particularly narrow alleyway, the imposter made a desperate attempt to evade capture. They overturned a stack of wooden crates, sending them tumbling into the path of their pursuers.

Holmes, with his lightning-fast reflexes, leapt over the fallen crates, barely breaking his stride. Watson, however, was not so fortunate. He stumbled, his foot catching on a splintered piece of wood, and he fell to the ground with a grunt of pain.

Holmes, torn between his desire to apprehend the suspect and his concern for his friend, hesitated for a split second. But Watson, ever the loyal companion, waved him on, urging him to continue the chase.

With a nod of understanding, Holmes pressed on, his determination renewed. He could hear the imposter's laboured breathing ahead of him, a sign that they were tiring from the relentless pursuit.

As they emerged from the alleyway onto a bustling main street, Holmes saw his chance. With a final burst of speed, he lunged forward, his hand outstretched. His fingers closed around the imposter's arm, and he yanked them to a halt, spinning them around to face him.

The imposter, their disguise now dishevelled and their face flushed with exertion, glared at Holmes with a mixture of defiance and fear. But the detective's gaze was unwavering, his expression one of grim satisfaction.

"The game is up," Holmes declared, his voice steady despite his own breathlessness. "It's time to reveal your true identity and face the consequences of your actions."

As the imposter's shoulders slumped in defeat, Watson, having recovered from his fall, joined Holmes' side.

Holmes reached for the hood that covered the imposter's face.

Chapter 12

Holmes pulled back the hood, revealing the face of Betsy, Mrs Henderson's maid.

"By Jove!" Watson exclaimed. "I was expecting to see you."

"Betsy," Holmes said, his voice gentle but firm, "are you the one who has been committing these thefts?"

Betsy's eyes welled up with tears, and she nodded, her voice barely above a whisper. "Yes, Mr Holmes. It was me. I never meant for it to go this far, but I was desperate."

Holmes said, "Tell us what happened. What drove you to such desperate measures?"

With a shaky breath, Betsy began her story. "It's my mother, sir. She's been ill for some time now, and the medical bills are piling up. I've been working as hard as I can to pay them, but it's never enough. The cost of her treatment is so high, and I didn't know what else to do."

Holmes nodded, his expression one of understanding. "And so, you turned to theft."

"I never wanted to be a thief," Betsy cried, her tears now flowing freely. "It started when I was visiting Enid, the maid at Mrs Baxter's house. I went upstairs to use the bathroom, and as I passed Mrs Baxter's bedroom, I saw some diamond earrings just sitting there. It was like they were calling to me, promising a solution to all my problems."

Watson said, "So you took them and pawned them to pay for your mother's treatment?"

"Yes," Betsy admitted, her voice filled with shame. "And it worked. I was able to pay for her medicine, but then she took a turn for the worse. I knew I needed more money, and that's when I stole from Mrs Henderson, my own employer. I'm so very ashamed, after all she's done for me. But I couldn't stop myself."

Holmes said, "And you stole from Mrs Thompson, too. How did you manage that?"

Betsy answered, "I had to deliver a message to Matilda earlier this week, and when she left the kitchen, I noticed some spare keys hanging up, so I took a set. I didn't want to, but all I could think about was Mum. She's the only family I've got and I can't lose her. I used those keys to get into the house when I knew Matilda would be out, and I took Mrs Thompson's brooch. I took her diamond necklace, too, just now. Matilda told me about it when we met at the shops earlier. I knew it would be enough to cover the rest of my mother's treatment. I told myself it would be the last time that I'd never steal again."

Watson said, "Oh, Betsy. I can't imagine the desperation you must have felt, but surely there were other options? Why didn't you ask for help?"

"I was too ashamed," Betsy said, her voice breaking. "I didn't want anyone to know about my mother's illness or our financial troubles. I thought I could handle it on my own, but it just got worse and worse."

Holmes said gently, "Betsy, I understand the desperation that drove you to these actions, but you must know that theft is never the answer. There are always consequences, and now you must face them."

Betsy nodded, her face streaked with tears. "I know. I'm ready to accept whatever punishment I deserve. I just hope that somehow, my mother will be taken care of."

Chapter 13

Later that afternoon, Sherlock Holmes and Dr John Watson returned to their lodgings at 221B Baker Street, their minds still preoccupied with the events of the day. As they settled into their respective armchairs, Mrs Hudson, bustled into the room, a look of concern upon her face.

"Mr Holmes, Dr Watson," she began, "have you solved the case yet? Or should I still be fretting about a thief lurking on our very doorstep?"

Holmes said, "I am pleased to say that the culprit has been apprehended, and the stolen items have been recovered."

Mrs Hudson exclaimed, "Oh, thank heavens! But who was behind it all?"

Watson answered, "It was Betsy, the maid who works for Mrs Henderson."

Mrs Hudson let out a gasp. "Betsy? That lovely young woman? No! Why would she do such a thing?"

Holmes explained, "Betsy's mother is gravely ill, and the cost of her medical treatment had become an overwhelming burden. In a moment of desperation, Betsy succumbed to the temptation of theft, believing it to be her only means of providing for her mother's care. She soon committed further thefts in order to raise more funds."

Mrs Hudson shook her head. "Oh, the poor dear. I can't imagine the desperation she must have felt to resort to such measures."

Watson said, "Indeed, Mrs Hudson. It's a tragic situation all around."

"But what will happen to Betsy now?" Mrs Hudson asked.

Holmes said, "That, I'm afraid, is for the victims of her crime to decide. They may take pity on her plight, but they might not, considering the value of the items stolen and the heartache it has caused them."

Mrs Hudson nodded, her expression thoughtful. "I suppose you're right, Mr Holmes. It's a difficult position for all involved."

Holmes continued, "Watson and I visited the pawnbrokers Betsy had used to sell the stolen items. Fortunately, they were still available for purchase. I informed the shop owner that the items in question were stolen property and needed to be returned to their rightful owners."

Watson chuckled. "The owner was none too pleased, but Holmes was quite insistent."

"Once we had the items in hand," Holmes continued, "we took Betsy and the recovered pieces to Mrs Henderson's residence and explained the situation. It is now up to Mrs Henderson and her friends to decide whether they wish to involve the authorities."

Mrs Hudson said, "Well, I do hope they show some mercy. Betsy's actions were wrong, of course, but her motivations were borne out of love and desperation."

Holmes said, "On a lighter note, one of the more satisfying aspects of this investigation was witnessing the dismissal of that dreadful milkman, Jimmy."

Mrs Hudson's eyes lit up. "Oh, yes! I heard about that from Vera next door. Apparently, many residents had lodged numerous complaints about his behaviour."

Watson said, "And rightly so. The man was an absolute menace."

Holmes said, "It seems that even in the midst of such a troubling case, there are small victories to be celebrated."

Mrs Hudson smiled. "Well, I'm just glad that the mystery has been solved and that our street is safe once more. Thank you, Mr Holmes, Dr Watson, for all your hard work."

Mrs Hudson left the room looking much happier than when she had entered.

Holmes said to Watson, "Of course, I am pleased we discovered who the culprit was, but the reasons behind the crime sadden me."

Watson said, "That aspect has been bothering me, too. As such, I intend to call upon Betsy's mother later today and offer my medical services free of charge."

Holmes' eyebrows rose. "You would do that? Watson, you are a gentleman in the truest sense of the word. I am proud to call you my friend. I am a fortunate fellow to have you in my life."

Watson cleared his throat. "Now don't get all emotional on me, Holmes. You know it doesn't suit you."

Sherlock Holmes burst into laughter. "You are right about that, but even I can let my emotions get the better of me sometimes." He smiled at his friend, a twinkle in his eyes. "I'll try not to let it happen again."

Book 5 - Sherlock Holmes and The Lamplighter's Mystery

Chapter 1

The rain pattered against the windows of 221B Baker Street, the sound a gentle accompaniment to the crackling fire in the hearth. Sherlock Holmes sat in his armchair, long fingers steepled beneath his chin, his grey eyes fixed on some distant point. Dr John Watson, as was his habit, busied himself with the day's newspaper, occasionally tutting at some article or another.

A sharp knock at the door roused both men from their respective reveries. Mrs Hudson, Holmes's long-suffering landlady, entered, her expression one of mild apology. "A Mr Percy Wentworth to see you, Mr Holmes. He seems quite distressed."

Holmes straightened, a glint of interest in his eye. "Send him in, Mrs Hudson."

Moments later, a man entered the room. He was in his early fifties, with a lean, agile frame that spoke of a life of physical labour. His clothes, though well-worn, were clean and neatly patched. He removed his cap, twisting it nervously in his hands.

"Mr Holmes, Dr Watson," he began, "I apologise for the intrusion, but I didn't know where else to turn."

Watson gestured to a chair. "Please, sit down, Mr Wentworth. Tell us what troubles you."

Wentworth sat, perching on the edge of the seat. "It's my job, sirs. I've been a lamplighter for nigh on thirty years, and I've never had a problem like this before."

Holmes leaned forward, his attention fully captured. "Go on."

"Someone's been sabotaging my work," Wentworth said, his hands clenching around his cap. "Lamps that I know I've lit, they're out again when I check on them later. And my tools, they go missing, or I find them broken. I'm falling behind on my rounds, and I'm afraid I'll lose my job."

Watson frowned. "Have you reported this to your superiors?"

Wentworth shook his head miserably. "What can I tell them? That I'm suddenly incapable of doing the job I've done for decades? They'll think I've gone mad, or that I'm too old for the work."

Holmes steepled his fingers once more. "You mentioned 'someone'. Have you seen this person?"

Wentworth hesitated, then nodded. "A few times, I've spotted a figure lurking in the shadows. Always at night, always when I'm on my rounds. But when they realise I've seen them, they run off. I've never got a clear look at them."

The detective's eyes narrowed. "And this, combined with the sabotage, has led to your current state of distress?"

"I haven't slept in days," Wentworth admitted. "I'm jumping at every shadow, expecting to see that figure. And the thought of losing my job, well, it's too much."

Watson, his face etched with sympathy, turned to his friend. "Holmes, surely we can help?"

Holmes was silent for a few moments, his gaze distant. Finally, he said, "Mr Wentworth, we will take your case. I cannot abide a mystery, and this one presents several intriguing points. The identity of your shadowy stalker, and the motive behind the sabotage. Yes, this is something we can help you with."

Relief washed over Wentworth's face. "Thank you, Mr Holmes. Thank you."

Holmes said, "Mr Wentworth, we will need more details about your work. Your nightly rounds, your duties, anything that might shed light on this mystery."

Wentworth nodded, a glimmer of pride entering his eyes as he spoke of his profession. "Of course. As a lamplighter, it's my job to ensure the gas lamps in my assigned area are lit at dusk and extinguished at dawn. I'm responsible for maintaining the lamps, too. Cleaning the glass, replacing the mantles, and making sure there's enough gas. It's not an easy job, sirs. We're out in all weathers, and the hours are long. But there's a satisfaction in it, knowing you're helping to keep the city safe and bright."

Watson, ever the empathetic listener, nodded. "I can imagine. And your rounds, Mr Wentworth? Do you follow the same route each night?"

Wentworth sat up a little straighter. "Yes, Dr Watson. I'm responsible for the lamps around the Downing Street area. Those streets are where many government offices are situated, and some people inside them work all hours, sometimes into the night. It's imperative that the lamps are in good working order. I've been doing that area for ten years now. It's one of the most important rounds in London. I know of many lamplighters who would love to be in charge of those lamps. Which makes this sabotage business even worse. I don't want to lose that round, not when I've worked so hard to make it mine."

"And your colleagues, your supervisors, what do they think of your work?" Holmes asked.

A touch of colour appeared in Wentworth's cheeks. "Well, I don't like to boast, Mr Holmes, but I'm well-respected in the company. I've always been diligent, you see. Never missed a shift, never had a complaint. I take pride in my work, and I think that shows. And I always make sure my record book is up to date. It's where I make notes about my rounds. The times when I lit and extinguished the lamps, and any repairs I had to make, that sort of thing. My record book is my most important possession and I take great care of it. My supervisors are always impressed with how efficient I am at keeping detailed notes." He fidgeted with his cap, his gaze dropping to the floor. "That's why this business has me so rattled. I can't bear the thought of them thinking I'm slipping, that I can't do my job anymore."

Watson reached out, patting Wentworth's shoulder reassuringly. "We understand, Mr Wentworth. And we'll do everything we can to get to the bottom of this."

Holmes, meanwhile, had risen and was pacing the room, his brow furrowed in thought. "The tools of your trade, Mr Wentworth, where do you store them when you're not using them?"

Wentworth blinked, surprised by the question. "In the alley behind my lodgings. There's a storage area at the end of it. It's where some of the other lamplighters keep their equipment, too. I keep my toolbox there, and my ladders as well."

Holmes nodded, a glint in his eye. "I see. And have you noticed anything unusual there? Any signs of disturbance or tampering?"

Wentworth frowned, thinking. "Now that I know of. My ladder is always where I leave it. And my toolbox too. Unless I've missed something obvious."

Holmes said, "It is possible that in your tired state, you may, indeed, have missed something. Perhaps some vital clue that the shadowy saboteur has left behind. This gives us a starting point. Mr Wentworth, I will need the address of your lodgings, and your permission to examine the storage area."

Wentworth, looking somewhat bewildered, nodded. "Of course, Mr Holmes. Anything you need. As it happens, I'm heading back home now."

"Excellent!" Holmes declared. "Then we shall come with you and start our investigation immediately. We will have your mystery cleared up in no time at all, Mr Wentworth."

Chapter 2

As the trio walked through the bustling streets of London, Percy Wentworth led the way, his shoulders hunched against the drizzling rain. Sherlock Holmes and Dr John Watson followed close behind.

After a brisk ten-minute walk, they arrived at a narrow, nondescript building tucked away in a side street.

"This is it," Wentworth said, gesturing towards a wooden door. "My lodgings."

He led them down a cramped alley that ran alongside the building. The space was barely wide enough for two people to walk abreast; the cobblestones slick with rain and grime. At the end of the alley, they came to a small, walled-off area.

"This is where we keep our equipment," Wentworth explained as he opened the door to the area.

Holmes stepped into the storage area, taking in every detail of the scene. It was cluttered with various tools and implements, such as ladders, toolboxes, coils of rope, and spare lantern parts. A low brick wall enclosed the space, but it would have been easy enough for someone to climb over, especially under the cover of darkness.

Watson, too, was examining the scene with a critical eye. "It doesn't seem very secure," he commented. "Anyone could access this area, especially if the door is left unlocked, as it was now."

Wentworth said, "There's never any need to lock it. We trust each other." He paused. "Or we used to, but I'm starting to think otherwise now, what with my damaged and lost tools."

Holmes crouched down, running his fingers over the ground. "There are several sets of footprints here. Difficult to distinguish with the rain, but it's clear this area sees regular traffic." Rising, he said, "Your ladder, Mr Wentworth. Which one is it?"

Wentworth pointed to a tall wooden ladder leaning against the wall.

Holmes approached it, running his hands over the rungs and examining the joints. "No obvious signs of damage or tampering," he said after a moment. "Now, where is your toolbox? I can see several here."

Wentworth said, "I keep mine tucked behind my ladder."

"Ah, yes, I see." Holmes examined the battered toolbox, which was locked. "Again, there are no signs of tampering. But that doesn't mean much. A clever saboteur would know how to cover their tracks. I assume your toolbox is always kept locked?"

Wentworth nodded. "It is." He gave them a wry smile. "But it's not the best of locks. I've had it for years and I think it's more rust than metal now."

Holmes shot him a smile. "Perhaps it's time for a new lock. Could we see your room? And the records you mentioned?"

Wentworth led them back out of the alley and into the building. They climbed a narrow, creaking staircase to the third floor, where he unlocked a door and ushered Holmes and Watson into a small, sparsely furnished room.

"It's not much," the lamplighter said apologetically, "but it's home."

Watson looked around, taking in the narrow bed, the washstand, the small table and chair. A single window looked out over the rooftops of London. It was a humble abode, but clean and well-kept.

Wentworth went to the table and picked up a leather-bound book. "These are my records," he said, handing it to Holmes. "Every lamp I've lit, every repair I've made, it's all in here. My route details are in it, too."

Holmes flipped through the pages, his eyes scanning the neat, precise entries. "You keep very detailed accounts, Mr Wentworth."

A hint of pride entered Percy's voice. "I have to. The Lamplighter's Office requires it. We have to submit our records every month for review."

Watson frowned. "And what happens if there are discrepancies? If a lamplighter falls behind on their duties?"

Percy's face darkened. "It's not good, Dr Watson. The Lamplighter's Office takes a very dim view of any failings. If a lamplighter isn't doing their job properly, they can be dismissed. And that's not all I have to worry about. I'm a member of The Lamplighter's Union, and they send inspectors around to check on our records, sometimes without any warning. And if the inspectors find anything amiss, they'll let the Lamplighter's Office know. Again, it could be a reason for dismissal."

Holmes handed the book back to Wentworth. "Now, if you could walk us through your nightly routine. Every detail, if you please. The more we know, the better equipped we'll be to unravel this mystery."

"Of course, Mr Holmes. It all starts when I arrive at the yard to collect my equipment. I make a note of what time I do that. Let me show you." Wentworth flipped through the pages of his record book. His eyes suddenly widened in disbelief. "This isn't right! Someone has been in my room, tampering with my records! Look, you can see how they've made it look as if I left for work later than I did, and that I returned too early. This isn't right at all! If an inspector turns up to look at this book without any warning, I'll be in real trouble, that's for sure."

Holmes walked slowly around the room. He examined the door and windows, searching for any signs of forced entry, but found none. The lock on the door was old but sturdy, and the windows were latched from the inside.

"No obvious signs of a break-in," he said, his brow furrowed in thought. "Which suggests that whoever did this either had a key or was let in. Mr Wentworth, I need you to think carefully. Is there anyone who might have a grudge against you? Another lamplighter, perhaps, someone who lives in this building or nearby?"

Wentworth hesitated for a few moments before saying, "Well, there's Horace Cuthbert. He's been a lamplighter for about ten years. He's always arguing with everyone, often for no reason at all. A real grumpy sort, and selfish too. And Horace has been after my route for years. He's made no secret of that. I get the feeling he's also jealous of how well-liked I am at the company."

Holmes nodded. "And where does Mr Cuthbert live?"

"Just down the street," Wentworth replied. "But surely it couldn't be him? I mean, Horace is a difficult man, but to go this far?"

Holmes held up a hand. "We must not rule out any possibilities, Mr Wentworth. Jealousy and resentment can drive men to desperate acts. We need to approach this carefully. If Mr Cuthbert is indeed behind this, we will need proof. Solid, irrefutable proof."

Watson added, "And we must act quickly. If those altered records are seen by someone in an official capacity by one of those inspectors you mentioned, well..." He didn't need to finish the sentence. The consequences hung heavy in the air.

Wentworth slumped down onto his bed, his face pale. "What am I going to do? I don't want to lose my job. It means the world to me."

Holmes turned to face the distressed lamplighter. "You're not going to lose your job, Mr Wentworth. I give you my word. We will solve this mystery. And soon. Do you have Mr Cuthbert's address?"

Wentworth said, "I do. He'll be starting his rounds soon. Shall I give you those details as well?"

"Please," Watson said.

Once they had the required information, Holmes said, "We will take our leave, Mr Wentworth, but we will be in touch soon." He tipped his hat in farewell and left the room with Watson at his side.

Chapter 3

Armed with the details of Horace Cuthbert's round, Holmes and Watson walked through the darkening streets of London.

The rain had lessened to a fine mist, but the chill in the air was palpable. As they walked, they noticed the lamplighters at work, their ladders propped against the lampposts, the soft glow of the gas lamps gradually illuminating the city.

"It's a thankless job," Watson mused, pulling his coat tighter around him. "Out in all weathers, ensuring the streets are lit for the rest of us."

Holmes nodded. "Indeed, Watson. And yet, for men like Percy Wentworth, it's a matter of pride. A job well done, a city kept safe."

Sometime later, they turned a corner onto the route that Cuthbert covered and heard a voice grumbling loudly. Following the sound, they soon came upon a man at the top of a ladder, his face twisted in a scowl as he worked on a lamp.

"Blasted rain," he muttered, his voice carrying down to the street below. "Freezing my fingers off up here. And for what? A pittance of pay."

Holmes and Watson exchanged a glance. This could only be Horace Cuthbert.

They waited patiently as the man descended the ladder, his movements stiff and jerky, whether from the cold or his own ill temper, it was hard to say. As he reached the ground, Holmes stepped forward.

"Mr Cuthbert, I presume?" he said, his voice pleasant but firm.

Cuthbert's eyes narrowed suspiciously. "Who's asking?"

"My name is Sherlock Holmes, and this is my associate, Dr Watson. We have an interest in the work of lamplighters and were hoping to have a word with you about your profession."

Cuthbert snorted, gathering up his tools. "What about it? I do my job, same as any other."

Watson spoke, "We've heard good things about your work, Mr Cuthbert. Your round takes you quite far afield, doesn't it?"

For a moment, the man's face softened, a glimmer of pride shining through. "That it does. All the way from here to the river, and back again. It's a long night's work, but I get it done."

Holmes nodded, his expression one of interest. "And what of your fellow lamplighters? We've heard that Percy Wentworth, in particular, has a rather coveted route."

At the mention of Wentworth's name, Cuthbert's face darkened, a sneer twisting his lips. "Wentworth? Ha! He's had it easy for years, with that cushy route of his. He's got much shorter distances than me. And lower lamps. It's a wonder he even needs a ladder! I'll be glad when he retires, I will. I've already put my name down for his round. It's about time someone else had a chance at an easy night's work."

Holmes studied the man. Cuthbert's resentment was clear, but was it enough to drive him to sabotage?

"I know who you are!" Cuthbert suddenly exclaimed, his voice laced with suspicion. "You're that detective, aren't you? I've seen your picture in the papers."

Holmes remained impassive, his expression giving nothing away. "My reputation precedes me, it seems."

Cuthbert sneered. "I get it now. It must be Wentworth who's been in touch with you, then. What's he been saying? Spinning some yarn about someone messing with his work? And pointing the finger at me?"

Holmes replied, "I'm afraid I cannot confirm or deny any client's business, Mr Cuthbert. I'm sure you understand."

Cuthbert let out a nasty laugh, shaking his head. "Oh, I understand all right. I heard Wentworth muttering about sabotage at the last Lamplighter's Union meeting. Load of old nonsense, that's what it is. Seems like he's seeing and hearing things, if you ask me. A sure sign he needs to hang up his ladder and retire, before he causes problems for the rest of us."

Watson frowned. "Problems? What do you mean?"

Cuthbert shrugged. "Well, if a lamplighter's not right in the head, who knows what could happen? He could miss a lamp, or he might not check the gas pipes properly and cause a leak. It's a matter of public safety, isn't it? Perhaps I should let one of the inspectors at the Union know about Percy's state of mind. They'd want to know if one of their lamplighters was losing his grip. Yeah, that's what I'll do. And I'll do it soon." He reached for his ladder. "Anyway, I've got work to do. Lamps won't light themselves, will they?"

With that, Horace Cuthbert turned on his heel and strode off into the misty night, leaving Holmes and Watson standing in the flickering light of the gas lamps.

Watson turned to Holmes. "Do you think there's any truth to what he's saying, Holmes? Could Mr Wentworth be imagining things?"

Holmes was silent for a moment, his eyes following Cuthbert's retreating figure. "It's possible. The mind can play tricks, especially under stress. But I'm not ready to dismiss Mr Wentworth's concerns just yet. There's more to this than meets the eye, I'm sure of it. But even so, we should speak to Mr Wentworth again now. Warn him about Mr Cuthbert's threat so he can prepare himself should an inspector turn up at his home. I have committed Mr Wentworth's route to memory from the information I saw in his record book. Let's head in that direction forthwith. Time is of the essence."

Chapter 4

As the evening settled over London, Holmes and Watson made their way through the winding streets, arriving at the trail of lit lamps that marked Wentworth's route. The flickering gas light cast an eerie glow, the shadows seeming to dance and twist with each step they took.

Up ahead, they spotted Wentworth using his long pole to ignite one of the lower lamps. His movements were practised and efficient, the result of years of experience.

But just as Holmes and Watson were about to approach him, a flicker of movement caught Holmes's eye. It came from one of the narrow alleyways that branched off the main street, a shadowy figure lurking almost out of sight.

Without a word, Holmes' hand shot out, grasping Watson's arm and pulling him into the shadows. They pressed themselves against the cold brick wall, their breath misting in the chill air as they watched the scene unfold before them.

The figure stepped out of the alleyway, their features obscured by the darkness. They seemed to be watching Wentworth intently.

Suddenly, as if sensing the eyes upon him, Wentworth spun around, his gaze locking onto the mysterious figure.

"Oi!" he yelled, his voice ringing out in the quiet street. "What do you think you're doing, lurking about like that?"

The figure startled, clearly not expecting to be spotted. In a flash, they darted back into the alleyway, their footsteps echoing off the cobblestones.

Holmes and Watson were in motion instantly, springing from their hiding place and giving chase. They raced down the alleyway, their coats billowing behind them as they ran.

The figure was fast, weaving through the labyrinth of side streets and back alleys with a clear familiarity. Holmes and Watson pursued, their breath coming in sharp gasps as they pushed themselves to keep up.

"Quickly, Watson!" Holmes called out, his voice tight with exertion. "We mustn't lose him!"

They turned a corner, expecting to see the figure ahead, but the alley was empty. They skidded to a halt, their eyes scanning the shadows for any sign of movement.

"Blast!" Holmes hissed, his frustration evident. "He's given us the slip."

Watson leaned against the wall, trying to catch his breath. "Who do you think he was, Holmes? Did you get a good look at him?"

Holmes shook his head, his brow furrowed in thought. "I didn't. But it's likely the person who is behind this sabotage business. Come, Watson. We must return to Mr Wentworth. He saw us take up the chase, and he'll want to know if we captured anyone."

Wentworth was waiting for them when they emerged from the alleyway, his face etched with worry.

"What happened?" he asked. "I saw you chasing after that man. Did you catch him?"

Holmes shook his head. "Unfortunately not. He knows these streets too well, it seems."

Wentworth's shoulders slumped, a look of defeat in his eyes. "So what now? Am I to spend every night looking over my shoulder, wondering when he'll strike again?"

Watson said, "We won't let that happen. Holmes and I are on the case now. We'll unmask that man, I guarantee you." He shared a look with Holmes before continuing. "I'm afraid we have some bad news for you. We spoke to Horace Cuthbert, and he's threatening to report you to an inspector at the Lamplighter's Union. Mr Cuthbert is going to claim that you are losing your mind, and that you could be a threat to public safety."

Wentworth paled. "He would do that? Then I'll lose my job for sure. There's going to be a meeting tomorrow morning at ten. I expect he'll do it then." He cast a wistful glance at the lit light above him. "This could be the last time I light these lamps."

Holmes said, "Don't give up hope yet, Mr Wentworth. It would be wise for Watson and myself to attend that meeting. It may give us an opportunity to speak with the other lamplighters and determine if anyone else has been the victim of sabotage. Then you'll know you're not the only one. May we have the address of where the meeting will take place?"

"Of course," Wentworth said, and he gave them the address.

Holmes took out his notebook and jotted down the information. "Excellent. Watson and I shall be there."

Watson, sensing the unease that still lingered in the lamplighter's demeanour, said, "Mr Wentworth, if it would make you feel more at ease, I could accompany you for the remainder of your rounds tonight."

Wentworth's face brightened at the offer. "That would be most appreciated, Dr Watson. Thank you."

Holmes nodded his approval. "A fine idea, Watson. I shall leave you to it and meet you back at Baker Street later."

As Holmes departed, Watson fell into step beside Wentworth, the two men making their way through the gas-lit streets of London. The rain had finally ceased, and the clouds parted to reveal a sky filled with glittering stars.

Around them, the city was settling in for the night. Families gathered in the warm glow of their homes, the sound of laughter and conversation drifting through open windows. Shopkeepers pulled down their shutters, securing their wares for the evening.

Wentworth moved from lamp to lamp. Watson watched, impressed by the man's dedication to his craft. Despite the weight of the situation bearing down on him, the man never faltered, ensuring that each lamp was lit and functioning properly.

As they walked, Watson engaged Wentworth in conversation, hoping to distract him from his worries. They spoke of their respective professions, the challenges they faced, and the satisfaction they derived from a job well done.

Time seemed to fly by, and before long, they had reached the end of Wentworth's route.

The lamplighter turned to Watson, gratitude shining in his eyes. "Thank you, Dr Watson. Your company has been a great comfort tonight."

Watson clapped a hand on Wentworth's shoulder, offering a reassuring smile. "Think nothing of it. Holmes and I will see you tomorrow at the Union meeting. I know this is a worrying time for you, but if you can, try to get a good night's sleep."

With a nod, Wentworth bid Watson goodnight and disappeared into the shadows, heading for home. Watson watched him go, a sense of determination filling his heart. Poor man. They would not let him lose his beloved job.

Chapter 5

Just before ten the next morning, Holmes and Watson arrived at the Lamplighter's Union building, a sturdy brick structure with large windows that allowed the morning light to filter through. They stepped inside, their eyes adjusting to the dimmer interior. The room was filled with the murmur of conversation as lamplighters gathered, some standing in small groups, while others took their seats at the long wooden tables that filled the space.

They made their way further into the room. Holmes's keen gaze swept over the assembled people, taking in every detail. He nudged Watson and inclined his head towards a corner where Horace Cuthbert stood, deep in conversation with another man.

"Let us move closer, Watson," Holmes said, "but discreetly. I believe their discussion may prove enlightening."

The two men casually made their way towards Cuthbert. As they drew nearer, Cuthbert's agitated voice reached their ears.

"It's not right, I tell you," Cuthbert hissed. "Percy's too old for the job. He's making mistakes. He's putting lives at risk. It's time for him to step aside and let someone else take over. Someone like me."

The other man, whom Holmes assumed was one of the union officials going by his smart attire, shook his head. "Now Horace, you know it doesn't work like that. Percy's still doing a fine job, and he hasn't given any indication that he's ready to retire."

Cuthbert's eyes narrowed. "But you promised me his round. You said it would be mine."

The official sighed, his patience clearly wearing thin. "I said no such thing. And even if Percy were to retire, his round wouldn't automatically go to you."

"What?" Cuthbert spluttered, his face reddening. "Then who would get it?"

"If Percy doesn't retire, his round will likely go to Miriam Reeves," the official said, his tone firm. "She's been doing an excellent job, especially considering she's only been a lamplighter for less than a year."

Cuthbert looked like he was about to argue, his mouth opening and closing like a fish out of water. But before he could speak, a bell rang out, signalling the start of the meeting.

As the lamplighters began to take their seats, Holmes and Watson spotted Percy Wentworth entering the room. They caught his eye and gave him a discreet nod, which he returned with a grateful smile.

Holmes and Watson found seats near the back of the room.

Holmes leaned close to Watson, his voice low. "It seems our friend Horace Cuthbert is not above using underhanded means to get what he wants," he said, his attention fixed on the disgruntled lamplighter a few rows ahead.

Once the last lamplighters had settled into their seats, the man who had been conversing with Cuthbert earlier took his place at the front of the room.

The man's voice carried easily through the room. "For any of those who don't know me, I'm Rupert Blackmore, the senior inspector with the Union. Thank you for turning up to this meeting. Now, let us begin."

Blackmore proceeded to cover the usual topics expected at such a meeting, discussing the importance of maintaining the lamps and ensuring they remained lit throughout the night. However, he also brought up a few complaints from some members of the public, which caused a stir in the seated lamplighters.

"It has come to our attention that some lights went out hours after they were lit," Blackmore said, his brow furrowed. "Unfortunately, it caused some people to lose their footing on the dark paths, and I regret to say, minor injuries were sustained."

A voice interrupted the meeting. It was Cuthbert, who stood up and demanded, "Whose round was it? Who's responsible for this negligence?"

Blackmore fixed Cuthbert with a stern gaze. "It is a private matter, Mr Cuthbert, and one that I will be discussing with the individual in question soon."

Cuthbert turned his head, sought Percy Wentworth, and gave him a pointed look. With a self-satisfied smirk, he sat back down.

The meeting concluded shortly after, and the lamplighters dispersed. Holmes and Watson, who had been observing the proceedings with keen interest, noticed Blackmore approaching Percy Wentworth. In perfect unison, Holmes and Watson stood and took a few steps closer to them.

They overheard Blackmore speaking in a low, concerned tone. "Percy, I'm afraid it was the lamps on your round that went out. This is highly unusual, especially considering your exemplary record. Is everything alright?"

Wentworth looked embarrassed. "I'm not sure what to make of it, Mr Blackmore. I always check them. I am so sorry this has happened, I really am."

Blackmore sighed. "I'm concerned, Percy. Not only about the lamps but also about some rumours I've heard regarding your state of mind. I fear for your well-being and your future employment if this continues."

"I assure you, Mr Blackmore, I'm perfectly fine. There must be some mistake. I'll double my efforts and ensure this never happens again," Wentworth said with as much confidence as he could muster.

Holmes and Watson watched as Blackmore walked away, leaving Wentworth standing alone, his face a picture of misery.

The two men approached their client.

"Mr Wentworth," Holmes said, "we are still investigating this matter thoroughly. We will find the culprit behind these troubling events. We overheard a conversation between Horace Cuthbert and Mr Blackmore before the meeting started." He gave Wentworth the details of that conversation.

Wentworth said, "I'm not that surprised, especially after you told me about his threat yesterday. I was half-hoping he wouldn't go ahead with it."

"And what of this Miriam Reeves that Mr Blackmore mentioned?" Holmes asked.

Wentworth's face softened at the mention of Miriam's name. "Ah, Miriam. She's a lovely young woman, one of the few female lamplighters in our area. I had the pleasure of training her when she first started, almost a year ago now."

Watson raised an eyebrow. "And how has she been performing in her role?"

"Oh, she's a quick learner, that one," Wentworth said, a hint of pride in his voice. "Keen to do well and always willing to put in the extra effort. She's been given a round near mine recently, and I've seen her checking the lamps multiple times throughout the night."

Holmes said, "Mr Wentworth, do you think it's possible that Miriam could be behind the sabotage?"

Wentworth shook his head vehemently. "No, no, I don't believe so. Miriam is a hard worker and has always been friendly and supportive. I can't imagine her doing something like this."

Holmes nodded, his expression pensive. "I understand your perspective, Mr Wentworth, but we must consider all possibilities. Could you provide us with the details of Miriam's round? We would like to speak with her, just to gather more information."

Wentworth hesitated for a moment, then nodded. "Of course, Mr Holmes. I'll write down the streets she covers and the times she usually starts and ends her shift."

Chapter 6

As the afternoon waned and darkness began to fall, Holmes and Watson headed through the misty streets of London, their steps purposeful as they sought Miriam Reeves. The gas lamps flickered to life one by one, casting an eerie glow across the cobblestones as the lamplighters began their nightly rounds.

They found Miss Reeves atop a ladder, her nimble fingers adjusting the wick of a lamp. She glanced down at the approaching figures, a flicker of recognition in her eyes.

"Mr Holmes, Dr Watson," she called out. "I saw you at the meeting this morning. I had a feeling I might see you again soon."

Holmes tipped his hat in greeting. "Miss Reeves, I presume. Might we have a word?"

She nodded, descending the ladder with ease. "Of course. I suspect this is about Percy and the trouble he's been having."

Watson said, "You've heard about the sabotage, then?"

"I have," Miss Reeves replied, her expression grave. "Percy's been talking to me about it for weeks now. He's convinced someone's out to get him, messing with his lamps and watching him from the shadows."

Holmes's eyes narrowed. "And what do you make of these claims?"

She sighed, her gaze drifting to the darkening streets. "At first, I thought it might just be his mind playing tricks on him. The night can do that, you know, especially when the fog rolls in. But I've experienced something, too. A shadowy figure, lurking in the alleys. Watching me as I work. Every time I shout at them, they disappear into the night."

"This is most concerning," Holmes said. "Miss Reeves, if Mr Wentworth were to retire, would his round be assigned to you?"

"I couldn't say, Mr Holmes. It would be an honour to take on his route, I can't deny that. But I wouldn't want Percy to retire, not because he thinks someone is out to get him."

Holmes said, "Do you have any suspicions about who might be behind these troubles?"

She shook her head. "I don't. I know Horace Cuthbert wants Percy's round. He's always going on about it. But I don't think he'd stoop so low. But there again, no one really knows another person, do they? Not really." She sighed heavily. "I hope you find out who is responsible. Percy's a good man, and he doesn't deserve this."

Watson said, "We are looking into this matter, and are sure we'll uncover the truth."

Miss Reeves smiled. "That's good to know. If you don't mind, I have to get back to my work."

Holmes and Watson bid Miss Reeves farewell and walked away.

A few minutes later, Holmes said, "Do you think she could be lying, Watson? It's possible that Miss Reeves is the one sabotaging Mr Wentworth's work."

Watson glanced at his companion. "But why would she do such a thing?"

Holmes replied, "She stands to gain from it. It's a coveted position, and one she clearly desires."

Watson nodded slowly, mulling over Holmes's words. "That may be true, but what about the shadowy figure we saw? Miss Reeves mentioned seeing it too."

"Ah, yes," Holmes said. "We saw a figure lurking in the shadows, but we assumed it was a man. However, you no doubt noticed Miss Reeves is dressed in trousers and a coat, not unlike a man's attire. In the darkness, it would be easy to mistake her for a male figure."

"Ah, yes, I see. And because she was trained by Mr Wentworth, she would be familiar with his tools and his record book, and where they are kept. If it is Miss Reeves, I wonder how she got into his room."

"Hmm, that's something we will find out in due course. It does trouble me that Miss Reeves could be behind this, considering how highly she thinks about Mr Wentworth. However, that could be an act. I suspect there is something we are missing; some truth yet to be revealed."

Watson said, "So what do we do now, Holmes?"

The detective's eyes gleamed with a familiar intensity. "We continue our investigation. If Miss Reeves is involved, we will uncover her deception."

Chapter 7

Inside 221B Baker Street the next morning, Holmes and Watson were deep in conversation when Mrs Hudson ushered in Percy Wentworth, who was in a highly distraught state. Mrs Hudson gave Holmes and Watson a swift nod before quickly leaving the room.

"Mr Holmes, Dr Watson," Wentworth began. "Something terrible has happened."

Holmes was on his feet in an instant. "What is it, Mr Wentworth?"

"It's my ladder. I think someone is trying to murder me. Could you come to my lodgings? It'll be easier to show you what's happened."

Without a word, Holmes grabbed his coat and hat, motioning for Watson to follow. The three men hurried through the streets of London and made their way to Wentworth's lodgings.

Once there, Wentworth led them to the storage area. With shaking hands, he pointed to his ladder, which lay propped against the wall.

Holmes and Watson examined the ladder, their eyes widening as they saw a deep, jagged cut that ran partway through the wood. It was clear that someone had deliberately sawn through the ladder, weakening it to the point of danger.

"I noticed it this morning. I came in here to check my toolbox and to see if anything was missing. I took your advice, Mr Holmes, and got a new look. My tools are all still there. I noticed that cut in that ladder when I was putting my toolbox back into its usual place. If I hadn't noticed it before my shift, I could have fallen and broken my neck. And I'm sure that shadowy figure has been following me more. I thought I saw him on the way to your home."

Holmes examined the ladder with a critical eye. "It's extremely fortunate that you noticed this cut, Mr Wentworth."

"That's not all, Mr Holmes. My record book, it's gone."

Holmes looked up from the ladder. "Gone? When did you last see it?"

"Last night, when I came home from my shift. I was so tired when I came in that I thought I might have put it somewhere else to keep it safe. I convinced myself I had, and that I would find it in the morning. But when I woke up and had a good look in every place possible, it was nowhere to be found."

Holmes suggested they have a look for any signs of forced entry to his room. After a thorough search, there wasn't any evidence of any illegal entry. The window was securely latched, and the door showed no signs of tampering. Holmes discreetly looked for the record book, in case Mr Wentworth, in his tired state, had missed it.

After their fruitless search, Wentworth said, "I don't know what to do. Without my record book, I'm finished. I might as well retire now and save myself the shame of being dismissed."

Holmes said kindly, "Nonsense, Mr Wentworth. We will not let this saboteur win. Watson and I will do everything in our power to find the culprit and clear your name."

"But I can't work without my ladder."

Holmes waved a dismissive hand. "Leave that to me. I have a neighbour, Ernest, who has a ladder. I'm certain he will be more than willing to lend it to you for the time being."

Wentworth's shoulders sagged with relief. "Thank you, Mr Holmes. I don't know what I would do without your help."

"We will sort this out, Mr Wentworth," Holmes said. "I promise you that. Now, let me go and speak with Ernest about that ladder."

Leaving Watson behind to offer comfort to Mr Wentworth, Holmes hastened back to Baker Street, where he immediately set about procuring a ladder from their neighbour, Ernest. The kind-hearted man was more than happy to lend his ladder to the distressed lamplighter. Holmes wasted no time in returning to Wentworth's abode.

Wentworth's face lit up with gratitude as he saw Holmes approaching with the ladder in tow. "Oh, Mr Holmes, I can't thank you enough," he exclaimed. "You've saved my livelihood, you have."

Holmes replied, "Think nothing of it, Mr Wentworth. We're happy to help in any way we can."

But even as Wentworth took the ladder and leaned it carefully against the wall, a shadow of worry crossed his face. "But what about my record book? I can't work without it. The union inspectors, they'll have my head if I don't have my records in order."

Watson, ever the practical one, reached into his coat pocket and pulled out a small, leather-bound notebook. "Here," he said. "This is a new journal that I popped into my pocket this morning in case I needed it. Your need is much greater than mine, Mr Wentworth. Besides, I have many more empty journals at home. You can use it to record your rounds for now, and then transfer the information to your official record book once we find it."

"Dr Watson, I don't know what to say. Thank you, truly." Wentworth gave him a smile.

Holmes said, "Try to keep your spirits up, Mr Wentworth. We'll find your record book, and we'll catch the scoundrel who's trying to sabotage you. You have my word on that."

Chapter 8

After leaving Wentworth's home, Holmes suggested to Watson they speak with Mr Blackmore about the relationship between Percy Wentworth, Horace Cuthbert and Miriam Reeves.

Holmes said, "Mr Blackmore knows these people better than us, and he may have some important information that will help our investigation."

Watson nodded in agreement, and together they returned to the Lamplighter's Union building and went inside. As they made their way down the hallway towards the offices, a movement caught Holmes' eye.

There, in one of the offices, was a furtive-looking Horace Cuthbert. He appeared to be rifling through some papers on the desk, his movements quick and nervous. As soon as he noticed Holmes and Watson, his face darkened, and he quickly rushed out of the office.

"Mr Cuthbert!" Holmes called out, his voice sharp. "What were you doing in that office?"

Cuthbert snarled, his eyes narrowing. "It's none of your business, Mr Holmes. Now, if you'll excuse me."

With that, he pushed past the two men and ran down the hallway, disappearing around a corner. Holmes and Watson exchanged a puzzled glance, but before they could pursue the matter further, a voice called out from behind them.

"Mr Holmes, Dr Watson! What a surprise to see you here."

They turned to see Mr Blackmore walking towards them, holding two steaming cups of tea.

Blackmore said, "I noticed you at our meeting the other day and was going to ask what your interest in lamplighters was, but alas, I never got the chance. Union business never stops." He looked into the office where Cuthbert had been, a frown creasing his brow. "That's odd. Mr Cuthbert was just here a few minutes ago, asking to speak with me about his promotion prospects. But it seems he's changed his mind."

Holmes said, "Mr Blackmore, we were hoping to speak with you about Percy Wentworth. As you may know, he's been experiencing some troubling incidents as of late."

Blackmore nodded. "Yes, I've heard. It's a terrible business, truly. Percy is one of our best lamplighters, and it pains me to see him going through such difficulties." He gestured for Holmes and Watson to follow him into his office. He set the cups of tea down on his desk and moved some papers to the side. "Please, have a seat. I'll tell you everything I know."

Holmes and Watson sat down, and Holmes asked if Blackmore could tell them about Mr Wentworth.

Blackmore said, "Percy has been with us for many, many years. He's always been a reliable and hardworking employee. I've never had any complaints about his work, and he's always been diligent about keeping his records in order."

Holmes asked, "And what about Mr Cuthbert and Miss Reeves? What can you tell us about them?"

Blackmore sighed, shaking his head. "Horace Cuthbert is a bit of a troublemaker, I'm afraid. He's been with us for about ten years now, but he's always been more interested in advancing his own position than in doing his job well. He's been angling for Percy's route for some time now, but I've made it clear that it will go to Miriam Reeves if Percy retires."

Watson said, "And how has Miriam been performing in her role?"

Blackmore's face lit up with a smile. "Oh, she's been a revelation. She's only been with us for about a year, but she's already proven herself to be one of our most promising lamplighters. She's hardworking, reliable, and has a keen eye for detail. I have no doubt that she'll go far in this profession."

"And have you noticed anything unusual in the past few weeks?" Holmes asked, "Any strange occurrences or suspicious behaviour?"

Blackmore shook his head. "Apart from Percy's lamps going out unexpectedly, nothing out of the ordinary, I'm afraid. But I'll keep my eyes and ears open, and let you know if I hear anything."

With that, Holmes and Watson thanked Blackmore for his time and took their leave. As they stepped out into the cool evening air, Holmes turned to Watson with a determined look in his eye.

"We're getting closer, Watson," he said. "I can feel it. We just need to keep digging, and we'll find the truth behind this mystery."

Chapter 9

Holmes and Watson stepped out of the Lamplighter's Union building and walked away.

Holmes suddenly stopped, his attention focused on the tall grass at the side of the path.

"What is it, Holmes?" Watson asked, looking in the same direction.

Without a word, Holmes strode over to the grass and reached down, his long fingers closing around a familiar object. As he held it up to the fading light, Watson gasped in recognition.

"Why, that's Mr Wentworth's record book!" he exclaimed, his eyes wide with surprise.

Holmes nodded, his expression grim as he examined the book. It was intact, but the cover was slightly damaged, as if it had been dropped or handled roughly.

"Indeed, Watson," he said. "And I suspect Mr Cuthbert may have had something to do with this."

Watson asked, "But why would Mr Cuthbert take that record book? And why would he drop it here, of all places?"

Holmes turned the book over in his hands. "It's possible he dropped it by accident on his way to see Mr Blackmore. Or perhaps he left it here on purpose, knowing Mr Wentworth would be unable to perform his duties without it."

"The scoundrel," Watson said with a shake of his head. "Speaking of Mr Cuthbert, what was he looking at in Mr Blackmore's office? And why would he run away when we confronted him?"

Holmes tucked the record book into his coat pocket. "I don't know. But I intend to find out. First, however, we must return this book to Mr Wentworth. Later, we will seek out Mr Cuthbert and speak to him again. Let's see if he's more forthcoming with information this time."

They set off walking again.

Watson said, "And what of Miss Reeves? Do you think she could be involved in any way?"

Holmes shook his head. "I doubt it, Watson. From what Mr Blackmore said, she seems to be an exemplary employee. But we can't rule anything out at this stage."

As they turned the corner onto Wentworth's street, they saw the lamplighter coming out of his building. His face lit up when he saw Holmes and Watson.

"Mr Holmes, Dr Watson!" he cried out. "Have you any news for me?"

Holmes reached into his pocket and withdrew the record book, holding it out with a small smile. "We found this, Mr Wentworth," he said. "Someone may have taken it from your lodgings and dropped it outside the Lamplighter's Union building."

Wentworth took the book. "Oh, thank you, Mr Holmes. I'm so relieved to have it in my hands again. But who could have taken it? And why?"

Holmes replied, "We have some suspicions. But we need to gather more evidence before we can make any accusations. In the meantime, I suggest you keep a close eye on your belongings and report any further incidents to us immediately."

Wentworth nodded. "I will, Mr Holmes. And thank you again, both of you."

After assuring Wentworth they would be in touch with him again soon, Holmes and Watson took their leave and headed back to Baker Street.

Chapter 10

Later on, as the sun began to set, Holmes and Watson set out in search of Cuthbert once more. They navigated the winding alleys and narrow passages, their footsteps echoing in the growing darkness. The air was thick with the scent of smoke and the distant sounds of the city settling in for the night.

As they approached the streets where Cuthbert conducted his rounds, they noticed the lamps were already lit, casting a warm glow across the pavement. They pressed on, their eyes scanning the streets for any sign of the lamplighter.

At last, they spotted him up ahead, perched on his ladder as he prepared to light the next lamp. But just as he reached for the wick, a shadowy figure emerged from the darkness and rushed towards the ladder.

Before Holmes or Watson could shout a warning, the figure purposely collided with the ladder, sending it toppling to the side. Cuthbert let out a cry of surprise as he tumbled from his perch, landing hard on the unforgiving stone below.

The shadowy figure darted away, disappearing into the night as quickly as they had appeared. Holmes and Watson raced towards the fallen lamplighter.

Watson reached Cuthbert first, kneeling beside him to assess his injuries. The lamplighter was unconscious, a nasty gash on his forehead oozing blood onto the pavement. Watson quickly checked his pulse and breathing, relieved to find both steady, if a bit weak.

"He's suffered a nasty blow to the head," Watson reported. "We need to get him to a hospital immediately."

Holmes nodded. "I'll go after the attacker," he said, already turning to give chase. "You stay with Cuthbert and summon a cab."

Watson nodded, watching as Holmes disappeared into the shadows in pursuit of the mysterious figure. He turned his attention back to Cuthbert, using his handkerchief to apply pressure to the wound on his head.

It wasn't long before Holmes returned, his expression frustrated and his breathing heavy from the chase. "They got away, yet again," he said, his voice tight with anger.

Watson said, "There's a cab waiting for us over there. Help me get Mr Cuthbert into it."

Together, they managed to place Cuthbert into the back of the cab. Watson got in with him.

Holmes said, "We can't leave Mr Cuthbert's ladder and equipment unattended. I'll take them to the storage area behind Mr Wentworth's house. With a bit of luck, I might catch sight of that shadowy figure on the way."

"This is getting more serious by the minute," Watson said. "First the sabotage, then the stolen record book, and now this attack on Mr Cuthbert. What could be the motive behind all of this?"

Holmes shook his head. "I don't know, Watson," he admitted. "Our priority at this moment is Mr Cuthbert's health. Let's not waste any more time. Get him to the hospital. We'll meet later."

With that, the cab clattered away through the darkened streets.

Holmes watched it go, feeling an annoying sense of frustration about the case. He hoped the mystery could be solved before anyone else was hurt.

Chapter 11

Next morning, Holmes and Watson sipped their tea as they discussed the events of the previous night. The attack on Cuthbert had left them both shaken and more determined than ever to uncover the truth behind the sabotage of the lamplighters.

"It's a dreadful business," Watson said, shaking his head. "Who could have pushed Mr Cuthbert off his ladder like that? And why? Could it have been Miss Reeves after all?"

Holmes replied, "I still don't believe Miriam Reeves is behind this. She has no motive to go after Mr Cuthbert, and from what we've seen of her, she seems to be a diligent and honest worker."

Watson nodded, taking another sip of his tea. "But who could it be? And what do they hope to gain by sabotaging the lamplighters?"

"That, my dear Watson, is the question we must answer," Holmes replied. "But there is one curious detail that may provide a clue. You mentioned Mr Cuthbert was mumbling something in his hospital bed last night?"

Watson sat up straighter, his eyes widening with realisation. "Yes, that's right! He kept repeating 'the Electric Illumination Company' over and over again before he fell asleep. I couldn't make any sense of it."

Holmes said, "I have read in the papers about plans to replace the gaslights with electric ones in certain parts of the city. It's possible that someone from the electric company might be behind these attacks, perhaps in an effort to prove the superiority of electric lighting over gas."

Watson frowned, considering the idea. "But why target the lamplighters specifically? Surely there are other ways to promote the benefits of electric lighting without resorting to sabotage and violence."

"Perhaps," Holmes mused, his fingers drumming on the arm of his chair. "But we must not discount any possibilities at this stage. I think it would be wise for us to pay a visit to the Electric Illumination Company and find out more about their plans. We need to determine how the introduction of electric lighting could affect the local lamplighters and their livelihoods."

Watson set down his teacup. "I agree. We should go at once. We don't want anyone else to get hurt."

The two men quickly gathered their coats and hats and stepped out into the bustling streets of London.

Holmes and Watson soon reached the gleaming new offices of the Electric Illumination Company. The building stood out amongst its neighbours, its exterior adorned with sleek, modern lines and large windows that allowed the bright glow of electric light to spill out onto the street.

The interior of the building was no less impressive, with polished marble floors and walls lined with the latest in electrical technology. Electric lamps cast a steady, unwavering light, banishing the shadows that so often lurked in the corners of gas-lit rooms.

The reception desk was manned by a young woman with a neat, efficient air about her.

"Good afternoon, gentlemen," she said, looking up from her work with a polite smile. "How may I assist you today?"

Holmes removed his hat and inclined his head in greeting. "Good afternoon, miss. My name is Sherlock Holmes, and this is Dr Watson. We were hoping to speak with someone about the company's plans for installing electric lights in the city."

The receptionist nodded, consulting a ledger on her desk. "Certainly, Mr Holmes. Mr Ranger would be the best person to speak with regarding that matter. However, he is currently in a meeting. Would you be willing to wait?"

"Of course," Holmes replied, and he and Watson took their seats in the waiting area.

As they sat, Holmes noted the way the electric lamps cast a steady, unwavering light, so different from the flickering glow of gas. He observed the people coming and going, their faces illuminated by the bright, modern lighting.

Suddenly, a familiar figure caught his eye. Descending the stairs was none other than Mr Blackmore, the inspector from the Lamplighter's Union. He was deep in conversation with another man, their faces animated as they spoke. The two men seemed on friendly terms, laughing and smiling as they reached the bottom of the stairs.

Holmes watched as Mr Blackmore shook hands with his companion, a broad grin on his face. The inspector seemed in high spirits, completely unaware of Holmes and Watson's presence in the lobby. With a nod, Mr Blackmore turned and strode away, leaving his companion to head in the opposite direction.

Holmes turned to Watson, his brow furrowed in thought. "Did you see that, Watson?" he murmured, keeping his voice low to avoid being overheard.

Watson nodded, his own expression one of surprise. "What could Mr Blackmore be doing here, at the electric company? And who was that man he was speaking with?"

"I don't know," Holmes replied. "But I intend to find out."

A short while later, Mr Ranger approached them. It was the same man who had been speaking with Mr Blackmore.

Mr Ranger greeted them warmly and asked, "Can I help you with something, gentlemen?"

Holmes stood, an eager look in his eyes. "You most certainly can, Mr Ranger. We have some questions for you."

Chapter 12

Holmes and Watson returned to the Lamplighter's Union building the very next day. They entered the meeting room and were greeted by Mr Blackmore, who looked at them with a mixture of curiosity and apprehension.

"Mr Holmes, Dr Watson," he said, shaking their hands firmly. "I must admit, I'm rather intrigued by your request to call this emergency meeting. What exactly do you plan to say to the members?"

Holmes gave him an enigmatic smile. "All will be revealed in due course, Mr Blackmore. Suffice it to say, it has something to do with a recent investigation of ours."

Mr Blackmore raised an eyebrow but said nothing further. As the members of the Lamplighter's Union filed into the room, he took his seat at the front.

The room buzzed with conversation as the lamplighters took their seats, their faces a mixture of confusion and curiosity. Percy Wentworth sat near the front, his face pale and drawn, while Miriam Reeves and a few others cast worried glances in his direction.

When everyone had settled, Holmes addressed the seated people, his voice clear and commanding. "Thank you all for coming on such short notice," he began. "I know you must be wondering why we've called this meeting. As some of you may know, my associate Dr Watson and I have been investigating a series of troubling incidents involving members of your union. Specifically, we have been looking into the case of Mr Percy Wentworth, who has been the victim of what appears to be a campaign of sabotage and intimidation."

Wentworth shifted uncomfortably in his seat as people looked his way.

Holmes continued, "Mr Wentworth has been an exemplary member of this union for many years, and yet someone has seen fit to target him, to undermine his work and threaten his livelihood. And he is not the only one. Just two days ago, Mr Horace Cuthbert was the victim of a vicious attack. He was forced off his ladder and seriously injured."

The room erupted in gasps and exclamations.

Holmes held up a hand for silence, and the room gradually quieted. "Thankfully, Mr Cuthbert is recovering in hospital. At first, Dr Watson and I believed these attacks might be motivated by jealousy or greed. After all, the position of a lamplighter is a coveted one, and there are those who might go to great lengths to secure a more favourable route or a higher standing within the union. But as we delved deeper into the case, we began to suspect that something else was at play. Something far more insidious than mere personal ambition."

The room was deathly silent now, everyone's attention fixed on Holmes as he spoke.

Holmes turned to face Mr Blackmore and said, "We believe the attacks on Mr Wentworth and Mr Cuthbert were not the work of a jealous colleague or a disgruntled rival. No, we believe they were part of a larger conspiracy, one that threatens the very future of lamplighters." He paused, letting his words sink in. "Mr Blackmore, would you care to explain to the members of this union why Dr Watson and I saw you shaking hands with Mr Ranger, a manager at the Electric Illumination Company, yesterday?"

Blackmore's face paled, and he shifted uncomfortably in his seat. "I... I don't know what you're talking about, Mr

Holmes. I've never met anyone from the electric company."

But Holmes was not to be deterred. "Come now, Mr Blackmore. We spoke with Mr Ranger himself, and he confirmed he had offered you a job at the electric company. A job which, I might add, you have accepted."

Cries of disbelief and anger rang out. Wentworth looked stunned, his eyes wide with shock.

Holmes pressed on, his voice rising above the din. "But that's not all, is it, Mr Blackmore? You see, we believe you have been deliberately sabotaging Mr Wentworth's lamps and his tools, to prove how unreliable human lamplighters can be."

Blackmore folded his arms. "You can't prove anything, Mr Holmes. This is all just wild speculation."

But Holmes was not finished. "Oh, but we can prove it, Mr Blackmore. You see, you chose Mr Wentworth's route for a very specific reason. It's the route that covers the streets where many of London's most influential politicians live. And you knew that if the lamps on those streets started going out, the politicians would take notice. They would question the reliability of the lamplighters, and would start to look for alternatives. Alternatives like electric lighting. And they are in a position to make changes happen quickly."

The room was silent now, every eye fixed on Blackmore. He looked around wildly, his face a mask of desperation and anger.

"But you didn't count on Mr Cuthbert finding out about your little scheme, did you?" Holmes continued. "He saw the documents in your office, the ones that proved you were planning to work with the electric company. And that's why you pushed him off his ladder. To keep him quiet. Perhaps quiet forever."

Blackmore said, "Okay! I admit it! But I did what I had to do for the future of this city. Electric lighting is the way forward, and the lamplighters are nothing but a relic of the past. They need to be replaced, and I was just doing my part to make that happen. And getting a job at that company secures my future."

Wentworth stood up, his face red with fury. "You traitor!" he shouted. "How could you do this to us? We trusted you!"

But Blackmore just sneered at him. "Trust? What good is trust in a world that's moving on without you? The future belongs to those who embrace progress, not those who cling to the past."

Holmes said, "And what about the lamplighters you have hurt, Mr Blackmore? Are they just collateral damage in your grand plan for progress?"

Mr Blackmore's face twisted into a mocking smile. "Progress always has its price, Mr Holmes. And if a few people have to suffer along the way, well, that's just the way it is."

His words caused people to leap from their seats and yell insults at Blackmore, a man they had trusted for years.

Holmes nodded to a couple of police officers at the back of the room who entered unobserved, especially by Mr Blackmore.

Holmes looked directly at Blackmore and said, "Your treachery has been exposed. There's no coming back from it. You won't be heading towards a bright future with the electric company. The only place you're going to is prison." The corners of his mouth twitched. "Which, at the present time, is completely illuminated by gas lamps."

The police led Blackmore away. The stunned lamplighters stood up and gathered in groups to discuss the shocking revelations.

Wentworth approached Holmes and Watson. "I can't believe it. I just can't. Mr Blackmore, of all people." He shook his head in disbelief. "Mr Homes, Dr Watson, thank you, for everything. I'll never forget what you've done for me. And for the other lamplighters as well. One thing still troubles me, though. How did Mr Blackmore get into my room without breaking in?"

Holmes said, "Knowing you would be on your rounds, Mr Blackmore visited your lodgings and spoke to your landlord. He claimed you had given him permission to enter your room at any time. The landlord had met Mr Blackmore frequently when he'd visited you and other lamplighters in the building, so he wasn't the least bit suspicious and let him in. After hearing the truth about Mr Blackmore, your landlord said he will never make that mistake again. He was most upset about what had happened."

"Ah, I see. That explains it. It wasn't my landlord's fault. He trusted Mr Blackmore. We all did." Wentworth sighed softly. "Well, I'd better get ready for my shift tonight. I'll call on Horace at the hospital first. See how he is, let him know what's happened. Thank you again, Mr Holmes, Dr Watson, you've saved my job. And my sanity."

Percy Wentworth walked away, looking much brighter and with his head held high.

"So, that's that," Watson said. "Holmes, do you think the gas lights of London will be replaced with electric ones?"

"It's highly likely," Holmes said. "The world is constantly evolving. Progress and innovation can't be stopped. But who knows, maybe some of those beautiful lamps will survive and cast their glow upon the people of the future, perhaps people even a hundred years from now."

Watson chuckled. "You're getting almost poetic, Holmes. May I say, even emotional?"

Holmes laughed. "It will soon pass. Come, Watson, I can sense there is another mystery waiting for us."

A note from the author

For as long as I can remember, I have loved reading mystery books. It started with Enid Blyton's Famous Five, and The Secret Seven. As I got older, I progressed to Agatha Christie books, and of course, Sir Arthur Conan Doyle's Sherlock Holmes.

I love the characters of Sherlock Holmes and Dr Watson, and the Victorian era that the stories are set in. It seemed only natural that one day, I would write some of my own Sherlock stories. I love creating new mysteries for Mr Holmes, and his trusty companion, Dr John Watson. It's not just the era itself that seems to ignite ideas within me; it's also the characters who were around at that time, and the lives they led.

This story has been checked for errors, but if you see anything we have missed and you'd like to let us know about them, please email mabel@mabelswift.com

You can hear about my new releases by signing up to my newsletter www.mabelswift.com As a thank you for subscribing, I will send you a free short story: Sherlock Holmes and The Curious Clock.

If you'd like to contact me, you can get in touch via mabel@mabelswift.com I'd be delighted to hear from you.

Best wishes

Mabel

Printed in Great Britain
by Amazon